THE INVISIBLE WEB

OLIVER BOTTINI

THE INVISIBLE WEB

A Black Forest Investigation: V

Translated from the German by
Jamie Bulloch

MACLEHOSE PRESS
QUERCUS · LONDON

First published in the German language as *Das verborgene Netz* by S. Fischer Verlag, Frankfurt, in
2010, and reissued by DuMont Buchverlag, Cologne, in 2017
First published in Great Britain in 2023 by MacLehose Press
This paperback edition first published in 2024 by

MacLehose Press
An imprint of Quercus Editions Limited
Carmelite House
50 Victoria Embankment
London EC4Y 0DZ

An Hachette UK company

A CIP catalogue record for this book is available from the British Library.

ISBN (MMP) 978 1 52940 921 5
ISBN (Ebook) 978 1 52940 922 2

This book is a work of fiction. Names, characters, organisations, places and events are
either the product of the author's imagination or are used fictitiously. Any resemblance to
actual persons, living or dead, events or particular places is entirely coincidental.

10 9 8 7 6 5 4 3 2 1

Designed and typeset in Minion by Libanus Press, Marlborough
Printed and bound in Great Britain by Clays Ltd, Elcograf S.p.A.

THE INVISIBLE WEB

Prologue

The last few kilometres in darkness before the radio tower appeared at the end of the motorway, a steel needle of muted yellow light. Mike Reuter loved this view and, even it if were safe for him to fly, he would always choose to travel by car. On this occasion he'd driven all the way across the country from the south-west. These few minutes in pitch-black Grunewald, at the edge of which the illuminated tower loomed, were pure magic. As ever when he came to Berlin, he was filled with anticipation and an indefinable longing. As if this virtually dead-straight road suggested everything could be different, as if he could embark on a new life.

The motorway then took the slightest of curves and the radio tower emerged – a beginning, perhaps even an end, but at any rate a promise, and for a few moments Mike felt something akin to happiness.

Mike left the motorway at the Konstanzer Strasse exit. He'd got used to driving without his satnav, memorising routes in car parks and service stations. Cross Hohenzollerndamm, left into Brandenburgische Strasse, the hotel immediately on the right. He drove past it slowly. A wide pavement with a group of elderly tourists sitting at white plastic tables. On the other side of the street was the café where Gretzki was waiting for him. A table by the outside wall, a glowing red dot that briefly described a circle in the air; Gretzki had seen him.

Mike parked the car a couple of blocks further down the street, then wandered back to the café by a circuitous route.

*

Three young men of Turkish or Arabic origin engaged in a loud conversation, two elderly women, a stooped old man with long hair and a small dog; and by the wall in the dark, as still as a statue, Gretzki.

Sitting down beside him he said, "I hope you're not thinking of giving up smoking."

"Don't worry," Gretzki chuckled, nudging the pack towards him. Mike lit a cigarette. The tourists' laughter drifted over and the tension grew, as it always did in the darkness. Too many blind spots, too many possibilities. Mike's gaze flickered from face to face, from movement to movement, from dark windows to lit ones, until he forced himself to stop.

"Relax," Gretzki said amiably.

They waited for the espresso to arrive.

While Mike stirred in some sugar, Gretzki began talking quietly. The plane had landed on time. To be on the safe side he'd taken two of his men along; after all, they'd only seen photographs of the target. No-one else was waiting at the airport apart from them. When Gretzki brought the cigarette to his lips, it lent his wrinkled face a reddish glow. The target had taken a taxi to the hotel, he went on, from Tegel to Wilmersdorf, not exactly the cheapest option. She'd arrived an hour ago and there'd been no sign of her since. No contact, no telephone conversations so far, not even during the cab ride.

They sat closely huddled, and Mike could smell the smoke that escaped from Gretzki's mouth when he spoke.

"Anything else?"

Gretzki shook his head.

Without letting the entrance to the hotel out of his sight, Mike took a sip of his coffee. The tourists got up and went to the curb where a large taxi had pulled up. Fat men in polo shirts and pleated trousers, middle managers of insignificant companies, their wives of a similar stature and similarly dressed with flashes of fake gold.

From the Ruhr or a small town far from any motorway. They squeezed themselves noisily into the taxi – time to see Berlin by night.

"You look tired," Gretzki said.

"Very busy."

"In *Freiburg*?" An affectionate smile: humour, Gretzki-style.

He didn't like Gretzki. A short, slender man in his mid-fifties with lifeless eyes, a shadowy individual, ideal for this sort of work, but too arrogant and smug. About a decade ago Mike's father had fished him out of a clique of former BND (foreign) and Verfassungsschutz (domestic) intelligence agents, and now he was running the Berlin office. There were no complaints, no mistakes. He had connections, experience, and Mike's father trusted him.

Nonetheless he didn't like Gretzki.

"What do I have to know?" Gretzki asked.

Mike turned to him.

They were listening in to Esther Graf's telephone calls and reading her e-mails. They'd known which plane she was going to take and which hotel she'd booked. But they still had no idea why she'd come to Berlin. At the beginning of October she'd made two calls from a phone box, during her lunch break. Maybe these had been about her Berlin trip, maybe not.

"Understood," Gretzki said.

Opposite, a hotel employee was clearing the tables of bottles and glasses. Mike could see the bar through the windows, empty apart from a lone customer. One of Gretzki's men.

"Is she important?"

"Important and useful," Mike replied.

"And if she loses her nerve we'll be busted?"

"Yes." He thought about the "we". Gretzki had nothing to do with the operation. He was only helping out because Esther was in Berlin for the weekend. Mike found the "we" too eager.

"Anyone else involved?"

Mike hesitated. "Hard to say."

Gretzki didn't probe further; he knew what this meant: keep your eyes open. He sat there motionless, an element of the darkness, superior, invulnerable, so it seemed to Mike. There had been times when he would have loved to have been like Gretzki.

"She's in room 34, you're number 35."

"Do the rooms face the street or out back?"

"Out back."

Mike sensed Gretzki's eyes running over him. It felt like leeches on his body.

"What if you bump into her in the corridor?"

"She's never seen me," Mike said.

He thought of the radio tower and the indefinable longing, one element of which was his desire not to be involved with individuals like Gretzki anymore. All those figures from the past, from East and West, the warriors who populated his life. Who were part of the "we".

"Bugs and cameras have been installed. The list of locations and the devices are in a suitcase under the bed."

Mike nodded, trying to ignore the conceited tone in Gretzki's voice. They'd fitted out the room even before Esther had arrived at the hotel.

No mistakes, bags of experience.

All of a sudden he felt the urge to hit Gretzki. Drag him into a side street and punch him over and over again. As if this might free him from everything Gretzki stood for.

"She's ordered a taxi from reception for nine o'clock tomorrow morning."

"Do you know where she's going?"

"No." Gretzki placed the room key on the table. "How long do you need us for?"

Mike took the key. "Until we know why she's here."

"Here's a theory. She's a pretty little thing, but uptight and lonely. She's come to Berlin to let her hair down."

Mike pulled the ashtray towards him and stubbed out his cigarette.

"Swingers club, lesbian party, gay bar. Or drugs." Gretzki's eyes gave him a bleak look.

"And?"

Gretzki felt for the pack of cigarettes without taking his eyes off Mike. "Or someone she's met online."

"We'll see."

"That's Berlin," Gretzki said.

Mike turned away and tried to control the anger brewing inside him. Maybe, he thought, he ought to do it – give Gretzki a thrashing.

The anger subsided when he pictured the Grunewald once more and the radio tower with its friendly light.

That, he thought, was Berlin.

A small room, wood-panelled, with curtains that stank of cigarette smoke and a huge water stain on the dirty carpet outside the bathroom door. When he sat on the bed he sank deep into the mattress. Whether or not the room had woodchip wallpaper, whether it was rundown or luxurious, with a hard or soft mattress, smelly or fragrant, it was always unfamiliar and always next to another, similar room where someone was staying who had no idea they were being watched.

He'd enjoyed this life in the early years. Being a stranger, invisible, but nothing happening that escaped his notice. He'd enjoyed the *power*.

The bedsprings creaked as he bent down and pulled out Gretzki's aluminium case.

One camera in the ceiling rose of the overhead light, one in a picture frame on the wall in-between their two rooms and one in the ventilation shaft above the door in the bathroom. Bugs in the telephone, beneath the desk and on the back of the heated towel rail. No blind spots; even a whisper would be audible – a perfectly prepared room.

Not for the first time Mike thought his father was right to have such a high opinion of Gretzki.

The lights in her room were switched off and it took a moment before he could see Esther in the dim glow of the moon on the small black-and-white monitor. She'd opened the window and was sitting on the sill, a cigarette in one hand and a glass in the other – red wine, probably, the only alcoholic drink she liked. She was wearing jeans and the light-blue blouse he really liked. Her hair was down, her legs outstretched and her head leaning back. In the large window she looked even more petite than usual. Her movements were slow and he imagined she was fairly relaxed.

She'd booked the hotel and flight from the office on October 20. Going to visit relatives, she'd told her colleagues. She didn't have any relatives in Berlin.

Esther hadn't made any phone calls to Berlin and hadn't written any e-mails relating to the trip, neither from the office nor at home. Two days passed during which they waited, scratching their heads. Then they hit on the idea of checking her movements prior to that point, which was when they came across the calls from a telephone box at the beginning of October. "We've rumbled her," his father said, and got in touch with Gretzki.

Movement on the monitor: Esther sliding off the windowsill. She stopped beside the bed and put on a sweater, then returned to the window with the bottle of wine.

When some clouds drifted across the moon she disappeared into a greyish-black haze. Then a hint of white – her cheek, her neck, her décolleté.

They could dismiss the likelihood that she'd already talked to someone. There'd been no meetings, no secret new acquaintances and no changes in her behaviour. But they couldn't discount the possibility that she'd come to Berlin because she'd been contacted – two short calls from a phone box: one minute fifty seconds and one minute ten.

They knew she was fragile. That's why they'd approached her seven months ago.

Making approaches at the right time and going into hiding at the right time was a fine art. They'd waited too long. No matter what happened in Berlin, they would have to drop her. Far too much was at stake.

Mike's mobile vibrated in his coat pocket – Gretzki. *Got everything you need?* he'd written.

This thought again: too eager for Gretzki.

He took off his right glove and wrote back, *Yes.*

The flash of a cigarette lighter on the monitor. They sat there, smoking in silence, connected to each other for the past seven months and yet not at all.

Esther in the bathroom, taking a shower, rubbing cream into her body, at the sink in a flowery nightie and socks. As ever when brushing her teeth, she supported herself with her left hand on the rim of the sink. Four minutes, two for the top, two for the bottom – the bug even picked up the beeping of the electric toothbrush. Then flossing, facial care, every evening the same economical movements, the same procedures, as if she were following a fixed plan.

Every evening and every morning since he'd known her.

Later, when she was sleeping, he picked up the little rucksack, left the room and went down to the ground floor. A threadbare rug muffled the sound of every footstep; pop music was coming from the bar. Through the glass of the double doors he saw Gretzki's man at the end of the bar – a huge, stiff body without a face; his head was outside the beam of light. For a moment he looked like a lurking reptile, and Mike cursed himself for having brought people like him and Gretzki into Esther's orbit.

He stepped out onto the pavement. Gretzki too would surely be somewhere close by still, in a car, a doorway – close enough, at any rate, to notice him. He turned to the right. Adrenaline tingled beneath his skin; his heart rate had quickened. All of his senses alert, taking in sounds, movements and reflections of light which could be important. No contacts, no phone calls, Gretzki had said, and nothing had caught their attention in Freiburg either. But he knew this meant nothing. He'd spent long enough observing people, getting informants to change sides, being part of a second or third ring around a target. No – an absence of contacts or phone calls meant nothing, and until they knew why Esther had come to Berlin, anything seemed possible.

Including that someone else was on to her – or on to him.

I've left the hotel, he wrote.

OK, Gretzki replied.

With the detector he discreetly checked to see if his car had been bugged in the meantime. Then he drove to Kurfürstendamm, headed into town, turned off and turned off again. He slowly coasted down cobbled streets, his eyes darting from the road to his rear-view mirror and back again. Faces caught momentarily in the headlights, indistinct movements out of the beams. Although he no longer wanted to be like Gretzki, he envied the man's serenity. Gretzki was what he did, which made him superior, and his superiority made him calm. He could cast off the shadows. He could forget, and maybe he was even able to trust other people.

After half an hour Mike was convinced that nobody was following him. Back onto Kurfürstendamm, where the traffic was at a standstill; a car had crashed into one of the yellow double-decker buses and was blocking the road. Tourists streamed down the pavements, and at the front of one building the blue neon letters of a cabaret club flashed on and off, always in the same rhythm. He thought of Gretzki's disparaging comments about Berlin. Mike, by contrast, liked everything about this city. The opportunities it offered, the rudeness, its vast size, the side streets lined with trees, even the sluggish buses and the sour faces of their drivers.

The fantasies that Berlin gave rise to, in which everything was possible.

Twenty minutes later he stepped into Brandenburgische Strasse and immediately sensed Gretzki's eyes on him.

Gretzki, who saw everything and knew everything, including what he was planning, of course.

Mike wandered slowly up to the café where he'd met Gretzki. The tables and chairs had been cleared away, and even the old man with the long hair and restless dog had disappeared.

When a light came on in a stairwell on the same side of the street as the hotel, he double-backed. A woman hurried onto the pavement; he caught hold of the closing door. In the narrow hallway that smelled of damp he watched the door click shut. Mike silently made his way up to the third floor and stopped at a window facing the street.

He took the night-vision binoculars from his rucksack when the hall light went out and began scanning the buildings opposite, window by window.

Five minutes passed without his noticing anything unusual. Then his mobile vibrated.

Left of café, Gretzki wrote. *Steps to basement.*

Mike put the binoculars to his eyes again. A building with wrought-iron railings, steps leading down to the basement, the windows partially hidden by the pavement. Not a blind spot, but plenty of darkness.

Now, Gretzki wrote.

The clouds parted to reveal the moon, and a woman's face appeared. Narrow glasses, concave nose, eyes focused on the hotel entrance. Her closed mouth was moving; she was chewing. Strap around the neck, maybe a camera, maybe binoculars. No ordinary citizen, that was clear to see. The consciousness of being on the government's side shaped people's faces and postures. A particular form of confidence that excluded any doubt.

Mike cursed silently. He was certain that the woman was there because of Esther. The avalanche had been set in motion and they hadn't noticed.

Can you find out who she is? he wrote.

We'll know tomorrow, Gretzki replied.

Mike kept looking at the woman for a while longer, then he put the binoculars back in his rucksack. He didn't get the impression she knew about him and Gretzki. The question was whether Esther knew about her.

On Saturday morning it was drizzling; the city was uniformly grey, as if all colour had been sucked from it. It won't change until April, Gretzki had said with a weary shrug, and Mike wondered whether this might be the weak point in Gretzki's armour of superiority: that he'd become tired of his home city.

Twenty to nine and they were sitting in Gretzki's Passat, fifty metres from the hotel entrance.

"Tell me," Mike said.

At one o'clock the woman with the glasses had been relieved by a man in a crumpled suit. Bad posture, carelessly shaven, a lacklustre officer lacking in ambition and style. Gretzki bet he was from East Germany. More likely Kripo or Verfassungsschutz than BND, he said, foreign intelligence has still the odd bit of self-respect.

Mike pondered how a Berlin government agency – whichever it was – had become involved in this. Were two short phone calls, without anything prior to those, enough to establish contact and make an appointment?

Gretzki seemed to have read his mind. "They don't know we're here. They're on to her, not us."

"Where are they now?"

Gretzki pointed to a blue Audi parked near the basement apartment on the opposite side of the street. Because of the rain it was virtually impossible to make out who was in the car. Two figures, driver and passenger, one holding a newspaper.

"The same as last night?"

"No, two new ones. The union makes sure they all get enough sleep."

Mike gave a polite smile.

The old man was pacing up and down outside the café, hands behind his back, followed by the dog. "Not a day goes by in this city without rubbing shoulders with a nutter," Gretzki said. "They study in Freiburg, then they come to Berlin and go crazy."

At that moment Esther came out of the hotel, her head and shoulders shielded by a bright-yellow umbrella with GoSolar written on it. She held the umbrella at an angle so she could keep an eye out for the taxi. Her hair was tied into a plait; a few strands had come loose and were sticking to her brow. She was pale and looked even more twitchy than normal.

"Do you want us to step in if she meets someone?" Gretzki asked.

"No."

"We could easily have her disappear for a few days. Then she'll reappear at Kottbusser Tor with the junkies, and the junkies will tell anyone who asks that she's been knocking around with them for a while, and because there's still a bit of heroin in her veins—"

"No," Mike interrupted. "We just need to know who she's meeting." For the first time he wondered if Esther was in danger. Maybe he'd misread his client's interests. Gretzki might not be the only one who would have her disappear for a few days. And many people had been killed for less.

The taxi arrived. Esther wanted to get in the front. "He's got his sandwich on the front seat," Gretzki said. Mike saw the taxi driver gesticulate and Esther quickly opened the rear passenger door. Gretzki giggled.

They drove in convoy – the taxi, the Audi, and he and Gretzki.

Gretzki's Berlin networks were in operation; the call came less than ten minutes later. He took the mobile from the hands-free dock and put it to his ear.

They were at traffic lights by the Grosse Stern, the taxi and the Audi concealed by other cars. The Victory Column, which shone so brightly when it was sunny, rose dully into the sky. Mike thought about how Berliners called the column "Goldelse", Kurfürstendamm "Ku'damm", the congress hall "the pregnant oyster", and what this said about them. Names that sounded at once affectionate and disdainful.

"Well, well," Gretzki said into the phone.

The lights switched to green. Esther's taxi headed north, followed by the Audi. Just behind, in the adjacent lane, was a small car with a driver who Mike vaguely recognised. Gretzki's reptile man.

The phone call came to an end.

"We were right," Gretzki said, plucking a cigarette from the packet. "Verfassungsschutz, Berlin office. Baden-Württemberg has asked for support."

Mike nodded. That changed everything. "Have you got anything else?"

Gretzki exhaled smoke. "The names of the investigators. And a copy of the request from Baden-Württemberg."

"I'll need that."

"There's not much in it."

"Does it say how long they've been tailing her?"

"No."

"Can you get me the surveillance records?"

"You'll have it all on Monday or Tuesday."

"And the conversation records, if there is a conversation."

They were now driving eastwards, passing a junction with a sign pointing to MITTE. Gretzki was frowning, seemingly wondering where Esther might be going. But then he said, "Keep in mind the thing with the junkies, Mike."

"No, that's not an option."

When the cold eyes fixed him, Mike suddenly realised that Gretzki knew everything there was to know about him and Esther.

Soon afterwards the taxi turned into a development of red-brick buildings and stopped. Gretzki stopped too, pointed to the buildings on either side and said, "Look. Charité Hospital."

"What illnesses do they specialise in?"

"All of them."

Esther got out. When the yellow umbrella sprang open the Audi cruised past. They watched in silence as she walked up to the main entrance. The Audi turned into a side road, but Gretzki's reptile man was suddenly there and entered the building right after Esther.

Two calls: one minute fifty, one minute ten. Enough time to arrange a doctor's appointment? Or to establish contact and fix as inconspicuous a meeting point as possible?

Two trips to the dentist in Freiburg in the last seven months. One visit to the gynaecologist, one to the internist. She'd been off work for a week with flu. And now the Charité.

"I need everything you can get me," Mike said.

"I'll have to make a few phone calls, then. Maybe meet someone."

Gretzki didn't move; Mike got the message. "Call me if you've got anything."

"Of course."

His eyes darted to the taxi which was still double-parked a few metres ahead of them. "And don't lay a finger on her, you get me?"

"Yes. It's not an option, Mike."

He got out. It was raining more heavily now and it felt cold.

A flight all the way across the country just for a hospital examination? He'd seen photocopies of Esther's medical file. No unexplained symptoms, no need for further tests. So why the Charité?

And since when had the intelligence service been involved?

Not sandwiches on the front seat, but newspapers and a well-thumbed book. And the driver was a woman, not a man.

On the smooth, light-coloured leather of the back seat, where Esther had put her umbrella, water droplets quivered with the unevenness of the road and ran when the taxi took a bend. Her scent still hung in the air.

Mike felt the driver's eyes on him in the rear-view mirror before she spoke. "What now? Have you made up your mind?" A torrent of hissing sounds, Swabian dialect uttered with fervour.

"Left again up there."

A shake of the head, a grunt, another hiss.

He made her pull over before the next junction and handed her twenty euros. "Keep driving straight until you've clocked up ten euros. The rest is a tip."

He got out and walked the few paces to the crossroads. Dark-red buildings that looked unbelievably sad in the rain, no sign of the Audi, and Gretkzi's Passat had vanished too. He resisted the urge to follow Esther and the reptile man into the hospital, crossing the street instead. Once more he felt eyes in his back, eyes that moved with him wherever he went. Which he couldn't shake off, not even when he slept; his dreams were full of eyes.

A bit further on he found a café. Self-service from the counter, half-hearted staff, pallid faces in the artificial light. Angry voices came from the kitchen. The espresso smelled as if it had been brewed twice.

He sat in a corner opposite the windows and door, and took out his mobile.

His father answered at once.

"We've got official visitors from Stuttgart and Berlin."

The click of a lighter, a deep inhalation. Eventually his father said, "We need to tidy up, then."

"Yes."

A moment's silence.

"Not a good time for visitors," his father said. "Do they know us?"

"Probably not, only our friend."

"Close acquaintances?"

"Doesn't look like it."

"Are you sure?"

"No, I'm not sure."

Two young women entered the café, ring notebooks sticking out of their shoulder bags – students. He'd heard stories of students who'd been recruited by one of the services in university corridors. But these two looked harmless; their giggling sounded genuine.

"When are you coming home?" his father asked.

Home, he thought. That meant Frankfurt, not Freiburg. "Tomorrow afternoon."

"Good. We need to make new plans."

The students left with their take-away coffees. The argument in the kitchen seemed to have died down, and pop music suddenly blared from the speakers.

"What about our Berlin friend?"

"A great help, as ever."

"Yes," his father said. "He's always reliable."

Mike put his mobile down on the table and picked up his espresso. The waiting had begun.

Gretzki arrived three hours later. The self-satisfied smile, the confident movements – he'd found Mike even here, in this nondescript café.

"Come on," Gretzki said amicably.

They left the café and got into the Passat.

"Referral from an internist in Freiburg," Gretzki said. "Suspected depression and anxiety neurosis. She had two appointments today, one with a behavioural therapist, the other with an anxiety specialist." He shook his head. "Amazing, what's on offer."

"Might they be bogus?"

"The appointments are genuine."

"What's the name of the Freiburg internist?"

Gretzki smiled patiently. "Köpfler."

Mike nodded. Köpfler had treated her flu in late summer. It was strange, though, that he hadn't noted any suspicion of a psychological disorder in her medical file, or the referral.

"On the other hand . . ." Gretzki said.

Their eyes met, and of course they were thinking the same thing. None of this necessarily meant anything – the Charité, the depression, the appointments.

They'd stay on Esther's tail until she was back on the plane.

Just after 2.00 p.m. she left the hospital and hailed a taxi. Reinhardt-strasse westwards, south to Strasse des 17. Juni, then back to the Victory Column. They followed fifty metres behind, this time on their own; the intelligence agents had vanished and there was no sign of Gretzki's reptile man either.

"I've got to get out of here, Mike," Gretzki said suddenly. "Out of Berlin."

Mike looked at him without offering a reply.

"I'll find someone for the office. And maybe you could use me somewhere else."

"Like where?"

"Freiburg wouldn't be bad." Gretzki gave an embarrassed laugh.

Mike nodded as he tried to dismiss the thought which had entered his head: that Gretzki's comment had something to do with Esther.

"Be nice to have some hills around, you know? It's all open here, in every direction, you feel . . . you feel like the stress is coming into the city from every direction."

"Stress?"

"Stress, filth. All the nutters and weirdos. If you've got a few hills around you, they stop all that, at least . . ."

". . . symbolically."

"Exactly." There was relief in Gretzki's smile.

"I'll have a word with my father."

"Thanks."

The taxi turned into Brandenburgische Strasse and stopped outside the café opposite the hotel. Esther stood beneath the umbrella, waiting for a break in the traffic, her face red. All of a sudden the old drunk was behind her, holding his dog, towering above Esther. Rainwater dripped from his head and nose. He bent down to her; Esther spun around and recoiled.

"Would you believe it?" Gretzki said in astonishment.

The old man offered her his hand and said something. His dog started yelping and flouncing. Esther shook her head and eventually the old man turned away. The dog jumped down and they plodded off together.

Gretzki laughed. "The Verfassungsschutz aren't recruiting nutters yet – it hasn't got that bad!"

Mike took his left hand off the seatbelt buckle and his right off the door handle.

Gretzki turned into Konstanzer Strasse and braked. "What now?"

"We'll keep on the case. If the Verfassungsschutz turn up again, get another two or three people. And have the old boy checked out."

Gretzki nodded. "Relax, Mike."

"Yes," he said, getting out and following the yellow umbrella into the hotel, Gretzki's eyes boring into his back.

*

The rain didn't stop, a constant drumming on the window. The same sound came more softly from the speaker. Ever since she got back Esther had been lying on the bed, dressed and curled up in a ball. At some point she'd fallen asleep.

At 4.00 p.m. a text message from Gretzki: *The nutter is just a nutter.*

At half past four it began to get dark. With every passing minute Esther vanished further into the darkness.

His mobile buzzed again. *We're alone*, Gretzki wrote.

By now the image on the monitor was grey and grainy. Mike switched from the camera in the ceiling rose to the one in the picture frame, and back again. He couldn't even see the outline of Esther's body.

Suddenly other sounds mingled with the pounding of the rain – footsteps in the corridor, getting closer. A man's footsteps.

Mike felt a tingling sensation and his heart was racing. He stood up, head bowed, the Walther already in his hand. Gretzki would move silently. The reptile man? Just a guest?

The footsteps stopped outside Esther's room. A faint jangling, maybe keys, maybe coins in a trouser pocket, a lighter. A knife, a pistol knocking against a wedding ring . . .

Mike lifted his Walther and knocked on the wall to Esther's room with the grip, once, twice. He heard a rustling through the speaker, then on the monitor he saw a light was on. Esther sitting on the bed, looking shocked in his direction.

Silence in the corridor.

Mike moved to his door without making a sound. More jangling, quieter this time. Now he could hear the man breathing.

The click as Mike unlocked the door sounded deafening to him. Just be quick, he thought, slipping into the corridor. A broad, expressionless face stared at him – not the reptile man, nobody he'd ever met before. There was no visible weapon; the man's hands were in his coat pockets. By the time he'd pulled them out Mike was already beside him, hitting the man with the hand holding the pistol, then again. The man shrank back with a whimper. Mike caught him when his knees gave way and shoved him towards the stairwell. The stench of sweat and frying oil assailed Mike's nose as he kept one hand over the wide-open mouth while the other pushed the back of the man's head. Mike saw tears in his eyes. Pressed closely together they stumbled to the door. Once inside the stairwell he pushed the man away, hit him again, then again and yet again.

The man collapsed, groaning.

As Mike was bent over him he felt a draught at his back. Within a split second arms were thrust around his chest like steel claws and a huge body was up against him. A voice in his ear whispered his name, then said, "You've got to get out of here, Mike."

He let the man pull him up.

The arms released him. "We'll look after this guy," the voice whispered. Mike turned around, looked at the reptile man and nodded.

"Is he alive?" asked Gretzki, who was standing in the doorway.

Blood from the split lip, from the broken nose, a dark-red pool beneath the head, the temples stained. Arms and legs twisted, no obvious signs of breathing.

The reptile man kneeled down and felt for a pulse. "Just about."

"Let's go, Mike," Gretzki said.

A quarter of an hour later he was back in his car. Brandenburgische Strasse, past the hotel, and after a few minutes he was sitting in Saturday-afternoon traffic on the city motorway. He'd thrown his things into the travel bag and left the hotel via the back entrance. Gretzki was going to dismantle the equipment, pay the bill and clean Esther's room tomorrow.

As he was leaving, Mike had taken one final look at the monitor. The light was off and Esther couldn't be seen.

"Don't forget," was Gretzki's parting shot, said with a smile. At first Mike didn't understand what he was getting at – Berlin, stress, Freiburg, the hills.

His mobile buzzed. Another text from Gretzki: *Hans Peter Steinhoff, Hamburg, freelance journalist. More soon.*

Mike didn't reply. He hadn't been expecting Steinhoff.

Everything seemed to be getting out of hand.

The radio tower – from the east this time – but he gave it a mere glance. Then he was on the motorway, crossing the Grunewald in dense traffic.

Steinhoff was alive and he would wake up in the lavatory on the third-floor corridor. If the police put the guest from room 35 on their wanted list they wouldn't get very far. The name was false, nobody had set eyes on him, and right now he was heading back into the darkness.

I

The Guardian Angel

1

The doorbell tore Louise Bonì from the dream that had haunted her every night since her return. Thirty-five jaded faces, seventy apathetic eyes, all gazing at her. She was standing by a green board, chalk in the white-dusted fingers of her right hand, staring at an oversized clock on the wall behind the police cadets, counting the seconds and dying of boredom. Nobody was saying a word, nobody was moving – hours passed like this. Wertheim in provincial Franconia had sneaked its way into her sub-conscious and refused to leave.

She threw back the duvet and sat up. It was 2.45 p.m., maybe Saturday, maybe Sunday already, but definitely November. Annaplatz was wreathed in mist, the church a dark shadow, and raindrops fell diagonally in the light of the streetlamps.

Since returning to Freiburg she'd been sleeping fifteen hours per day. Some days she found two editions of the *Badische Zeitung* outside her door. More than one dawn was followed immediately by dusk. Two months of boredom perverted the very course of time.

An attempt to make atonement. In summer, while on duty, she'd hit a rapist in custody. Rolf Bermann had talked her out of reporting herself – if found guilty she would have lost her job – and worked hard behind the scenes. In the end he'd been able to convince Marianne Andrele, the public prosecutor, and Reinhard Graeve, the Kripo head, that Louise hadn't been thinking straight due to exhaustion and shock. The compromise they reached was a few weeks' leave and Wertheim.

If she'd had an inkling that she might die of boredom in provincial

Franconia, she might have not let herself in for it. The weekends with Ben in Freiburg were her salvation.

She staggered into the hallway, wearing Ben's favourite T-shirt and shorts. On the floor were dust balls, shoes, clothes, newspapers, pizza boxes, and in the mirror she saw a ghost moving beneath a jungle of dark hair. A few months without the glaring neon-lit corridors of Kripo, stressed colleagues, everyday tension, and her entire life was in chaos.

The doorbell rang again, then a tentative voice from the past said over the intercom, "Louise? It's us."

Two short, bashful males, one now hanging around her neck, the other holding flowers and cakes, unsure where to put them.

"What about your mama?" Louise whispered.

"She's a little bit sick," her brother whispered back.

"She sends her regards," her father said.

"What's wrong with her?"

"Oh, just a cold."

"She's sad," her brother whispered.

"Women are sad sometimes," she whispered. "And now you get down."

The dark locks flew back and forth, the thin arms tightened their grip around her neck. "Not the sadness with blood."

"Louise, where . . .?"

She turned to her father. "In the kitchen."

Together they watched him, cheek to cheek, the big sister, the little brother whose name she still found it difficult to say out loud, even after two years. Like the dark locks and wary eyes, the name belonged to her other brother, her real one. Who'd died in a car accident in 1983 and who'd been replaced without much ado in 1996, insofar as that was possible with another woman.

Ever since, there had been two Germains – a dead and a living one, who couldn't help it that the first was dead. Or that it had taken their father seven years to tell Louise about his new family.

"Had you forgotten we were coming?" her father called out from the kitchen.

She didn't reply. Germain, who refused to let go, her father amidst the mess in her kitchen – all a bit much for these sluggish moments after waking up from her Wertheim dream.

Louise had a good yawn.

Noises were coming from the kitchen. Something rattled and was pushed across wood. Rustling. Cupboard doors closing, water running. Drawers opening, closing. A clearing of the throat, silence. Then water again and the amusing gurgle of the almost empty plastic bottle when you squeezed out the last of the washing-up liquid.

With a sigh she closed her eyes and pictured her father at the sink. He rolled up his sleeves fastidiously, then his small, flaccid hands plunged into the water. And this was only right, she thought; her father ought to atone too. For the rest of his life, if she had a say in it.

"Alright, then," she said, dragging the new Germain into the bathroom with her and shutting the door.

The flowers arranged in a vase on the dining table, a lit candle, the aroma of fresh café au lait. Plus half a dozen slices of cake and pastries, which looked as if they came from the French president's private confectioner. When it came to food and drink, the French element in her father, which he'd been trying to eliminate for forty years, still came to the fore. His accent was polished, his German smugness well honed, his French family ignored, and all this merely to forget the 1960s and '70s, the arguments with her mother, the failure of his life plan, and of course Germain's death a few years afterwards.

They ate in silence; it was becoming increasingly difficult to talk to her father. Some things couldn't be discussed in the presence of the new Germain – the fact that there'd been another Germain, his mother's sadness, but not the sadness when she bled – while other things weren't her father's business – Ben, *the problem*, Wertheim.

He meekly pointed his fork at a note beside the vase. "Are you flying to Berlin?"

She frowned and picked up the note. Words jotted down and flight info for Monday – tomorrow. From Karlsruhe/Baden-Baden to Berlin-Tegel. Vague memories formed in her mind. A call from Rolf Bermann one morning – perhaps *this* morning – a request from their colleagues in Berlin for help with an investigation. A trail that led to Freiburg.

"Looks like it."

"For work?"

She nodded.

"With your gun?" Germain asked.

"You're not allowed to take guns on aeroplanes," her father said.

"Louise is."

"No, I'm sure not even Louise is allowed to do that."

"The police can do anything."

"Not *any*thing, Germain."

"*Any*thing."

"Louise, would you please—"

"Do you have to arrest a killer in Berlin?"

"Germain . . ." Her father broke off. She saw resignation in his eyes and for a moment she almost felt sorry for him.

Then she couldn't resist a smile. It had taken him years to accept that she'd joined the police. One child dead, the other with Kripo – could there be anything worse for someone like him?

The fact that his new child was fascinated by the police.

Because Germain insisted on hearing it all in detail, she told him, to her father's visible chagrin.

No, she wasn't going to arrest a killer, but to talk to a man who'd been beaten up by another man in a Berlin hotel and threatened with a gun. Because this other man had registered at the hotel under a false name and nobody had seen him, her colleagues in Berlin were at a loss and—

"And because they don't know what to do they ring Louise," Germain said, raising his eyebrows in triumph.

"It won't be quite like that," her father said.

"It is."

"Well, they checked the other guests," Louise said, "and staying in the room outside which one man attacked the other one was a woman from Freiburg. But she's got no idea what was going on. And because the whole thing's rather strange and my colleagues don't know what to do, they get funny ideas . . ."

"And *that's* why they call Louise," her father muttered.

For a moment there was silence. Then Louise began to laugh and her two short men joined in.

They relaxed. Germain talked about school, her father about acquaintances in Kehl whose names and stories she immediately forgot. When Germain was in the bathroom, her father said quietly, "What about . . . the problem?"

That was the end of the relaxation.

"The problem?"

"You know, your problem with the um . . ."

Splaying her fingers defensively on the table, she said, "There isn't a problem."

"That's good to hear."

"There used to be one, but there isn't one anymore, OK?"

"Yes. That's . . . that's great."

"How's Karin?"

"Oh, she's got a really nasty cold."

"That's rubbish, Papa."

Her father gazed at her in surprise, then lowered his head and began pushing cake crumbs with his fork from the edge of the plate to the middle until he'd made a small brown pile. When there was nothing more to push he looked up. "Would you like another café au lait?"

"Is she cheating on you?"

"*No*, Louise!" He got up quickly and held out his hand.

She let him stand like that for a moment before passing him her cup.

"What does your new boyfriend do?"

"Have I got a new boyfriend?"

"I thought . . . Didn't you mention someone called Ben Liebermann recently?"

"That's old news, he's been on the scene almost a year."

"*That* long?" Her father forced a smile which seemed affectionate and desperate in equal measure. "Your mother will have met him, then." Without waiting for an answer he went back into the kitchen.

Yes, Ben and she had gone to Provence for a week in August. Wonderful days with Ben, rough days with her mother, who also had problems with police officers, albeit for different reasons than her father. In the 1960s and '70s "the state" had been the worst of enemies as far as she was concerned, and the wars of the past were not easily forgotten. Because Ben had left the force voluntarily in 2004, in the end she was prepared to give him a chance. But she would have preferred an incensed ATTAC official, a disillusioned social worker or an honourable failure of an existentialist bicycle courier to a former Kripo officer.

In the bathroom the flushing of the loo, in the kitchen the buzzing of the milk frother. Then her father was back, cup in hand. "I thought we might meet him today."

"He's not in Freiburg right now."

"Where then?"

She didn't reply.

He put the cup in front of her and sat down. "You look tired."

"And you look unhappy."

"No, no, Louise, it's just . . . You know, the age difference, thirty-four years, you've got to understand that people have different interests and needs."

"Kick her out if she cheats on you."

"Kick her . . .?" He didn't finish his sentence. They looked at each other in silence, and for a moment Louise felt a connection. Father and daughter, both – if her hunch was correct – with unfaithful spouses, and in the end both humiliated fools.

She cleared her throat. Time for a few frank words between fellow dupes.

But her father put a finger to his lips: Germain was coming back.

"Who's that man in the loo?" Germain climbed onto his chair and sat on it cross-legged. "In the photo."

"A . . . a friend of Louise's," her father replied.

"He looks like me."

"No, Germain, that's just your imagination. Do you want another hot chocolate?"

"But he *does* look like me."

Her father reached for Germain's mug. "I'll make you another one, OK?"

"What's the man in the loo called?"

Her father froze, returning her gaze, panic in his eyes. Tell him, Papa, she thought, or I'll do it. Not a friend, but a dead man.

"Err . . . Klaus," he replied. "Isn't it, Louise?"

"That's funny," Germain said. "Like Mama's friend."

Louise sighed. Nothing had changed. Just like herself and the dead Germain, the new brother was growing up with secrets and lies. With a fake story.

And, as in the past, she sensed she couldn't tolerate it.

*

At around five o'clock her father and brother put on identical green anoraks and identical blue woolly hats. Whereas one of them already had his hand on the doorknob, the other had his arms around her neck again, pressing his cheek to hers.

"Can I sleep at yours tonight?" he whispered.

"No," she whispered.

"Why?"

"I've got to go to Berlin tomorrow, remember?"

"Can I sleep at yours tomorrow, then?"

"No, but soon. OK?"

His locks flew in every direction. "Tomorrow or today."

"That doesn't work."

"You could look after me once in a while."

Louise said nothing. Words she fancied she'd heard for years in her father's reproachful silence, especially after Germain's death.

She put the new brother down and kissed him as affectionately as she could on the cheek. "Sometime, but not now."

Then the two of them had gone, whereas the secrets and lies, and all the conflicting feelings that these had a habit of unleashing within her, would remain a while longer.

Louise went back to the sitting room. Cleared and wiped the table, washed the plates and cutlery, leaving only the flowers as a reminder of her old and new relatives from Kehl. She sat on the sofa. As ever in moments like this she felt the urge to pour herself a glass or two. Drink away the past, just as her over-fussy father seemed to wipe it away with a damp kitchen cloth.

The latter might work, the former wouldn't.

At half past six Rolf Bermann called and asked how the afternoon with the "Kehl crew" had been. She replied it was just how you'd imagine an afternoon with people from Kehl: slightly dull.

He laughed. In the background children were yelling – the

Bermanns had ended up with five of them – dogs were barking – two – and television voices were blaring away – at least four. An idyllic Sunday at the Bermanns'.

"Quiet, the lot of you, I'm on the phone!" Bermann boomed.

Louise went over to the balcony door and tried to look past her reflection into the misty darkness, but only saw herself, the reflection of the lights in the sitting room and the streetlamps.

The children and dogs had fallen silent.

"I was on the phone to Berlin earlier," Bermann said. "The colleague looking after the case is called Rohwe. You'll like him, he has hunches."

"What's he saying?"

"'I've got a funny feeling somehow,'" Bermann said in a thick Berlin accent.

"Anything more specific?"

"'A kind of hunch, you *know*? I've got a kind of hunch.'" Bermann gave a contented laugh. On his lovingly curated list of people he couldn't stand, Swabians were in the top spot, followed by homosexuals, headstrong women, intellectuals and psychologists. In seventh or eighth place, above politicians and Islamists, were Berliners. First place on the list of things he liked was shared by children and compliant women, and in third place was whatever new car he'd just acquired.

That, at any rate, was how Bermann's official behaviour could be classified. Unofficially things looked different, but because there were at most five minutes per week when he didn't have his unofficial dark recesses under control, this was irrelevant. In any case the contradictions would have been hard to put up with, for him and for everyone else – since she'd stopped drinking and now looked attractive again, Louise was close to the top of *both* lists.

"You *know*?" Bermann said fervently, still in his ham Berlin accent.

"That's why you're sending *me*," she said, "because of the hunches."

"Got it in one."

She'd wandered over to switch off the lamp and now went back to the balcony door in the dark. Outside, the mist enveloping the streetlamps was almost white, it was drizzling, and in some window on the other side of the square she could make out the first Christmas decorations shining a golden-yellow colour. She was looking forward to returning to Kripo life in a few hours, albeit via the Berlin detour. The boredom at Wertheim police academy, the visit from relatives, the racket of Bermann family life and now also the reminder that Christmas was around the corner – too much idleness for her taste.

"Everything just the same, eh?"

Bermann laughed. "I'm too old to change."

"Thank God," Louise replied and hung up.

2

Rain and grey skies in Berlin too, with a sharp wind to boot, driving the droplets beneath the canopy covering the entrances to Tegel. Boni hurried alongside Eberhardt Rohwe – mid-thirties, detective chief inspector at police HQ 2 – to the car park in the centre of the ring of buildings, feeling tiny; Rohwe had to be at least two metres tall.

He pointed to a black car and held the door open for her. As she put on her belt he said, "Coffee at the station, crime scene or straight to the hospital?"

"Crime scene, hospital and then coffee at the station."

Rohwe nodded, started the engine and drove off. He wasn't a handsome man but she liked his eyes, his clear, intelligent look that made you realise a mass of serious thoughts were swirling in that brain of his.

And she liked his uncompromising Berlin vernacular.

"Been here before?"

"One or twice for a couple of days. And on a school trip, of course, in the late seventies."

"With the obligatory visit to the other side."

"A few hours in Alexanderplatz."

Rohwe chuckled. He was ducking to avoid hitting his head. His hair was barely longer than his stubble and there were lots of moles on his cheeks damp from the rain. "Is there anyone in this country who didn't go on a school trip to Berlin?"

She shrugged. "State education policy."

"What do you remember about it?"

"Do you really want to know?"

"Too much booze?"

They'd left the airport and were now on the city motorway. The grey of the sky seemed to match the grey of the road and of the capital as a whole. She thought that winter in Berlin must be unbearable – the cold, the wind and all colours anaemic, without lustre. Not her sort of city.

"Wrong topic," she said to Rohwe.

"Berlin or too much booze?"

"Alcohol."

"No beer at the station, then."

"I haven't touched a drop in two and a half years, it's going to stay that way and we're not going to say any more about it. Put some music on, Eberhardt."

"Not Eberhardt, please. Only my ex-wives call me that."

"What, then?"

He switched on the CD player and turned down the volume. Element of Crime, one of their German albums: *Die schönen Rosen*. Ben's favourite band and favourite album. "Rowi or Ebbe."

"OK, Ebbe then."

"Shall I tell you about Saturday or do you want to see the crime scene first?"

"First I want to answer your question. About what I remember."

Rohwe shot her a glance. "I'm prepared for anything."

"Sex in a museum loo."

He laughed. "I understand – state education policy. Which museum?"

"I've forgotten. Now you can talk. I particularly want to hear about your hunches – I'm into hunches."

She knew most of it already from Rolf Bermann, although now Rohwe was talking about two suspects and an attempted murder. Hans Peter

Steinhoff, the victim, could only recall *one* man – a man who'd come out of room 35, attacked him for no reason and threatened him with a pistol. But in the pool of blood in the stairwell, where Steinhoff had lost consciousness, forensics had found traces of shoeprints, and in the toilet cubicle, where he'd come round, others that weren't identical to the first lot. For one thing the patterns of the soles didn't match, but also the substance was different – not blood this time, but remnants of wet dogshit. As Steinhoff was alone when he regained consciousness, the prints couldn't have been from some random helper. It couldn't have been someone going to the toilet either because the prints were too obviously concentrated around the spot where Steinhoff had been lying. They'd been wondering, of course, Rohwe said, why only one of the suspects had attacked Steinhoff if two had been present.

"Well? Any ideas?"

He shook his head. "Nothing conclusive. All we know is that the second person came via the stairs, as there were traces of shit on the carpet."

"If Steinhoff didn't see him, he must have turned up later than the other guy."

"Correct. Maybe even after the first man had left."

"What's the name of the guy from room 35?"

"Friedrich Müller. According to his ID Müller lives in Dortmund. And indeed there is a man of that name who lives in the street he gave as his address. But the man can prove he wasn't in Berlin that weekend. He's a bus driver and was working on the Saturday."

"False name, false ID," Louise said.

"Yes."

They left the motorway at Kaiserdamm, headed towards MITTE / BRANDENBURG / REICHSTAG, then turned off to the south. City motorway, Damm, Chaussee – as if this city were trying to demonstrate at every moment how large, important and confusing it was. Certainly

41

not a city for her; she needed brightness, the sun and clarity. From any point in Freiburg you could see the hills to the north, east or south, and you knew that whichever direction you drove in you could be out of the city in ten minutes if need be. Ten minutes here merely got you through three sets of traffic lights and you were still surrounded by concrete and masses of people.

If Ben moved to Berlin in the spring he'd have to go without her. People can't live off affection and bread alone, especially not Freiburgers. She definitely needed a few hills around her, even if she didn't climb them but just enjoyed the view from time to time.

She gathered together the hair at the back of her neck and tied it with a band. "Was Steinhoff staying at the hotel?"

"No, he was looking for the bathroom."

"On the third floor?"

"The one downstairs was occupied."

"Hmm. I would have waited until it was free."

"Maybe he's got prostate issues."

She smiled. "Anything stolen?"

"Wallet, mobile."

"So the fake Friedrich Müller beats up Steinhoff, the second man finds him, drags him into the toilet and robs him? Unlikely."

"This is Berlin," Rohwe said.

"That's hard to forget. But this isn't just an attempted murder and theft."

"No?"

"You wouldn't have called for me otherwise."

Rohwe didn't contradict her.

"Which finally brings us to your hunches, doesn't it?"

"Not yet. Only to a rumour."

From some pocket in Rohwe's light-blue denim jacket, Queen's "We Will Rock You" suddenly blared out. He frowned, pursed his lips and made no move to answer it.

When the mobile fell silent Louise said, "What sort of rumour?"

"That Steinhoff does the occasional bit of work for foreign intelligence."

Hans Peter Steinhoff was one of those reporters whose name had briefly been mentioned in connection with the BND's journalist scandal. In 1993, foreign intelligence began monitoring writers who were critical of the service, and also recruiting informers to gather information on colleagues as well as BND intelligence officers. Supposedly this was the service's way of finding out which internal sources had been leaking insider information to journalists. One of these informers, it was claimed, had been Hans Peter Steinhoff.

"What's that all about again?"

Rohwe looked at her in amazement. She shrugged. This summer, two months' teaching at the academy in Wertheim, almost paralysed by boredom. It was inconceivable that she'd buy newspapers, let alone read them, and who could bear listening to Franconian voices reading the radio news?

He grinned. "Supposedly the BND's plutonium affair. Back in the nineties, remember?"

"Vaguely. Was Steinhoff involved at the time?"

"We don't know."

Leaning back in her seat she looked out of the window. Attempted murder of a former BND informer, investigations in Berlin – this wasn't how she'd envisioned her return to work. "Have you spoken to him?"

"Yes."

"And asked him about the BND thing?"

"Yes. He's refusing to comment on it."

"And you just left it at that?"

"Correct. I always behave properly, at least when I'm on duty."

"I don't, especially when I'm on duty."

"I know, your reputation precedes you." That case with the terrorist hunters a few years ago, Rohwe said, got his Berlin colleagues very excited for a while. A female police officer from the provinces actually trying to apprehend a handful of trained Islamist killers! Marching up a mountain on her own and putting a pistol to the commander's head! Getting knifed in the stomach and surviving! "You've got a fan club here."

"My picture as desktop wallpaper, that sort of thing?"

"We've had stickers made."

They laughed.

"So you know about the alcoholism too?"

Rohwe stopped outside a hotel and switched off the engine, but didn't get out. His clear eyes were fixed on her. "Unofficially."

"So you wanted to know officially."

"I don't pay much attention to rumours, especially not when they're about colleagues."

"*Very* proper indeed."

He raised an eyebrow. "Back to Steinhoff. He's not cooperating. He's pressed charges but he's not saying more than the bare minimum. He must have been in panic at the beginning, but when I spoke to him there wasn't any sign of that. No, he was . . ." Rohwe hesitated, "monosyllabic."

"We'll see. Baden charm can move mountains."

A hint of sternness flashed in Rohwe's eyes. "Just don't get me into trouble, OK? I've got children, two ex-wives and expensive hobbies."

"Hospitals have canteens. You go and have a coffee while I talk to Steinhoff."

He shook his head. "Forget it."

"If only it were that simple."

"It is, Louise. This is our city, you're our guest and you're going to play by our rules."

"Sounds like a threat."

They laughed again, but Rohwe's eyes remained stern.

"'Guest' isn't quite right. You requested me here."

"Well," Rohwe said slowly.

"Well?"

An unpleasant suspicion took root in her, and Rohwe confirmed it. Rolf Bermann had thought it a good idea for "our colleague Boni" to take an excursion to Berlin "if you're alright with that". Everyday life in Freiburg was really depressing for such an energetic investigator as her; a trip to the capital would be just the ticket in late-autumnal provincial Germany, where nothing happened. A smile darted across Rohwe's face. On the phone, in-between various instructions to the kitchen – "I want the egg cooked for exactly three minutes, please, darling", "Double espresso today, please, darling" – Rolf Bermann had gone beyond the remit for assistance with the investigation by saying that Freiburg would interview the victim in Berlin. "'You'll be delighted I'm sending you the best person,' he said."

Louise shook her head in disbelief. Bermann's games were getting stranger and stranger.

Once again "We Will Rock You" sounded from the depths of Rohwe's clothing; once again he ignored it.

"Persistent girlfriend?"

"Let's move on . . . What else do you want to know?"

"What did the witness from Freiburg see or hear?"

Rohwe rocked his head from side to side. Esther Graf didn't have much to say either. She was woken by a "commotion", heard some footsteps and sounds coming from the neighbouring room, then she lay down again. The patrol units, who were the first on the scene, asked her about Steinhoff, as did the Kripo officers who turned up later. But she didn't know him. Rohwe himself hadn't questioned her. When he took over on Sunday afternoon she was already back in Freiburg.

He put a hand to his mouth and cleared his throat. So, what they had was a case of attempted murder, two suspects nobody had seen, a victim who was reluctant to talk, and a witness who hadn't seen anything and not heard very much. All this, combined with the rumour about Steinhoff, was obviously cause for suspicion. "Which brings me to my hunches. Any experience with the BND?"

"Not much. Sometimes they help out, sometimes they obstruct."

Of course Berlin Kripo occasionally had contact with the BND, Rohwe said. Thousands of politicians, diplomats, secret service agents, the hooligan problem, quite apart from the fact that Berlin was one of the major centres of organised crime besides London and New York . . .

"Keep it short, Ebbe."

He paused. "Since I found out that Steinhoff might be working for foreign intelligence, I've been expecting my boss to call me off at any moment. You know, bury the case."

It took a moment for the penny to drop. "Those calls," Bonì said.

Rohwe gave a grim smile. "He's a big Queen fan."

"Christ! What are we waiting for?"

Louise got out, hurried across the pavement in the pouring rain and entered the hotel. A different city, the same game. Some government agency pulled the strings, someone was swayed, and the case was no longer a case.

She stopped in the lobby. To the left was the reception, to the right double doors, open, that led to the bar. She couldn't see anyone in there. In the background the drone of unbearable German pop – and suddenly a squawked "We Will Rock You".

"Louise," Rohwe said behind her. He had the singing telephone in his hand. "I have to answer this. If there's anything else you want to know, ask now."

"Which room numbers?"

"The woman in 34, the suspect in 35."

"Are the rooms still cordoned off?"

"No, but they're not going to be available to guests until tomorrow."

"Will I get the forensics report?"

"When you're back in Freiburg."

She rolled her eyes. Rohwe just shrugged.

"Which hospital is Steinhoff in?"

"Martin Luther hospital in Caspar-Theyss-Strasse. If you, erm, urgently need to see a doctor, take a taxi. It isn't far."

"What do you know about the weapon?"

"Nothing. No idea if it was real gun or a blank."

Rohwe put the mobile to his ear. The conversation was brief and one-sided; he barely uttered a word. As he slipped the phone back into his pocket he nodded. "Arson in Schmargendorf. Nice to have met you." There was regret in his eyes.

Louise swallowed her anger and took his outstretched hand.

"I need to keep your boss posted. What should I tell him?"

"That I'll take a look around Alexanderplatz and wallow in my memories."

Rohwe smiled then left, a scrawny, hunched man two metres tall who couldn't do what he wanted, and accepted this too willingly for her liking. All the same she suddenly felt the urge to go after him and beg him not to leave her alone. We don't have to go up to the third floor, we could have a coffee in the bar, chat for a few minutes longer . . .

She stared stiffly at the glass entrance door that was just closing. The urge became ever more pressing; she felt a tightness in her chest and fear in her head. Louise laughed out loud in anger. She knew this feeling, she thought she'd got over it. It was from those pre-Jägermeister days, pre-marriage days, from her wild Stone Age when vast oceans of apathy would sometimes fill her entire body.

She took a deep breath. Stay calm, Bonì.

Move, Bonì.

She went over to the reception. Amongst the keys hanging from hooks behind the counter were those to rooms 34 and 35. She'd been looking forward to returning to work, being in a team, getting stuck into puzzles, working fourteen-hour days with colleagues. And now this. As so often she'd been outmanoeuvred and now she was alone. Worse still: in this huge, depressing city.

Louise grabbed the keys, hurried to the stairs and took two at a time. Her legs were slightly unsteady and her temples throbbed. Quite clearly the demons hadn't been driven away and were still lurking inside her, waiting for the right opportunity.

Yes, she thought, there is a problem, Papa – it hasn't been solved for good yet.

She felt better when she was standing in the third-floor corridor. Anger, action and determination had often helped in the past too.

And an investigation, of course.

A Hamburg journalist, who possibly worked for the BND, had been threatened with a weapon and beaten up, but didn't want to cooperate. The suspect had booked into the hotel under a false name. A second person had appeared on the scene and dragged the victim from the stairs to the toilet. A witness had heard something, but hadn't seen anything. A chief of police had taken a phone call and moved his investigator to a different case. Too many strange circumstances, considering not very much had actually happened.

She groaned. Nothing concrete and yet thousands of loose ends. Not to mention the fact that she was poaching on unfamiliar territory and that there was no case.

In room 35, a wardrobe, a bed, a desk with a television set. One wood-panelled wall, a water stain on the carpet outside the bathroom. A hotel room like so many others: anonymous, random, unlovingly furnished.

Room 34 was the mirror image and equally depressing.

The stairs again, then the toilets. The pungent smell of detergent everywhere. The blood and shoeprints had been cleaned up. She knew she wouldn't make any progress here. First forensics, then the chambermaids. If one lot had missed something, the others would have found it.

She kept going down the corridor and turned the corner. Eight more rooms. According to Rohwe, six of them were booked on Saturday afternoon, but the guests weren't in the hotel. The two rooms opposite 34 and 35 were empty.

Bonì returned to where the attack had taken place. Four people involved: one victim, two suspects, one witness.

And maybe the BND.

The suspects had vanished, she wouldn't be able to question foreign intelligence. Which left the victim and the witness.

And the anxiety, somewhere deep in her bowels.

Downstairs the old hits were still playing, but no employees – a hotel without staff and without guests. Only the ghosts of Roland Kaiser or Roberto Bianco, or whatever those crooners were called.

She put the keys back on the hooks. On the way out her mobile rang. "No playing silly buggers, alright?" Bermann said without a greeting.

A day of strict bosses.

For a moment she was on the verge of hurling abuse at him down the phone. On her very first day of work after three months he'd got her out of the way and sent her packing to Berlin . . .

But it was good to hear his voice.

"You're interrupting my work, Rolf."

"Go to the Turkish market on Maybach-Ufer."

"And do what?"

"Buy salad, buy neck scarfs, eat a doner. Do things normal women do. Then go to the airport and buy some make-up."

"Have the BND called you?"

"No, just my Berlin colleague, you *know*?"

She was still in the foyer, listening to the sound of his voice. Bermann was a reliable yardstick for her state of mind. The worse she felt, the more welcome he was.

Movement on the other side of the glass door made her look up. A woman and a man entered the hotel. The woman took off her glasses and dried them with a tissue. The man glanced at Louise.

"So, no silly buggers, OK?"

"Coming from you," she said, hanging up. As she walked past the woman and man, he briefly looked at her again.

She stood outside the hotel and waited. After twenty years with the police you could recognise colleagues.

Ten seconds or so passed; neither of them emerged.

3

On the way to the hospital she picked up the loose ends again. Only one thing seemed to be clear: Hans Peter Steinhoff was at the centre of it all.

And her fellow officers? Eberhardt Rohwe is taken off the case, then an hour later two investigators turn up. But from which agency?

"Visiting a patient?" said the taxi driver, a small old man with tufts of white hair sprouting from his ears.

"Yes, sort of."

"A relative?"

"No."

"Bad?"

"Not yet."

"Let's hope for the best."

"For me?"

"For the patient."

"I'll pass that on."

She took her mobile from the pocket of her anorak. Nothing from Ben. He'd been in Sarajevo for a week and they'd last spoken the day before yesterday – both of these seemed an eternity ago. A visit to his past, and probably also an attempt to shake off the frustration of Freiburg. For the first four months he'd worked as a night watchman at a little-used car park in St Georgen, and he'd been unemployed ever since. The Baden-Württemberg police wouldn't open their doors to him again and he wasn't interested in working as a security guard for a supermarket chain or as a bouncer at a disco in Karlsruhe.

Then, in October, the enquiry from Potsdam had come via a former colleague: an administrative job with the federal border force, which a few months earlier had been renamed the "federal police". Department 4, "International affairs, European cooperation" – Ben's specialist area. Desk work for a year or two, then see what might happen. Why not go back to Bosnia–Herzegovina as part of the European Union Police Mission? The State Investigation and Protection Agency was still far from being able to stand on its own two feet.

Sarajevo – great, she said.

We'll see, Ben said.

Don't imagine for a moment that I'll accompany you and fill my days hanging around with the other appendages.

What about Berlin?

I'd have to check it out first.

Now she had checked it out, and she knew she wouldn't go with him to either Sarajevo or Berlin. A long-distance relationship was looming. But maybe that wouldn't be such a bad thing. Distance prevented you from getting lost in excessive intimacy. Which was a danger in her relationship with Ben; she'd got very used to having him around.

The taxi driver stopped. "Ten euros thirty."

"Eleven."

"Receipt?"

"No, thanks."

She placed two banknotes in his shaky, hairy hand and he gave her change.

"Bye-bye, then."

Bonì got out and followed the taxi with her eyes. Through the side window she could see only the top half of the driver's head and his hands. A bizarre sight in a bizarre city.

She turned towards the entrance to the hospital. Officially Kripo was off the case, but some authority was still investigating it. There was one positive aspect about this whole affair, though, she thought: the good guys were represented in abundance.

Then things became even more mystifying: Hans Peter Steinhoff had discharged himself early that morning, against the advice of the doctor.

Two nurses could tell her no more than this, then a junior doctor said that Steinhoff had left on his own; nobody had come to pick him up. Allowing himself to be buttered up by Baden charm, the doctor showed Louise the medical file. A laceration to the back of the head, a broken nose, two teeth knocked out, bruises all over the left side of the face. Admitted unconscious, woke up on Sunday morning. He wasn't in a critical condition, but they wouldn't have discharged him before the beginning of next week.

The night sister on the ward had gone home in the morning. Louise asked the junior doctor for her phone number. He shook his head and told her to see the medical director, the head of nursing or the chief executive.

Louise began her search with a sigh.

But she had no luck. The director was on holiday, the head of nursing in a staff meeting and the CEO was having lunch out.

This city and her – they didn't get on.

When she was outside she called Rohwe. "It's getting stranger and stranger, Ebbe."

He sighed.

She told him about the investigators at the hotel and about Steinhoff. When Rohwe said nothing she leaned against one of the narrow columns by the entrance and waited in silence.

Puddles on the pavement reflected the white building. Raindrops distorted the image.

Say something, Ebbe.

"Hmm," Ebbe said. "Steinhoff called earlier."

"What, he called you?"

"No, the station. I . . . um . . . I wasn't there."

She snorted. The Berliners listened to their bosses – the case had been buried.

"And? Did your colleague say what Steinhoff wanted?"

Rohwe laughed uneasily. "He didn't fully understand him."

"I might have known. What did he understand, then?"

"Apparently Steinhoff wanted to withdraw the charge."

"He can't do that." Attempted murder was a crime that had to be prosecuted by law. At any rate Kripo should have continued the investigation and called in the public prosecutor.

"I expect he doesn't know that."

"Or your colleague misunderstood him."

"We're assuming it's the latter."

"So you're going to clear that up when Steinhoff calls back?"

"Exactly."

"And until then you'll be dealing with the arson attack in Schnackendorf."

Silence.

"Is that why you joined Kripo? To look away?"

He cleared his throat. She was expecting a protest or some unintelligible Berlin curse, but nothing of the sort happened. All he said was "Schmargendorf".

The rain had grown heavier. She peeled away from the column and moved further into the shelter of the canopy.

Say something, Ebbe.

"Let's say . . ." Ebbe said, then broke off. His voice sounded distant but not unfriendly. She could clearly sense his dilemma: play along or hang up?

"Let's say *what*?"

"That you're not focusing on the key question."

"Which is?"

"Why Steinhoff was in the hotel."

He was right. Twelve rooms on the third floor, eight of them booked. But there were guests in only two of the rooms on Saturday afternoon: Esther Graf in 34, the suspect in 35. What if Steinhoff wasn't the central figure in all this, but Graf? Or the man from room 35? If that's why Steinhoff was in the hotel?

"Do we really know nothing about the guy in room 35?"

"We?"

"Alright, then – *you*."

"No, nothing."

"Come on, Ebbe. You must have something."

Rohwe took a deep breath. "Give me five minutes."

He called back less than four minutes later. His voice was almost drowned out by the noise of the traffic; he was standing outside. If what he was doing wasn't proper, she thought, then at least he wasn't being improper in the hallowed halls.

The first details about room 35 had come in from forensics around lunchtime. "No fingerprints, not on the door handles, the bathroom fittings, the flush plate or the loo seat."

"The chambermaids did a thorough job."

"And wiped the door handles?"

"I mean, we *are* in Berlin. Everything's possible here, isn't it?"

Rohwe didn't laugh. "False ID, no fingerprints . . . The room was cleaned professionally."

"That's a bit fanciful."

"We didn't find any fibres, hair or skin particles either. Not on the pillows, sheets or duvet. *None*, Louise. The room was cleaned. The question is, by whom? The suspect himself, after beating up Steinhoff? He wouldn't have taken the time to do it. By the second man, then. He gets the victim out of the way then he removes all the traces from room 35."

"OK, so we can assume we're dealing with professionals."

"We?"

"You."

"No," Rohwe said. "Not we. You – on your own."

Four hours till her flight. Enough time for MITTE / BRANDENBURGER TOR / REICHSTAG. But Louise and sightseeing didn't get on, especially not in this city that could only offer concrete and clouds. So she took the bus to Tegel, grabbed a curry sausage with chips, then a latte macchiato, and afterwards wandered three times through the terminal, thinking to herself. Wertheim, the relatives from Kehl, the uncertain future. The big picture.

There was no doubt her life had improved since her treatment for addiction in Oberberg and her withdrawal at the Kanzan-an more than two and a half years ago, but something wasn't quite right; something was missing. She'd thought she would be stable by now, but that was clearly a misapprehension. There was nothing in her life apart from work, as well as Ben for the past year. Hardly any friends, no desire for a holiday, no passions. No goals, no prospects. Like her mother at seventy, Louise was still waging war on all fronts, as if she could sense her existence only in the act of resistance. No pausing, no relaxing.

No, something wasn't right.

Maybe, she thought when she was finally sitting at the gate, the decision to marry Mick, the booze, the self-sacrifice at work, the constant battle against everything and everyone were merely attempts to run away – from whatever it was.

Herself, probably.

She landed in Karlsruhe/Baden-Baden at around seven in the evening. No more November rain, no mist; instead it was surprisingly mild and all traces of anxiety and doubt had gone. In good spirits she fetched her car key from the police office at the airport. A few unstable hours in Berlin . . . that could happen, don't blow it out of proportion. She was a southerner – in the north, body and soul got out of step.

But it was better to stay on your guard. Maybe it was time for another coffee with Katrin Rein, her favourite blonde psychologist.

Bermann rang as soon as she got into her car.

"Where are you?"

"In Karlsruhe."

She heard a satisfied muttering. No extra day in Berlin, no bosses annoyed, no complaints from the capital in the offing.

"How was the Turkish market?"

"Wonderful, thanks for the tip."

"I knew you'd like it. Buy anything?"

"Bagsful. Blue neck scarves, red neck scarves, heart pendants, cuddly toys, that sort of thing."

"You must show me sometime."

"Tomorrow, if you like."

"Good girl."

She laughed reluctantly. Perhaps this was Bermann's new strategy: no longer getting worked up.

"We've got a burglary for you."

"How lovely."

"A villa in Günterstal, you know your way around there." She heard him chuckle. In 2003 the Asile d'enfants case had taken her to Günterstal, to Richard Landen. She was attached to Landen for a while – a year and a half, to be precise. She still wasn't sure what Bermann hadn't liked about this – the fact that Landen was an intellectual or that she'd fallen for him.

"I'm going to talk to Esther Graf tomorrow, Rolf."

"Esther who?"

"Esther Graf. The witness."

She switched on the ignition and put her mobile in the speaker cradle. "Just to close the case. Esther Graf is in Freiburg."

"Speak up, I can't understand what you're saying."

She didn't respond.

"What witness?"

"See you tomorrow, Rolf."

"Half seven, bright-eyed and bushy-tailed."

"Don't forget to bring your second along."

Another chuckle. There was no doubt that someone had missed her.

An hour or so later she entered her apartment. No messages on the answerphone, and the two rooms were emptier than usual. Sometimes Ben was there when she came home from work, reading the paper, a book, or checking out job advertisements online. As he cooked he would say things like, "I went for a walk by Lake Constance today" or "I was in Gérardmer watching your uncle drinking absinthe". Occasionally he would let slip a "darling" or "sweetheart" and the two of them would laugh in surprise.

She sat on the sofa and ate the two slices of cake left over from the day before. Twinkling behind all those unanswered questions about Berlin was one thought she still couldn't grasp. Only when she put the plate in the shiny sink did she put her finger on it. Not a thought, but another question: When had rooms 34 and 35 been booked?

Louise started her laptop and looked up the hotel's telephone number. It rang nine times before she heard a half-hearted male voice. Not a Berliner this time, but a Bavarian. He muttered and grumbled for several minutes before the Baden charm triumphed. Maybe a wheat beer had just gone flat.

What the Bavarian told her from the booking software made all the trouble worthwhile. Esther Graf had booked by e-mail on October 20. Room 35 had been reserved two days later. A note on the booking said that Friedrich Müller had specifically requested that room and would not be put in another.

A regular guest?

No. It was his first stay.

She hung up.

Why had the unknown man asked for room 35? She could only think of one answer: to be beside Esther Graf.

She checked the time. Just after nine – early enough to pay a visit to a witness who claimed not to have seen anything and to have heard very little.

At least when she was interviewed in a very proper way.

4

Esther Graf lived in Littenweiler, on the eastern outskirts of Freiburg. From the B31 Louise followed a road up the hill that seemed to lead straight into the forest, but curved sharply just before. Beyond the bend she noticed steps; ten metres above the road stood a small house. She parked the car and briefly indulged in some memories. Kirchzarten was less than five kilometres from here, and not much further to the south was the Grosse Tal, from where she and Thomas Ilic had climbed the face of the Rappeneck in that hot summer of 2003. It had begun with a small barn on fire and finished with several people losing their lives.

And Illi so traumatised that he was on sick leave for several months, and now had taken early retirement.

Another friend and ally gone.

Many old colleagues had left, many new ones had arrived and this was the nub of the problem. She was finding it increasingly difficult to get used to the new ones.

Boni got out. Lights were on in the house, all the windows lit up. The steps were slippery; climbing them carefully in the dim glow of a distant streetlamp, she recapped what she knew about Esther Graf.

Not much.

At the top of the steps a paved path led to the house. Beside the door was a yellow umbrella; only the surname was on the bell. She rang, heard footsteps on the other side of the door, followed by an anxious-sounding woman's voice.

Boni said her piece.

The door opened and a dark-blonde woman appeared. Early thirties, hair tied back, slim, one metre sixty to sixty-five, a face that was very pretty but looked pale and exhausted.

One glance at those lifeless eyes in their dark cavities was enough. Louise knew that a lot of things here weren't right, something was missing.

She entered the hallway. After Esther Graf had closed the front door, she said, "What do you want?"

"I'd like to sit down and have a chat with you."

"Is this about Berlin?"

"Yes."

"But I've already told your colleagues—"

"I know."

They sized each other up in silence. One of them was waiting for questions, the other to be taken into the sitting room. Louise suppressed a smile. Stalemate.

The hallway was narrow, the ceiling low, and it smelled of hot oven and burnt dough. One door led to the kitchen, the other to a room – both were open. From a row of hooks hung blazers, two or three coats and scarves, all chucked on top of each other. Beneath these lay a muddle of shoes, and on one of the stairs that led to the upper floor a pile of dirty washing.

"I'm not . . . prepared for visitors."

"That's OK. My place doesn't look much different."

"I don't think I can help you further."

"It'll only take a few minutes. May I?" Louise said, hanging her anorak on top of a dark-blue coat.

Esther Graf sighed. "Alright, then. Follow me."

The sitting room was like a dark cavern, a claustrophobe's nightmare. Black-brown bookshelves lined two walls and the rest of the furniture was in a similar colour. Mahogany, but probably this was just the paint; the stuff looked as if it came from IKEA. Hanging in front of the two windows were red-blue patterned curtains screening the room from prying eyes.

Esther pointed to a chair and sat on the sofa. Between them, like a sort of barrier, stood a coffee table with the leftovers from supper: red plastic mat, a plate with the crusts of a frozen pizza, a half-filled glass of red wine, a crumpled cloth napkin and a remote control. Esther picked it up, switched off the muted television and asked again, "What would you like to know?"

"Basically the same as my colleagues in Berlin."

"But surely there must be—"

"A report? There is." Louise smiled.

Esther looked at the remote control in her hand and, abandoning her resistance, told Louise what she already knew, nothing more, nothing less.

"What precisely do you mean by 'commotion'?"

"It sounded like a tussle. Punches, groans, stifled cries. Rapid footsteps."

Louise nodded.

"Later there were normal footsteps. Somebody in the room next to mine."

"How much later?"

"I don't know, I went back to bed a few minutes afterwards."

"So you heard sounds from the room next door?"

"Yes."

"What sort of sounds?"

"Nothing unusual. The sorts of sounds you'd hear in any hotel room. Then the room being hoovered."

Louise thought of what Eberhardt Rohwe had surmised: hoovered, cleaned – professionals.

"Were you afraid?"

"Yes."

"Why didn't you notify anyone? Hotel staff, police?"

Esther shrugged. "I didn't want to get involved. I mean, I didn't know what was happening."

"Do you know now?"

"No, I . . . not exactly. A man was beaten up, wasn't he?"

"You could put it that way."

"What are you calling it?"

"Attempted murder."

"Attempted . . ." Esther broke off.

"Did you notice anything else? Before or afterwards?"

"No."

Saw nothing, heard barely anything. Louise believed Esther Graf and this wasn't like her.

She got up, went to the dining table and leaned against it. The cluttered walls and low ceilings were like a closed shell around the room, which seemed almost like a prison.

Esther appeared to be comfortable in her prison.

"Did the commotion in the corridor wake you up?"

Esther wasn't sure. There was also, she said, a muffled knocking or hammering coming from the room next door. That must have woken her.

"A knocking or hammering?"

"As if someone was knocking a nail into the wall."

"In a rented hotel room?"

A vague shrug of the shoulders.

"The wall between your room and the neighbouring one?"

"Yes."

Louise pictured room 35. Wood panelling rather than a plastered wall. "Someone hits the wall, you wake up and then the commotion in the corridor begins?"

Esther nodded. Two blows then a few seconds' silence before the door to the room next door opened and . . . another shrug.

Louise frowned. Her gaze fell on the plate with the pizza crusts. She pointed to it. "May I?"

Esther raised her eyebrows in astonishment.

"I'm hungry," Louise said, smiling.

As she ate the cold pizza leftovers she asked further questions, beginning with a few innocuous ones that Esther Graf answered hesitantly. No husband, no children, she lived on her own. Not currently in a relationship, she simply didn't have the time. Commercial training, employed for the past six years at GoSolar AG, a solar energy firm, where she was the assistant to the head of research and development.

"In Haid?"

"What I don't . . . Yes, in Haid. What I don't understand is . . . you're acting as if the whole thing has something to do with me. What happened in Berlin."

Louise put the plate down on the table and ran the sleeve of her jumper over her lips. Esther's expression and voice had changed, but only very slightly: she seemed tense. Bonì was puzzled to note that this change had aroused her sympathy rather than suspicion. "Is that a possibility?"

"I don't know how. I mean, I . . ." Graf paused and looked down again at the remote control, which she placed carefully back on the coffee table. Her hand was shaking.

"The man we're looking for, the suspect, was staying next door to you because he'd specifically asked for that room. He wasn't a regular at the hotel. We must entertain the possibility that he knows you."

Esther looked at her. "Impossible!"

Louise said the false name, Friedrich Müller, Dortmund. It didn't ring a bell with Esther.

"Who knew you were going to Berlin?"

"My boss and a few of my colleagues."

"And why were you in Berlin?"

Esther Graf leaned back and stared at Louise with wide eyes. She swallowed and shook her head.

Then the tears flowed.

Louise had sat on the sofa, one hand on Esther's shoulder. Any more would have been intrusive, but the hand was necessary and it didn't seem to bother Graf. A quarter of an hour went by without a word being spoken. Louise didn't probe and clearly Esther didn't feel the need to confide in her. She sobbed quietly, occasionally blowing her nose and patting her cheeks dry. Eventually she cleared her throat and said she'd had appointments in the Charité's psychotherapy department. Louise nodded, even though she didn't really understand why you would fly eight hundred kilometres to get psychological help; it would be hard to find anywhere in the world with more psychotherapists per square metre than in Freiburg.

Esther seemed to have registered Bonì's surprise. Her GP, she said, had a brother-in-law at the Charité who was eminent in his field. Besides, she'd been worried about bumping into someone she knew in Freiburg. A friend, a colleague. She'd been worried it might cause her difficulties.

"Difficulties? At work?"

"At work, with my landlord, at the bank. If I ever need a loan and they know that I . . ." Esther faltered.

"That you what?"

"That I've got problems."

"What sort of problems?"

Esther shrugged.

"Depression?"

No answer, and Louise didn't say anything either. She understood the fear of getting into difficulties, at least as far as work was concerned. She'd been through it herself.

"And then the gossip . . ."

"How's it going to continue? You can't fly to Berlin every week."

"No."

"What are you going to do?"

"I . . . I don't know yet."

"What did the doctor say? The one at the Charité?"

Once more Esther didn't reply.

"Inpatient therapy?"

"I . . . they've recommended a place in the Black Forest."

No, it can't be, Louise thought.

"The Oberberg clinic," Esther Graf said.

Soon afterwards Louise got up to leave. That evening Esther was neither willing nor in a state to answer any more questions. She sat there on the sofa apathetically, making no move to see Louise to the door. Although she wasn't crying anymore she was firmly in the grip of some demon or other.

Louise hated these moments when the gulf between professional necessity and human decency was so wide. If she wanted to find out more, she would have to hassle Esther. And if she hassled Esther she would push her over the edge. Whichever way she looked at it, Bonì bore responsibility.

"Can I leave you alone now?"

"Yes," Esther said, eventually standing up.

In the hallway Louise put on her anorak. "Do you have any idea who the man in room 35 might have been?"

Esther Graf shook her head. She leaned against the wall with her arms crossed. Her eyes were small now, almost disappearing in the black cavities.

"Someone from work? An ex-boyfriend who can't get you out of his head?"

"I . . . I don't know."

"Are you being threatened?"

"Not at all . . ." Esther put the tissue to her nose. Her eyes were welling with tears again.

"I can't go easy on you," Louise said. "I'd very much like to, but I can't. I have to know what happened in Berlin. Why it happened."

Esther Graf didn't respond, but her face said it all – please leave and never come back.

She sat in the car for several minutes, gazing at the bright windows of the little houses that ran all the way down the hill to the centre of Littenweiler. Now and then shadows slithered through the light, somewhere it went dark and somewhere else light. Three people and a dog on the road, a couple in a car, their heads close together. For years she'd been pleased she no longer belonged to a community of whatever sort, in which her autonomy would be compromised and there was the risk of dependency. But since Ben had moved to Freiburg she'd found it increasingly difficult to be on her own. One of the many pillars of resistance within her had collapsed, a little voice whined at hourly intervals, *call him/move in with him/marry him* and that sort of nonsense. The soul was an inexhaustible reservoir of new forms of sentimentality.

Who would have thought it? As you got older life didn't become simpler, but more difficult.

She automatically glanced at her mobile. Still no message from Sarajevo.

Call him, the little voice whined. Shut your trap, Louise thought.

She was convinced that Esther Graf was withholding information from her, whether intentionally or not. Information that might explain why she, Steinhoff and the unknown man were all in the same hotel that same Saturday afternoon.

The chain of logic was flawed, but it seemed to point in only one direction. The unknown man, who insisted on the room next to Esther Graf. Hans Peter Steinhoff, who wasn't staying at the hotel yet had gone up to the third floor. The violent attack, which may have been attempted murder and was later disguised as theft. The accomplice who'd cleaned room 35.

Had both men been waiting for Steinhoff? Was Esther Graf a sort of decoy to lure him to the hotel? But then there was the question of why both men hadn't attacked him together. And why the knocking on the wall just prior to the attack? A sign for Esther? If so, she wouldn't have mentioned the knocking to Louise.

Or was it all just coincidence and Bonì was getting carried away again?

A noise interrupted her thoughts – a front door being closed. A few metres above the road the yellow umbrella appeared. Esther Graf was hurrying down the steps. When she got to the road she started going uphill. The umbrella lit up beneath a streetlamp, the only flash of colour in the darkness.

Soon afterwards it had vanished between the trees.

Louise took hold of the door handle, then changed her mind. She wasn't going to follow her. Esther had a right to be alone with her demons.

Back home, the empty rooms, the silence and a feeling of paralysis. All of a sudden the tightness was back in her chest. And a familiar, loathsome thought: how about a snifter?

She frantically looked for the Element of Crime CD that Ben had burned for her. When the music was finally on it felt a bit better.

Bonì reached for her mobile and called Eberhardt Rohwe. After fifteen rings a wall of pub noise; the jumble of bawling voices and loud rock music molested her auditory canal. When detectives clock off for the night . . .

"Professionals," she said. "You were right."

Rohwe didn't reply. She heard a creaking door close, then silence.

"Am I interrupting?"

"How could you be interrupting? I've just sunk a few beers." There was laughter, cigarettes and drunkenness in Rohwe's voice. Four beers, she guessed, maybe more. A two-metre-tall man could take a lot.

"I went to see Esther Graf."

He gave a snort that sounded like a laugh. A friendly sound.

She told him about her visit to Littenweiler. The prison-like sitting room, her impression that Esther knew more than she was letting on. And: two knocks on the wooden wall, Ebbe. He warned her. What about? Steinhoff?

Rohwe was silent but she got the feeling he was listening to her.

"I need the photos from forensics."

A grunt, less friendly this time. "I've no idea where they are, I'd have to look for them first."

"Did they photograph the wall?"

"What wall?"

"The one between 34 and 35."

"I see . . . No."

He laughed in disbelief.

"Do we actually know what Graf got up to on Saturday afternoon? Did she leave the hotel at all?"

Rohwe groaned. "My God, you don't stop, do—"

"Tell me, Ebbe."

No, Rohwe replied, sounding sober all of a sudden. They didn't know, he hadn't asked her. "I don't understand what you want, Louise. If you keep on like this you'll jeopardise our colleagues' investigation. You might put people's lives in danger. Don't you care about that?"

She sighed. Of course she cared. But when you got stuck into things it wasn't easy to simply let go. It was what she was like – they knew it in Freiburg and since 2003 they ought to have known it in Berlin too. The facts of the case were just too tempting for someone who liked to get stuck in. Steinhoff, who was working for the BND; the BND, which didn't want Kripo to investigate; a false name, a fake

ID; an attempt to withdraw the charges. All of this reeked of manipulation, an intrigue that would help someone and harm someone else. Did Kripo have to make itself the BND's henchman?

Admittedly, it might just be the empty rooms, the silence and the tightness inside her chest.

"I'm going back in now," Rohwe said.

"Will I get the photo?"

"Only if you take it yourself."

"Shit."

"I'm afraid I won't be able to pick you up from Tegel this time. By the way . . ." The door creaked, voices and music surged again. "Although Steinhoff has done the odd bit of work for the BND, they're not involved in this case."

"Who, then?"

"The Verfassungsschutz." The pub noise was abruptly replaced by the engaged tone.

Not foreign intelligence, but domestic intelligence. Not Pullach, but Berlin or Stuttgart – which extended the palette of possible backgrounds to the case. Far-right and far-left extremism, Islamism, extremist activity by migrant organisations. Spying, Scientology, betraying state secrets and a few other little things.

From her memory a name popped up, then another, and another until the list comprised a dozen people. Former Kripo colleagues, those she'd been on courses with at the academy, fellow students at Villingen-Schwenningen. All had one thing in common: they'd gone to work for the Verfassungsschutz's regional office in Stuttgart.

Louise found BND officers to be pathologically secretive, pompous spies, amoral saviours of the world. You'd happily throw a spanner in their works. By contrast, those in the Verfassungsschutz were colleagues you respected.

The game was over.

*

That night, Wertheim again – the same dream, the same pairs of apathetic eyes. At around four in the morning she sat bolt upright, bathed in sweat.

The obligatory glance at her mobile. No missed message.

Louise went to the bathroom to have a pee. For minutes she stared in the mirror at the jungle of hair that was becoming increasingly alien. Back when it was all about the booze and fighting her addiction, she'd felt herself to be a whole, as clearly defined matter. Now she was dissolving and running in all directions.

In this foggy moment between sleep and waking she suddenly understood why: she was worried about losing Ben.

Was it possible that she *loved* him.

She might have expected that it would come to this one day. And yet it was still a shock.

The question remained as to whom it was a greater shock for – her or him.

She went back to bed and lay awake until half past five. When she'd finally made up her mind to get up, she fell asleep again.

5

The troops had marched out, the corridors were deserted. Her heart stirred by a few friendly words from the porter, Gregori, Bonì entered her office at half past nine, the office she'd shared with Thomas Ilic until the summer. At the end of July he'd cleared his desk and soon afterwards she went off to Wertheim on furlough. Some sensible individual who seemed to know her well had seen to it that Illi's desk wasn't assigned to anyone else while she was away. Maybe that same sensible individual had put a vase of flowers on her desk – albeit a dozen yellow chrysanthemums. They couldn't have been working for Freiburg Kripo a year ago – if they had, they would have steered clear of chrysanthemums. In 2004 the Merzhausen case had taken her to chrysanthemum-festooned Lahr, from Lahr into the abyss, and from there to Croatia and Bosnia.

She picked up the phone and dialled the extension of the Holiest of Holies on the fourth floor. While it was ringing she booted up her computer.

"Welcome back," Reinhard Graeve said.

"Thanks. Are the flowers from you?"

"I wanted lilies, but Rolf said you liked chrysanthemums."

She grinned. How wrong you could be. Not a sensible person, but a senseless one. "Where is he?"

"Arresting two suspects." Graeve gave her the lowdown on the burglary in Günterstal. They had a witness and a registration number. Bermann and the investigation team had set off an hour ago with a search warrant.

Louise felt relieved to have been spared that.

"He didn't fancy waiting any longer," Graeve said.

"Fine by me." She opened her e-mails. Seven messages, probably personal ones, forwarded early this morning by a colleague who'd managed her inbox in her absence. An eighth e-mail had just come in – Eberhardt Rohwe from a gmx address, so a personal message. Subject heading "The Wall", a few lines of text and two photographs in an attachment.

"Would you like to come up for a few minutes?"

"Of course."

"Cup of tea."

"Yes, please. But don't let it brew for too long."

Graeve laughed and hung up.

She opened the attachment. Two photos of the panelled wall – a shot with the desk and a close-up. There were two visible indentations in the wood, about one and a half centimetres apart. As far as she could make out they were two centimetres in height and two and a half centimetres wide. The one on the left was slightly higher up.

Bonì clicked back to the text.

One metre sixty-five from floor, some sort of pattern. Splinter of wood on carpet behind desk, looks new. Best of luck – a fan.

The timestamps showed that the photographs had been taken half an hour ago. After firing off a quick answer – *Thanks a million!* – she enlarged the picture of the wall.

Despite being pixelated, the indentations were relatively easy to make out. A hard object in the form of a hammerhead, riffled horizontally, the sides smooth. The gap between the lines got narrower from the bottom upwards. In both indentations the lower part was clearer than the upper; the object must have hit the wood at an angle.

She sank back into her chair and stared at the slightly fuzzy image on her monitor. What was the suspect holding in his hand before he attacked Steinhoff?

Louise opened a desk drawer and took the Heckler & Koch out of its holster. No riffling on the underside of the grip, but a deep groove and a circular cut-out in the middle. But that didn't mean anything; she knew that there were pistols with riffling. But which models? A question the in-house armourer or the forensics lab would be able to answer.

She wrote to both, attaching Rohwe's close-up, and left the office. Even if the game was over as far as Kripo was concerned, a few more pieces of information couldn't hurt anyone.

The tea was ready and Louise was met by the aroma of East Frisian cosiness. Reinhard Graeve, late forties, born in Hamburg, and Kripo boss in Leer for many years, put on his jacket that he only ever took off when he made tea, even in summer. His suit and tie were the only symbols of authority he used. She'd never met another man who was so restrained and yet exuded such unassailable power.

"Cream?"

"A dash."

He lifted a tiny jug and poured a touch of cream into her cup. "Kluntje?"

"What?"

Graeve pointed at a bowl with white rock sugar.

She put up two fingers. "Say that again."

"Kluntje."

"Sounds sexy."

"But all it does is ruin your teeth." With a pair of sugar tongs he dropped two rocks into the cup. "What is it with the chrysanthemums?"

She picked up the cup and wandered over to the window. Old town, minster, Schlossberg in the rain. You couldn't see far today. But there was a hint of brightness in the grey. "They bring up unpleasant memories. A case before your time."

"Which one?"

"Merzhausen."

Graeve nodded. He seemed to know about it.

"Handsome Bob lived up here back then," she said. "Now he's idling away his days in the provinces. Don't-make-mistakes-Bob made mistakes."

"We're all worried about making mistakes," Graeve said.

"I'm more worried about doing the wrong thing."

"Is there a difference?"

"What constitutes a mistake is relative. What's right and wrong isn't relative."

"So the chrysanthemums were a mistake but not wrong?"

"Sort of."

Graeve stood beside her and they drank their tea in silence. How often she'd stood here with Almenbroich. Some things changed, some repeated themselves, and somehow that was reassuring.

"Rolf and his games," she said.

"Signs of his affection."

"For you or me?"

"For you. He's delighted to have you back, but of course he can't admit it to himself. That's why he sends you to Berlin and why he suggests I buy chrysanthemums."

Bonì shrugged. She had experience of Bermann covering up his affection. The fact that his delight at her return was felt all the way up to the fourth floor did not bode well.

"Tell me about Berlin."

She raised the cup towards the window. "Give me a few more minutes."

She'd assumed that Graeve was thinking along the same lines as Bermann – a case that isn't one? It's of no interest to us; we're not even responsible. To her surprise she discovered that she was wrong. Graeve wanted her to stay on Esther Graf's case.

He was concerned about the unknown man from room 35. If there was a link between that man and Graf, they must anticipate that he would turn up in Freiburg or might already be here. If a brutal, armed professional, using false papers and suspected of attempted murder, was wandering around Freiburg, would Kripo sit there doing nothing? No way. They would request the protocol of the victim's interview from Berlin and launch a local manhunt using the description of the suspect.

"Should I speak to Graf again?"

Graeve pondered this. "Do some research into her but stay in the background. Get a couple of colleagues from D24 and have her . . . how should I put it? Observed for a while. For your protection, you understand."

Louise nodded. The necessary legal requirements were not in place for more thorough surveillance. "What about the Verfassungsschutz?"

"I'll make a few calls. If the agency really is conducting an investigation, we need more precise information as to how we should act and how to avoid getting in our colleagues' way. But most importantly we need a guarantee that they've got the situation and the suspect under control."

"Talk to Rohwe's boss."

"Which office?"

She took Rohwe's business card from her trouser pocket. "HQ 2 – VB II 5. I'm assuming he's the Kripo boss." She gave Graeve the card. "He's a big Queen fan."

"What a coincidence," Grave said, smiling.

"Let me guess: you *love* Queen."

"Ever since I was a boy."

"Don't tell him that. They only got together in 1970."

Back in her office, Bonì put the vase of chrysanthemums on the windowsill so they weren't in her line of sight. She spent a few minutes wiping her desk, basin and shelves to remove the dust that had accumulated in spite of the cleaners. Then she checked for new e-mails.

Neither the armourer nor the lab had replied. She wasn't expecting much from the former as he wasn't fond of her. Unlike William Brenner, firearms expert at the forensics lab. She couldn't say what he fundamentally liked about her, but his specific interest was more definite. For the past two and a half years his nineteen-year-old son had been taking meditation classes from a Japanese Zen master, which had shocked the parents, sending them into a panic for months. Louise had been reassuring. No druggy trances, no perverted sexual practices. Just sitting there, thinking of nothing.

It's urgent, she wrote to Brenner, copying in the armourer.

Then she googled GoSolar, which threw up more than sixty thousand hits. The company's website was full of green and yellow, as well as smiling employees. The present was wonderful, the future blossoming. A medium-sized flagship German company, the eighth largest producer of solar cells in the world. She skimmed the blurb and soon she'd had enough of environmental paradise.

Then she remembered Ernesto Freudenreich.

The financial investigators in D31 had their offices on the same floor as Bonì's department, D11. Three minutes later Louise was with Freudenreich, who was more like a deer than a human being. If you spoke to him he recoiled in shock. If you put a hand on his shoulder he fled behind a chair or a table. If you made to hug him he took refuge in the lavatories.

Not that anyone would seriously consider hugging Freudenreich. But his departmental colleagues occasionally delighted in pretending that they were going to. Maybe because he was responsible for D31's internal nickname: the "Felt-Slipper Department". Every morning Ernesto Freudenreich, around forty years of age, would change out of his street shoes and into lilac felt slippers.

Before joining Kripo he'd worked for years as a qualified economist at a private bank, gathering dust behind plastic ferns in windowless number dungeons and cultivating his fear of other people, especially other people's bodies. Then the bank went bust. A week after his last day at work Freudenreich contracted glandular fever and wasn't able to get out of bed for five months. He would probably still have been lying in it today if he hadn't had an uncle by the name of Christian Almenbroich.

Almenbroich forced his nephew to do a special Kripo course for those joining the police from business, and promised him a windowless office of his own, plastic ferns and a whole lot of numbers, thereby probably saving him from death by loneliness. He'd kept this promise apart from the window.

"Don't worry," Louise said, holding up her hand.

"I haven't got time," Ernesto mumbled, glancing at her terrified through his nickel-framed glasses.

She pointed at the chair by the desk. "May I."

A shake of the head.

"Where then?"

"Not there."

There was another chair by the sink. "How about there?"

"No. *There*," he said, indicating the side wall. Three chairs, lined up like in a doctor's waiting room. She sat down.

"No time," Ernesto whined.

"I know," Louise said.

Because officers in D31 rarely did field work, they were called "desk worms". An affectionate joke between colleagues, but in Ernesto's case it was on the button. A perturbed, pink, squirming paper worm.

And yet, he knew everything that had anything to do with the German economy, whether it be criminal or not.

Everything.

*

"It's not part of my remit."

"What?"

"That sector."

"The solar sector?"

Ernesto nodded. For a few seconds he looked relieved, but when Louise stayed in her chair the relief vanished and the tension returned. "I'm afraid it's not part of my remit," he reiterated.

"I understand." She crossed her legs. "But I'm sure you know where to look."

"I'm not qualified in that area, I'm afraid."

She smiled.

"Not to mention totally uninformed."

"Ernie, I don't want physical explanations, just a few numbers. OK?"

"It's Peter's sector."

"He doesn't like me."

Ernesto stared at her. Louise was expecting professions of solidarity with Peter Schöne, the head of department. But then he said, "Ulf. He's an expert in energy."

She rejected the idea; Ulf didn't like her either.

"Annemarie."

"Come on, Ernie. Seeing as I'm here."

"But I know nothing about it."

"It's like going to the dentist. The sooner you start, the sooner it's over."

Ernesto furrowed his sweaty brow and frenetically ruffled his mop of curly hair. Then he hunched over and disappeared behind his screen. His fingers flew across the keyboard almost silently and the printer began throwing out pieces of paper. She noticed the lilac slippers beneath the desk, the two big toes rubbing together. The printer by the wall opposite whirred and whirred.

Eventually he said, "That should suffice," and his head popped above the top of the screen.

She got up and took the sheets of paper from the printer tray. "Thanks."

"Hmm."

"If I need anything else I'll be back."

"No time," Ernesto said gloomily and hid behind the screen again.

Bonì went down to the ground floor, bought a can of mineral water and some crackers from the machine, and returned to the third. Those daily routines, how she'd missed them.

And yet she felt strangely despondent. She barely took notice of the colleagues she bumped into, thinking instead of those she wouldn't see anymore. Illi with his blue notebooks, Alfons Hoffmann with his chocolate croissants, and not forgetting soft but strict Almenbroich.

If only Bermann were back . . .

Longing for Bermann, now that was something quite new.

Dark clouds had gathered in paradise. GoSolar's current figures looked miserable.

Louise was sitting on the sill of the second window, eating crackers with one hand and leafing through the printouts from Freudenreich with the other. She'd successfully overcome the first hints of tiredness, but more were on their way. Percentages, balances, business – not exactly her great passion.

In the third quarter GoSolar's turnover and profit had fallen by twenty per cent. And this following a prognosis from the first quarter suggesting growth of at least twenty per cent by the end of the year. Which corresponded to the assessments of financial journalists – in early summer GoSolar was still seen as the flagship company of the German solar industry. Their expansion of production capacity was hailed as "smart because it's cautious". A hidden champion with excellent prospects and innovative products. The newest coup was the "DriveSolar" project: solar cells specifically designed for the roof and bodywork of cars.

But in June GoSolar lost a big order from a Spanish client. In addition, two or three smaller intermediaries had popped up this year, while several regional and national government bodies had put their orders on ice. If the experts were to be believed, this was down to the negative rumours that had been doing the rounds publicly since April – insider trading, financial straits, decline in quality. As a consequence the share price had fallen steadily, currently standing at thirty-five per cent below what it had been in April.

With a yawn, Louise looked up. In the west, above the Vosges, was a broad band of light blue. Over Freiburg the leaden gloom was gradually assuming some colour. A grain of light seemed to be growing inside the blanket of cloud, as if it were about to explode at any moment.

She put the printouts to one side.

A witness with secrets, a mysterious attack in Berlin, rumours about GoSolar. Perhaps these were connected, perhaps not. Whatever the truth, the next step would be to have a nose-around at GoSolar, if only to rachet up the pressure on Esther Graf. But this was not an option until Graeve had talked to Stuttgart.

She grinned. Reinhard Graeve's calm authority even worked on her.

Shortly afterwards she got an answer from Wilhelm Brenner at the lab. As ever it was thorough and meticulous, with five photographs attached.

The impressions made in the wood panelling of room 35, Brenner said, suggested a 9mm Walther P5. The contours of the underside of the Walther's grip were quite distinct and, so far as he could tell from the photographs, matched the marks on the wall.

Brenner had got hold of a Walther P5 from the armoury at the regional headquarters, pressed the underside into some plasticine and photographed the impression. She compared the image with Rohwe's close-up. Brenner was right; it was a match. So now they knew the make of pistol the man from room 35 was carrying, which he'd used to bash against the wooden wall.

He'd booked room 35 and he'd woken or warned Esther Graf. He *knew* her. How? And what was his interest in her?

Graf had readily told her about the knocking on the wall. It would have been more prudent to keep quiet about everything pointing to a connection to her mysterious guardian angel who, after all, was suspected of attempted murder and falsifying documents. Assuming there *was* a connection.

Was it possible that he knew her but she didn't know him?

With a sigh Louise stood up. In the mirror above the basin she saw a pale face with two shiny cheeks and bags under the eyes. She'd only been back at work for two days, back in this familiar environment that gave her life meaning – but you couldn't tell by looking at her. Chaos before, during and after Wertheim. If she were being honest, the battery had been running on reserve for years. She was punishing both body and soul.

Boní washed her face with cold water and wondered when she'd last felt fresh and recuperated for any length of time. The answer was sobering: two and a half years ago, between April and July 2003, when she'd stayed at the Kanzan-an in the woods of Alsace and weaned herself off alcohol. Therapeutically quiet, solitary months. A Japanese Zen monk, a grey cat, a stubborn inspector and many silent, friendly trees which had patiently put up with emotional outbursts.

She dried her face and returned to the photographs, Brenner's e-mail and the puzzles.

Once more from the beginning.

A shady journalist who might have been a threat to Esther Graf. An unknown, extremely brutal guardian angel, who'd warned her.

The Verfassungsschutz, who'd put a stop to the Kripo investigation. How to piece it all together? One possible answer was that the guardian angel was an undercover agent for the Verfassungsschutz. She dismissed this idea. An undercover man who'd become so wrapped up in his fake identity that the boundaries had become blurred and he was now guilty of attempted murder?

What if he'd changed sides and the service was now trying to capture him?

She rubbed her temples. None of this was important for the moment, she thought. The key was the current whereabouts of both Steinhoff and the unknown man. In Freiburg, near Esther Graf?

One out to get her, the other to protect her again?

Hans Peter Steinhoff hadn't gone home. Colleagues from Hamburg Kripo, who Louise had phoned for help, went to Altona. His wife had opened the door. She said that Steinhoff's work in Berlin was dragging on and he wouldn't be back before the end of the week. She gave the name of a hotel in Kreuzberg, which Hamburg Kripo called. Originally Steinhoff had booked to stay until Sunday, but he hadn't been at the hotel since Saturday afternoon. On Sunday evening he sent a taxi driver to collect his things and pay the bill.

It took Hamburg Kripo two hours to find the driver, then they rang him. The telephone call took another half an hour as the driver was from Ghana, barely spoke a word of German and was distraught. The German police! A passenger helped out. At the end of the conversation they found out what Louise had already suspected: Steinhoff's things had been taken to Martin Luther hospital.

She notified Richard Graeve.

The local manhunt for the unknown suspect was already underway. Now Steinhoff's name was added to the list. Although the suspicion that he might be after Esther Graf wasn't enough, Graeve had been convinced by another argument: wherever Steinhoff was, his attacker might be too. If they found one of them they would possibly get their hands on the other as well.

And surely Steinhoff would be easier to track down. Given the injuries he'd been dealt in Berlin, he was bound to stick out in a peaceful city like Freiburg.

"What about Stuttgart? Got anything out of them?" Louise asked.

Graeve laughed grimly.

He told her he'd called Eberhardt Rohwe's boss and been given the name of a departmental head at the Berlin Verfassungsschutz office. He'd rung this man's secretary and been given the name of a departmental head at the Baden-Württemberg office. He'd spoken to another secretary, who said the departmental heads were in a meeting but she would pass on his request to be called back. There had been nothing yet.

"Lucky for us," Louise said. "Which department?"

"Four."

She racked her brains. "Counter-intelligence and all that other stuff, right?"

Graeve laughed. The other stuff was security of information, sabotage prevention, identity checks and Scientology.

"A small step forwards, at any rate," he said.

"But in which direction?"

"Please hold back until they tell us."

"You know I'm not very good at that."

Graeve sighed. "Who doesn't?"

In the afternoon the scanned report of Steinhoff's police interview by Chief Inspector Eberhardt Rohwe finally arrived from Berlin. It didn't contain anything new apart from a vague description of the suspect: around 1.85m tall, between thirty and forty, extraordinarily quick and strong, close-cropped dark hair, stubble.

She went to her colleagues in surveillance with this description along with a photo of fifty-one-year-old Steinhoff taken a couple of years back, which she'd found online. The data was fed into the computer, as was the order not to approach either of the two wanted men if they were spotted. Report at once and just keep watching.

Then Bonì instructed two officers to keep a watch on Esther Graf. One she knew from summer 2003: Kilian, late twenties, casually dressed in a cool way, shoulder-length hair, one of the wild, new Kripo generation. She'd never seen the other officer before. Marc was slightly younger than Kilian, but a copy style-wise. Two men you would more readily imagine with surfboards under their arms.

"Let's go, then," Kilian said, taking his leather jacket from the back of the chair. For the first time Louise noticed that he had breath-takingly beautiful, regular eyebrows. She recalled Richard Landen's brows, interrupted by a little patch of grey. She'd fallen in love with this patch before falling in love with the rest of the man.

"What?" Kilian said with a relaxed smile.

She pointed at his eyebrows. "Do you pluck them?"

The smile grew broader. "Allow me to have my secrets."

"I'll tell you mine."

"I know them already."

"You do?"

He rocked his head from side to side. "The important ones at any rate."

"Tell me."

"I will at some point over a glass of water and some ćevapčići."

She stopped short, then laughed as she opened the door.

"So we're just watching, not doing anything?" Marc said.

"That's right."

They went into the corridor.

"What if something comes up? What side are we on?"

"The most important thing is to protect Esther Graf. Everything else depends on what happens."

"What might happen?"

She thought for a moment.

"We've got a victim, Steinhoff, who might pose a danger to Graf. We've got a suspect who's brutal, but might also be Graf's guardian angel. We've got the mystery-mongers from Stuttgart who might be on to one of the three, or all of them." She shrugged, "I've no idea what might happen. Maybe nothing at all."

"Off we go, then," Kilian said, giving her a sunny smile and bounding down the stairs with his hand on the rail.

Fellow officers welcomed her back. They chatted, ate crackers and drank coffee. She found out the latest gossip – an affair, a divorce, and did you know Tito's gay?

So what?

Of course, so what. But who'd have thought?

Just family tittle-tattle. It mitigated the unfamiliarity but didn't help the tiredness.

After the gossip had been dealt with, conversation turned to appraisals. Every two years officers were given an appraisal by the Kripo head as well as the boss of HQ. The maximum score was five points, but only thirty per cent of officers in each rank got four or five. Louise had been appraised by handsome Bob in 2004, scoring three points, and everyone knew that she would always be stuck on three points. They discussed others' chances. Rolf Bermann, people were saying, was a five-point candidate this time. His behaviour had been notably friendly these last few months.

When they were done discussing appraisals, they moved on to the upcoming football World Cup, which was increasingly tying up resources and had been dominating day-to-day life at police HQ for a long while.

The very idea of football brought on a new wave of tiredness. "Guys, I've got a lot to do," she said, yawning.

"Are you going to have a flutter?"

"Get out, now."

In a quiet minute she phoned Graeve.

Still no call from Stuttgart.

"For God's sake. How are we meant to work like that?"

"Stay calm," Graeve said.

"It's easy for you to say. You're not me."

Graeve didn't respond. He knew she had to do something. Wait and hope that surveillance got a lucky break while Steinhoff and the unknown man were in action? Rely on Kilian and Marc preventing what might happen? Not a good plan.

"Maybe they're not in Freiburg at all, Louise."

"Graf is in Freiburg."

Graeve sighed. "Another tea?"

"No, thanks. I'm going to pay another visit to the desk worms."

"Poor Ernesto. Go easy on him."

But she wasn't thinking of Ernesto Freudenreich. She needed a wolf, not a worm.

"Well, well. Look who it is," the wolf growled.

She went into the office and shut the door. "I need your help."

"I see."

Peter Schöne, head of the financial crime department, sat bent over documents, a sheer colossus in a room that was far too small. Deep furrows in his brow, and bags beneath small, staring eyes. Over the years some colleagues had developed an aversion to Louise, whereas some hadn't liked her from the outset and over the course of time felt their judgement vindicated. Schöne was one of the latter.

"Are you looking into GoSolar?"

"Are you prowling around my department?"

She leaned against the door and returned his stare. Schöne looked down again and turned over a page.

"Have you heard from Berlin?"

He didn't look up. "Hysterical again, Bonì?"

Suppressing her pride and frustration, Louise told him about Berlin, Esther Graf and GoSolar. Schöne glanced up once or twice, but then returned to his files and flicked through the pages. When she'd finished he said, "Send me Rolf. Let's see what he thinks."

"Rolf isn't here."

"I know."

She waited a moment, maybe for the anger to come, maybe for Schöne to change his mind. When neither materialised she left.

At around six Louise gave in to her tiredness and frustration. This wasn't her day. Bermann might have been able to salvage it, Ben certainly, but one wasn't back yet and the other still hadn't got in touch.

"Alright," Graeve said. "There's not much we can do, anyway."

"Keep me updated," she yawned into the phone.

Bonì printed out the photographs of the hotel wall and the pistol grip, as well as the picture of Steinhoff, and gathered up all the documentation she had relating to the case. Material for the night if she were kept awake with fear of having another Wertheim dream.

When she went through the glass door into the stairwell she heard voices echoing in the distance, and could pick out those of Bermann and Marianne Andrele, the public prosecutor. They seemed to be surrounded by a large entourage; other voices rang out as did a tangle of footsteps. Bermann laughed; it must have been a successful excursion.

Louise paused and considered saying hello, but then went on her way. The interrogations were about to begin, so she would just be getting in the way.

Once outside the chaos in her apartment immediately came to mind, the empty rooms, the empty fridge. The answerphone without any messages.

Bonì got into her car. A few questions to Esther Graf remained unanswered and more had cropped up. As hard as she tried, she couldn't push these to the back of her mind.

She checked the time.

Half past six – the pizza might still be warm.

6

The road into the woods, the steps and the brightly lit house above. Although Kilian and Marc were nowhere to be seen, there were others she recognised from the day before: the couple in the car twenty metres down the road. Louise toyed with the idea of wandering over for a quick chat amongst colleagues. But a junior minister in Stuttgart might end up choking on their dinner.

Bonì thought of Steinhoff and the unknown man, wondering if they were nearby. Her hand automatically felt for the holster, then she remembered that she'd put it back in the drawer that afternoon.

She got out, climbed the steps and rang the bell.

"You?" Esther Graf said, resting her head against the doorframe.

In the corridor Louise saw the same disorder as on the previous evening. The doors to the kitchen and sitting room were open, and all the lights were on. Again Louise could smell oven heat and burnt dough.

She hung her anorak on the same hook, on top of the same blue coat.

On the coffee table in the sitting room were the red plastic mat, a plate with two quarters of frozen pizza and crusts, a glass of red wine and a crumpled cloth napkin. The curtains were drawn, the television on. What a life, Louise thought, in the prison of whatever emotions.

Esther pointed to the chair and sat on the sofa. After switching off the television she nodded towards the pizza. "Hungry?" Her movements looked weary and she spoke in a monotone. Beneath her eyes black shadows shimmered through cover-up cream. She looked as if she hadn't slept for days.

"I'm always hungry."

"But it's gone cold. If you don't mind . . ."

Louise smiled, gave a dismissive wave of her hand and took a slice. Salami and mushroom, not her favourite toppings, but beggars couldn't be choosers. She bit into it.

"It's still ongoing, then."

"Like I said, I'd love to spare you all this, but I can't."

Esther motioned to her to carry on.

"What were you doing on Saturday night?"

"Nothing. I mean, nothing in particular."

"Did you leave the hotel?"

"I . . . I went for something to eat."

"On your own?"

Graf nodded.

"Where?"

"In which restaurant, do you mean?"

"Yes."

"Why do you need to know that? Why are you treating me like—"

"Like what?"

"Like a suspect."

"Am I?"

"That's what it seems like."

Louise wondered if she should mention her hunch that Hans Peter Steinhoff and the unknown man might have come to Freiburg – one to do what he hadn't succeeded in doing in Berlin, the other to prevent this from happening. That everything which had happened in Berlin and elsewhere was linked to her, Esther Graf. That she might be in danger.

She decided against it, for now at least. "Maybe because I get the feeling you're not being straight with me."

Esther took her eyes off Louise and stared at the coffee table instead, the remote control in her hand. She sat slumped, her face a picture of exhaustion and distress.

"Which restaurant were you in, Esther?"

"I can't remember the name."

"Where is it?"

"Somewhere close to the hotel."

"Describe the route there."

"I . . . I took the underground, a few stops. I got out somewhere and—"

"Which station?"

"I don't know."

"How many stops did you go?"

"I didn't pay attention."

"Where did you get your ticket?"

"From a machine."

"And on the way back?"

"From another machine."

"Have you still got it?"

"No, I . . . I don't hold on to my tickets."

"What about the restaurant bill?"

Graf shook her head.

"Did you pay by card or cash?"

"Cash."

"Was the restaurant right beside the underground?"

"Yes . . . er, I don't know. I might have walked a bit."

"When did you get there?"

"Around . . . half eight."

"What did you eat?"

"Pasta and salad."

"Pasta with what?"

"Pesto."

"Italian restaurant, then?"

"Yes."

Louise eyed up the second slice of pizza on the plate in front of her. Could she really eat Esther's pizza while she was cornering her?"

"So, an Italian restaurant, probably very close to an underground station. What line?"

Another shrug.

"The hotel is on the U7," Louise said. "Which means you were in an Italian restaurant that's likely to be close to a U7 station. There can't be many of those."

"Yes," Graf mumbled.

"Who did you meet?"

"I told you, I was on my own," Esther said, putting the remote control on the table. "Maybe it was a bit of a walk."

"From the underground to the restaurant."

"I think . . . I think I went up the stairs then wandered through the streets for a few minutes. And somewhere I found the restaurant."

"A few minutes from the underground?"

"Yes."

"You had an appointment, didn't you?"

Esther didn't respond.

"Who did you meet?"

Silence descended on the room. Then Graf abruptly got up and walked out. Louise heard her go up the stairs, the only sound a faint scraping when her slippers came into contact with the carpet.

Upstairs a door was opened and closed.

Then silence again.

Five minutes passed; Esther didn't come back down.

Graf was lying and she wasn't well. Louise knew this but nothing else. Not which side her witness was on, whether she was in danger or represented a danger to anyone else, or both. Whether she was suspected of espionage or whether she was merely being investigated by the Verfassungsschutz as part of a routine check. And sabotage or Scientology? She couldn't imagine Esther Graf involved in either.

No sound from above.

She called Kilian. Nothing unusual in the vicinity of Graf's house, just a pair of lovers who'd been sitting in a car for a couple of hours, kissing each other without much passion.

"They were there yesterday too. Our friends from Stuttgart."

"We thought as much."

"Call me if anything happens."

She hung up and dialled another number. Again it rang for ever and again she got the unfriendly Bavarian. At least he seemed to agree that the police had to be helped, even Baden police. Grumbling, he looked through the telephone list for the previous Saturday. Yes, Esther Graf had been called in her room, at 19.11. The call had lasted just under eight minutes.

Did he by any chance know if or when she'd left her room?

No. He could hardly see through thousands of walls from Prenzlauer Berg.

Louise refrained from passing a sarcastic comment. After all, they might need to call on this Bavarian again.

She got up and went into the hallway. The entire house was completely silent. She climbed the stairs past a pile of washing. Upstairs were three doors, two of them open with lights on in the rooms. A bathroom that hadn't been cleaned in weeks, a small spare room. Unlike the rest of the house, this was neat and tidy. Was it because Esther was expecting a visitor, or because nobody ever came to stay?

Bonì opened the closed door. The bedroom. Graf was sitting in a chair by the window. The curtains were drawn here too.

"Esther," Louise said, touching her shoulder. "Please talk to me."

"I can't," Graf whispered.

"Who called you in Berlin? Who did you meet?" She kneeled

beside the armrest and lay a hand on Graf's arm. "People from the Verfassungsschutz?"

"I really can't—"

"Was it about your company? GoSolar?"

"Just go and leave me alone. *Please!*" Graf had closed her eyes and was fighting back the tears.

Louise waited a moment, then got to her feet. She gently stroked Graf's shoulder. "Look after yourself. And go to Oberberg. It's not so bad. I was there for a few weeks myself."

When Esther didn't respond, she left.

No sign of Kilian and Marc, nor the "loving couple" – the car was empty. Four officers keeping a house under surveillance. That ought to be sufficient protection, assuming Graf needed it.

Rather than head down to the B31, Louise drove via the Waldsee and along the Sternwald. As she waited at a railway crossing she called Reinhard Graeve.

He'd now spoken to Stuttgart. The agency was up in arms – Freiburg Kripo, particularly Louise Bonì, was jeopardising a protracted investigation into a highly complex case and stirring up a catastrophe. For God's sake call your people off before they screw it all up.

"We're staying out of it, Louise."

She bit her lip. "Why don't they want to cooperate?"

He didn't know. Basically he knew nothing. The Stuttgart domestic intelligence office didn't think it necessary to fill him in about the highly complex case.

"What about Steinhoff? The suspect?"

"They're dealing with him."

"Is he still on our wanted list?"

Graeve hesitated. "Not officially, but unofficially yes. But in no circumstances are we to apprehend him. Are you still at Esther Graf's?"

"How . . .?" She broke off.

"Stuttgart," Graeve explained.

They're quick, Louise thought.

She told him about her conversation. Graeve agreed with her that Graf was hiding something. But if she had met with the Verfassungsschutz in Berlin, he said, they ought not to worry. Because presumably it meant she was on the side of the good guys.

Louise wondered if he was thinking the same as she was: don't mention the two officers keeping watch in Littenweiler. What wasn't mentioned could be forgotten. People who were forgotten could stay where they were. Do a bit of surveillance, just in case.

"See you tomorrow," Graeve said.

"Yes," she replied, relieved.

Back home a little red light glowed, filling the room with friendliness and warmth. Then came a familiar, albeit distant voice, and life returned to her apartment. A couple of days ago Ben had lost his mobile in the mountains above Sarajevo, and because he didn't have a head for figures he couldn't remember any of her numbers off the top of his head, and because he'd been out all day and this was Bosnia, it had taken a while to get hold of her number and now she wasn't in.

"I miss you," the familiar, distant voice said.

Come home, then, she thought.

Home, how that sounded. A home in that sense didn't exist. She lived in Wiehre, he in Stühlinger. And Freiburg was definitely not Ben's home; he already wanted to leave.

"Call when you've got the time," the familiar, distant voice said, giving the number of a hotel.

Well, she had the time – and the desire – but all of a sudden she didn't fancy phoning him. The problem was always the same, even if you were no longer young and inexperienced, even if you were careful: the moment you fell in love you were at risk of collateral damage. Your own apartment seemed empty when your other half wasn't there. You slept worse when you slept alone, you ate without any enjoyment when dining on your own, you didn't know what to do with your spare time if you couldn't share it. You sacrificed your independence and autonomy just to love a little and be loved. You became panicky.

"I love you," the familiar, distant voice said.

Click, the answerphone went.

That night no dreams came for a simple reason: she couldn't get to sleep. The love question was bothering her. It was sobering that at the age of forty-five she basically still hadn't learned how to be stable, either with a partner or without one. What was the point of all those battles she'd fought with herself, all the victories over her demons if her stability only existed when she wasn't in love?

Or was she loving in the wrong way?

She kept turning from one side to the other, but the questions remained the same.

In a doze early the next morning she heard a mobile sing, go quiet, then start up again. It took her several minutes to realise that the singing was coming from her sitting room. As she made her way towards it the melody stopped and her landline began to ring.

Kilian.

"We need you," he said.

Esther Graf had tried to kill herself. The guardian angel had saved her.

7

On the short drive to the hospital she called Kilian back.

Esther Graf had slashed a wrist.

"I fucked up," Kilian said.

Louise wanted to reply but no words came out. The traffic light turned red, she accelerated. She wiped tears from her eyes with her sleeve then put the mobile back to her ear. But still she couldn't speak.

The tightness was back in her chest and the fear inside her head.

"Shit," Kilian said.

At the next red light she put her foot down again. She hung up; the hospital was straight ahead.

Kilian was waiting on the pavement by the main entrance. Louise double parked, put on her hazards and got out.

"How is she?"

"No change."

"Christ, Kilian, she's going to make it, isn't she?"

"Yes." His hands were in his coat pockets and he stared at her with tired eyes. "Do you want to see her?"

"Talk to me first."

He took a deep breath. "There's not much to say."

Marc and he had taken turns to sit in the car or wander around. They hadn't noticed anything unusual. At around two in the morning an ambulance turned up. They got out and went up to the house with the two paramedics.

The front door was open.

They found Esther Graf in bed in a dressing gown, unconscious and with a bandaged wrist. Someone must have attended to her because she'd done it in the bathtub. Given the loss of blood there was no way she could have got out alone. The water was red, the tiles spattered.

Kilian paused, rubbed his eyes, then said, "Thank God she wasn't lying in it."

"Keep going, Kilian."

The floor tiles were awash, the carpet on the landing and in the bedroom damp. Whoever it was had lifted her out of the bath, stopped the blood, applied the bandage, put her in a dressing gown and carried her into the bedroom.

Then he'd called an ambulance.

"Do we have a name? A number?"

"No name but a mobile number. It must be his mobile because Esther Graf doesn't have one." Kilian handed her a piece of paper. "The number's being checked."

"Have you requested forensics?"

"Not yet."

"Do it. As soon as they get to HQ in the morning they should go straight to Littenweiler. Until then nobody's to enter the house. He will have left traces."

Kilian fished his mobile from his pocket.

"Wait," Louise said. "What about the Verfassungsschutz?"

"They arrived at the house shortly after us."

"The couple in the car?"

"Yes."

Kilian and the woman – Antje Harth – agreed to sort out the jurisdiction later as there were more pressing matters to deal with. They examined the rooms together, they left together and sealed the door together.

"Where are they now?"

Kilian shrugged. When he left with the ambulance he briefly saw the Stuttgart agents by their car, both on the phone. They hadn't turned up at the hospital.

"And Marc?"

"He stayed in Littenweiler. Oh God, Louise . . ." He put his head on her shoulder.

She stroked his hair, which comforted her slightly too. *She'd* fucked up, not Kilian.

Then she pushed him away. "It's my fault, Kilian. I ought to have anticipated something like this."

He smoothed his unruly hair. "The light in the bathroom was on. From eleven to two. Three hours. Nobody spends three hours in the bathroom."

"Stop beating yourself up."

"I saw the light but didn't twig. I watched carefully but still didn't notice him. He must have—"

"Stop it, Kilian!"

But he couldn't stop. The man had been close to the house, somehow he'd got in and bandaged Esther Graf – and he, Kilian, had stood around failing to notice anything.

"Make the call now, Kilian. Tell them I want Lubowitz. And ring Marc. He must make sure that nobody enters the house before Lubowitz has been."

Kilian nodded. She heard him talk but didn't listen to what he was saying. She thought of the unknown man who'd saved Esther's life and wondered where he might be. Did he wait for the ambulance somewhere close to the house, then follow it?

Bonì let her eyes wander over the parked cars and the street; it was quiet at night. A streetlamp and the orange of her hazards provided a little light. There appeared to be no-one here apart from her and Kilian. But what did that mean? Four investigators were watching Esther Graf's house, but none of them noticed the man.

Kilian had stopped talking and their eyes met. His free hand reached for the holster; he'd understood.

As he went out into the road she tried to order her jumbled thoughts. In Berlin Esther was warned by the man from room 35. They were assuming that the same man had come to her rescue tonight. If this was true, he'd been very close by in the key moments, and yet had remained invisible – to Esther as well.

She beckoned Kilian over. If the man was still here, he'd be somewhere inside the building, not outside.

Close to Esther.

Esther Graf was in intensive care. They only got as far as the security door and weren't even allowed to take a look at her. The young night sister sitting in a small room behind a pane of glass seemed to have been given clear instructions.

Ten minutes later the doctor in charge – Bertram Faller, a short, burly man with a beard – came over to them and said, "No visits, no conversations."

"I have to talk to her as soon as she's awake," Louise said.

"No," Faller said, shaking his head resolutely. "She may well be a key witness, but she tried to commit suicide." When she regained consciousness there would be only doctors and psychologists around her. As soon as she was physically stable, she would be transferred to the psychiatric ward. He'd ended up with her by chance, and he was going to look after her and protect her to the best of his ability. Which meant no talking to Kripo, no stress. "Do you understand?"

Faller was bursting with energy and Louise sensed that tonight she didn't have anything to offer in opposition. "Dr Faller—"

"No." He raised his hands and was about to go.

"Hey," Kilian said wearily.

"Wait," Louise begged.

She told him about the man who had probably saved Esther's life.

That he was wanted for attempted murder and might be here in the hospital, close to Esther.

"But he wouldn't do anything to her, would he?"

"*He* probably wouldn't. But somebody else might."

"Does she need protection?"

"We have to assume so."

"Then arrange it." Faller started wandering away, but again Louise called him back.

"One more question."

"Yes?"

"Did she do it . . . properly?"

Faller raised his eyebrows and nodded.

"What with?"

"A razor blade."

"Can you tell when, roughly?"

"Five, ten minutes before she was bandaged up. Is that it?"

"Not yet." Louise rubbed her temples. Buzzing on the ceiling above her was a neon tube light, a constant, high-pitched sound that she couldn't block out. "Has the Verfassungsschutz already been here?"

"The . . ." Faller screwed up his eyes.

"Like I said, she's important."

"Is that why she did it? Because the police think she's important?"

"Nonsense," Kilian said.

"If the Verfassungsschutz turns up I'll tell them the same as I've told you: no talking." With that, Faller opened the door to the intensive care ward and vanished.

Kilian called the control centre again and asked for four constables. According to the night sister the intensive care ward had two entrances, both of which had to be guarded. A nun in a white habit took Kilian through the stairwell to the other security door.

Louise got a chair, but she was too unrelaxed to sit and instead wandered down the empty corridor. The buzzing of the light followed her, remaining at a constant volume, even when she'd reached the other end of the corridor. She put her hands over her ears but it didn't help; the noise was still there, the noise and the sight that Kilian had described: the red water in the bath, the blood-spattered tiles.

At the far end of the corridor Bonì turned around. She heard voices and footsteps coming from the stairs; the constables had arrived.

Two colleagues stayed at the security door here, the other two followed the nun back into the stairwell. The night sister brought more chairs.

Louise resumed her pacing. The buzzing inside her head had grown louder. She saw Esther lying in the bath, eyes closed, hair swimming around her face. Her wrist slashed, she thought, puzzled. The aggression, the physical side of it didn't add up. If Esther was going to attempt suicide in the first place, surely she'd take pills rather than butcher herself like that.

She went back to the night sister's office. "Get me Faller."

The sister picked up the telephone. Seconds after she'd hung up, the security door opened and Faller was there. Kilian was with him.

"You've got to ask her something," Louise said.

"What?"

"Whether she did it herself."

"Are there any doubts?"

"It's just not like her. To slit her wrist, I mean."

Faller disagreed. If the decision was a spontaneous one, the psychological strain big enough and there was nothing else to hand – pills, a gas oven, a car – even suicidal people who might seem incapable of it could slit their wrists. Besides, Esther Graf had only slit one wrist rather than both. Perhaps her shock, disgust and pain had been greater than her determination. "Hoping she's done enough, she lies back and closes her eyes. At some point she loses consciousness . . . I could mention a dozen cases like that."

"All the same, ask her, would you?" Louise handed him her business card. "And change that bloody neon light. It's broken, can't anybody else hear it?"

Faller glanced up at the ceiling, then grinned as he took a step towards the security door. "You should go home and get some sleep, Frau Bonì. You look very tired."

"Not yet. Could you get us a plan of the building?"

Kilian held out a photocopy.

"Call me," Louise said.

Faller nodded and went back into intensive care.

"Attempted murder?" Kilian asked softly.

She knew what was going through his mind. Not only had the guardian angel slipped unnoticed into Esther's house while Kilian was standing outside, but a potential murderer too.

Louise patted his shoulder. "Just a thought, don't get worked up, OK?"

He stretched out his arms and let them drop – it's alright for you to talk, you're not the guilty one.

"Kilian, I really can't deal with this now. Show me the plan."

He handed her a floor plan, a jumble of lines, figures and words beneath the heading "NEW BUILDING". Three floors plus a basement, dozens of corridors, various stairwells, all that she could make out. But her mind wasn't able to process anything else. "Where are we?"

"Here," Kilian said, pointing at a corridor on the second floor.

"Good, let's begin. Pay attention to the floor too. There might be blood on his soles."

"Before you get any ideas, we're sticking together."

She shrugged. "I don't have a weapon anyway."

"The sight of you will frighten him to death."

She smiled. At least one of them was able to crack jokes.

*

Starting with the kitchenette they worked their way slowly up the corridor. The electric buzzing followed Louise, becoming ever more excruciating. "Can you hear that?" she asked.

"Yes."

Two doors further down. "Can you still hear it?"

"Vaguely."

Another two doors down. "What about now?"

"Not anymore."

"Shit, it's inside my head."

Doctors' offices, a cleaners' closet, staff toilets, a restroom for orderlies, but no patient rooms in this wing according to the plan. They skipped rooms behind locked doors; the night sister had refused to give them the master key until they got a search warrant – which no doubt wouldn't be forthcoming.

Now and then they bumped into people on night shift, some wearing habits, others not. One nun was sleeping in the restroom, while in the toilets they waited tensely by one of the cubicles, then a constable came out. Faller passed them a few times in the corridor; from the expression on his face, it looked as if he thought they'd lost it. He was probably right, Louise concluded; their search was anything but promising. If Esther's guardian angel didn't want them to find him, they wouldn't.

If he was here at all.

Twenty minutes later they turned into another corridor. Louise put her hands over her ears but the buzzing persisted.

"You're just tired," Kilian said.

"Rubbish, I'm wide awake."

"Two minutes' break?"

"Alright, then." She sat on the ground and leaned her shoulder against Kilian's leg; he was still standing. What had Faller said? Esther had been bandaged five minutes – ten, at most – after slitting her wrist. Which meant either her saviour had been in the house the whole time, or he'd coincidentally slipped in at that moment, or he'd noticed the light on in the bathroom and had drawn the right conclusion.

None of these possibilities seemed especially plausible.

A thought she'd had earlier entered her head again: close to Esther at the key moments and yet always invisible. Unlike the Kripo surveillance officers and the Verfassungsschutz, who'd also been invisible but had missed the key moment.

Cursing, she put her head in her hands. From the beginning again. The unknown man. The surveillance officers. A network of observers. Five minutes, ten tops.

She held up her arms and let Kilian pull her to her feet. "Call Marc."

He was holding his mobile. "I haven't got any reception in here."

"Her house is bugged, they're listening in on her. They've probably installed cameras too."

Kilian looked at her incredulously. "Who?"

"No idea. Him."

"But bugs? And cameras?"

"He must have *seen* it, Kilian. That's how he got there in time."

And he had seen *her* twice – at Esther's – and heard her conversations with Kilian and the Berlin-Bavarian. Bonì shuddered. The idea that she might have been observed and listened to without noticing it . . . And yet she prided herself on her intuition.

Louise dismissed this unsettling feeling and got moving. Kilian's mobile worked in the stairwell. A message had arrived – a voicemail from Marc. Kilian put his other hand on her arm as he listened. "He says there are people who want to get inside the house."

"Shit!"

"Two men. He's asking what he should do."

"Call him!" Louise began to run, as far as that was possible in her state and on a staircase. She tugged her mobile from her trouser pocket. As she waited for a connection she heard Kilian say, "Speak up, Marc," then, "Shit, I can't understand what you're saying," then, "He hung up."

"Try him again."

The officer at the control centre answered her call. Bonì requested more patrol cars, and for regional HQ to be asked if a SWAT team could be mobilised at once. She gave the location and a brief outline of the situation.

"Engaged," Kilian said.

"And get Rolf Bermann out of bed," Louise said.

"Oof," the control centre officer said.

They'd reached the ground floor and were sprinting to the exit. The buzzing in her ears had got louder and a few tones higher. It now sounded more metallic than electric, and it almost felt like an object, a solid block of steel going straight through her hearing and sitting heavily in the centre of her head.

Kilian said something but the words didn't get past the block.

"What?" she called out.

"If anything's happened to him . . ."

"Rubbish."

She shoved open the door and leaped outside. Once again Kilian's words were obstructed by the block. "Speak up, for God's sake!"

"Steinhoff!" he cried.

She knew what he meant. Steinhoff had been brutally beaten up and was perhaps only alive now because he'd been saved by some lucky turn of fate. Why should it be any different with Marc?

She shook her head. Don't think about it, Kilian . . .

Her mobile rang – the officer from the control centre. The SWAT team was on its way. But they hadn't managed to get in touch with Bermann on any of his numbers. "Shit!" she said, putting her mobile away. Adrenaline pumped through her blood vessels along with pure fear. Just don't break down now, don't think about Esther and Marc, about the fact that she was responsible for what happened, that a little sip, a little glass, a little bottle would make this burden bearable. Concentrate on the fact that a life existed outside this work, a little brother, Ben, remember that love is wonderful, you just have to work at it properly, then it becomes beautiful and manageable.

But she wasn't able to think of Germain or Ben; all she pictured in her mind was Esther Graf in a bath full of red water, and Marc on the run from two shadows.

8

Bonì felt better in the car. Focusing on the road dispelled those images and the engine drowned out the noise in her head. But the weight was still there, from one ear to the other.

Kilian tried Marc again; it just rang and rang. She dictated a text message: *There soon, get in touch.*

No reply.

On Schwarzwaldstrasse they were overtaken by half a dozen patrol cars with sirens blaring and blue lights flashing. Louise accelerated to keep up with the convoy. Kilian rang the officer in charge and asked them to turn off the sirens.

They raced through Littenweiler.

"Shit, it's switched off," Kilian said, putting his mobile in his lap.

The road leading to Esther's house was deserted. They passed the car Kilian and Marc had arrived in late the previous afternoon. The Stuttgart agents' car had gone.

No lights were on in the house.

With the other police officers they hurried to the car of the officer in charge, an old acquaintance from Freiburg South: Helm Brager. Two years ago he had led the operation in Merzhausen. Louise offered him her hand.

"Your case?" Brager said.

"It's all a bit vague. The Verfassungsschutz is involved too."

Brager frowned, but said nothing.

Louise didn't know much about him, apart from the fact that he'd been battling cancer for years. As in November 2003, the signs were visible – sunken, hairless face, forehead and cheeks covered in a film of sweat. She even remembered the eyes narrowed at the corners. His voice sounded softer than before.

Louise filled him in: three people, probably armed, one officer from D24, perhaps a hostage, the situation unclear. Their last contact with their colleague was at 3.11, nineteen minutes ago. They didn't know what had happened in the meantime.

"What sort of people are they?" Brager asked.

"No idea, but professionals for sure."

"Verfassungsschutz?"

"Don't think so."

Brager opened his mouth without saying anything. His eyes became small and he seemed to be holding his breath. In the frenzied reflection of the blue lights his bony features looked as if all life had been drained from them.

"Are you OK?" she asked quietly.

He nodded. "Let's go up."

"We'll secure the area then wait for the SWAT team."

Louise stood with Kilian and Brager in the shelter of a small wooden shed at the bottom of the steps, about fifteen metres from the front door. Although they weren't anticipating an exchange of fire, they didn't want to risk anything. Two uniformed colleagues wandered around searching for Marc; his mobile was still switched off. Other officers were dotted around the house at a distance.

No movement through the windows.

"There's nobody in there," Brager said.

She thought of the unknown man who came and left without being noticed. Who was there without anybody seeing him.

It was 3.35 a.m. The SWAT team would be here at any moment. Bonì glanced at the road, down the hill. In the distance she saw blue lights approaching rapidly. She counted four cars. Eight men plus

Brager's officers, Kilian and her. Around twenty-five of them in total, up against two or three suspects. In normal circumstances this would be enough. In a hostage situation things were different.

"We need a megaphone," she said to Brager, taking the mobile from her pocket to call the SWAT commander.

"Louise . . ." Kilian muttered.

She put her mobile down. The front door had opened, but there was nobody to be seen.

With the radio to his mouth, Brager said softly, "Movement up at the house, door opened. We're waiting."

Louise stared at the black rectangle. In her head she saw the narrow hallway, the hooks with the muddle of clothes, and below them the disarray of shoes. Armed individuals lurking in the darkness.

Then a voice shouted, "We're coming out! Don't shoot!"

"Marc," Kilian said.

Brager spoke into the radio. At the periphery of her vision Louise detected movement. The uniformed officers were getting into position, finding makeshift cover behind trees, a fence, an elevation in the ground. In the light of the moon there was the occasional glint of a star on an epaulette.

Then Marc came staggering out. His hands were behind his back, his mouth stuck with tape, his ankles tied together with rope that prevented him from taking anything but the tiniest of steps. Right behind him was a masked man. One hand was on Marc's arm, the other pressing the barrel of a pistol to the side of his head.

"Hold back!" Louise said.

Brager passed on the order.

Marc and the man stopped a few metres from the house. Two other people appeared in the doorway, stepped out and stopped. They too were wearing heavy masks with eye slits and wielding pistols. Both had rucksacks on their backs.

"Jesus Christ," Kilian said. "Who the hell *are* they?"

Louise didn't reply. She wondered if it was significant that both men's weapons were pointing to the floor rather than being aimed at someone. As if they were trying to avoid unnecessarily aggravating the situation.

It was now almost completely silent. Apart from the buzzing in her head, Brager's shallow breathing and the call of a night bird in the woods, not a sound could be heard.

"We've got to do something," Kilian said.

"No way."

"Are you going to wait for them to shoot him?"

"They're not going to shoot him, Kilian." Out of the corner of her eye she could see that the blue lights of the SWAT vehicles had reached the centre of Littenweiler. Now she could hear the engines too. A couple more minutes and they would be here. A dozen officers trained for situations like this and a commander who had the responsibility for deciding what happened from now on. No snipers, but the SWAT team would act the moment an opportunity presented itself. The cool-headed words of a chief inspector with a dubious reputation didn't carry much weight here.

"Are you going to let them leave?" Kilian asked.

Before she could reply they heard a metallic click. The masked man behind Marc had cocked his pistol.

"Shit, I told you!" Kilian hissed.

"Just shut up!"

Holding her breath, Bonì stared at the pistol pointing at Marc's head. What if she were wrong, would it happen again? Blurred images from her past flickered in her mind – a similar situation two and a half years ago: endless police officers, the SWAT team in position, a hostage-taker holding a gun to a colleague's head in a clearing . . . and shooting.

"They're waiting for something," Brager said.

Finally Louise understood. "Give them room." She retreated from

112

the steps; Brager and Kilian hesitantly followed her. As if they'd been waiting for this signal, the men started moving, approaching them slowly. Marc led the way with short steps. His head bowed, he looked more ashamed than afraid.

"Are you OK?" Kilian called out.

Marc nodded without looking up.

"Don't put up any resistance, do you hear me?" Louise said.

He nodded again.

She gazed at the weapon pressed to his head. Up until two years ago Freiburg Kripo had used that same model – a Walther P5.

The pistol the unknown man in Berlin had been carrying.

Louise looked at the man behind Marc, trying to recall Steinhoff's description. Around one metre eighty-five, between thirty and forty years of age, strong. What she saw matched the description.

His eyes stayed on her as he walked past. Dark, expressive eyes that gave her the feeling he'd recognised her.

Bugs and cameras . . .

"We need to talk," she said. "You know who I am. Call me."

The man didn't respond.

Having reached the steps, he went down them with Marc, followed by the other two men. Once on the road they turned towards the woods. Now the two men with rucksacks went ahead, Marc and the third man advancing more slowly, as if they had all the time in the world.

Kilian touched her arm. "I've got to follow them."

"They're not going to touch him."

"They did Steinhoff."

Louise wiped sweat from her brow and cheeks. "With Steinhoff there must have been a reason. There isn't one with Marc."

"He's seen their faces, maybe he's heard something. I'm responsible for him, Louise."

"And I'm responsible for you. You're staying here."

On the road below them the first SWAT officers were getting out of their cars, wearing protective vests. Boots were opened, visor helmets and machine pistols handed around.

"Make sure nobody goes into the house," she said, trotting down the steps.

The commander came up to her. "Are you Bonì?"

"Yes."

"Do you have a hostage situation?"

"Not anymore." She summarised what had happened.

"Are you going to let them go?"

"Only for today."

Louise went back to Brager, who was waiting at the top of the steps. He was wiping his head and face with a tissue. She looked at him and sensed that he was at the end of his tether, not just tonight, but in general. He'd battled long and hard, and now all his energy was depleted.

"You need a break, Brager."

He didn't respond to this. "Sorry about your colleague."

"Thanks."

She asked him to leave four of his officers at the house; she didn't need any more than that. No roadblocks and no manhunt until Marc was safe.

Brager nodded and said something. She cupped a hand to her ear. "I've got such a noise inside my head, I'm hearing really badly."

He forced a smile. "Both of us could do with a break."

"Yes."

"I've got a message for you?"

"Who from?"

"Kilian."

She turned to the house. Brager's officers were standing around on the paved path, but there was no sign of Kilian.

He would have passed her down on the road, so he must have

gone into the woods from up here. Ten metres away was a low wooden fence. Behind it, already in darkness, lay a strip of meadow, beyond that a thicket of trees and shrubs.

She looked at Brager again. "What's the message?"

"Don't call him. He'll get in touch with you."

Louise had expected anger, but instead only felt exhausted and old. A year ago, it struck her, she would have gone after Kilian, maybe she would have been the one to insist they follow the hostage takers. In her state neither was conceivable now.

She could only hope that Kilian would be content to keep watch and not try to free Marc.

"OK, then, Louise," Brager said, offering his hand. "See you next time."

"All the best, Helm."

Louise chatted to the officers who remained and walked around the house while trying to grasp some of the thoughts that had got caught in the tangle of her exhaustion: the cameras, the bugs, five minutes, ten tops . . . She went over to the fence by the slope and peered down at the houses.

If the guardian angel had arrived on foot after Esther's attempted suicide, he must have stayed close by. How many metres could you cover in five minutes? Four hundred if you walked. Fifteen hundred if you ran?

A hiding place in a radius of one and a half kilometres.

When she was sitting in the car she concluded that exhaustion and age were irrelevant. She'd lost the feeling of invulnerability that had carried her through all these years, along with the understanding of what was right and wrong.

Bonì started the engine and drove off.

One of the reasons Esther had seen no other way out apart from suicide was that Louise had put her under pressure. That was what this was about, nothing else. For the second time in her life, she was guilty.

115

II

The Web

9

The morning meeting began at eight o'clock on a sparkling blue day. The mood in the Holiest of Holies was tense, at least so far as Louise could judge. She'd slept barely two hours and took in only one word in three. Things that did register were "Football World Cup" and "Coalition negotiations", while there was also talk of a new, hitherto unknown species of damselfish discovered off the coast of Fiji, and the elegant leather sofas they were sitting on.

The secretary had served tea and biscuits. Reinhard Graeve led the discussion along with Henning Ziller, head of department 4 at the Stuttgart Verfassungsschutz office. Also present were Rolf Bermann, the last to arrive, and the two agents who'd been watching Esther Graf's house, Antje Harth and Michael Bredik, who both looked bleary-eyed too.

When the chat about the sofas came to an end there was silence.

"This tea . . ." Henning Ziller said. Rapture was writ large on his face. On his left wrist, like a drowsy insect, was a pilot watch, its silver metal strap a perfect match for his rectangular glasses. Whenever he moved his hand the links of the strap clicked. Ziller's tinted hair made him appear forty, but in view of his position he had to be at least fifty.

"East Frisian," Reinhard Graeve said.

"Quite exceptional. It's made my day."

"Thanks."

"Normally my sons do this when we have breakfast together in the mornings. Half an hour that fills the rest of my day with joy."

"How old are they?"

"Peter's five, Moritz is three."

Another moment's silence. Everyone apart from Louise and Ziller himself seemed to be trying to work out how old he was when he became a father for the first time.

Bonì was beginning to get restless; there was no end to the small talk.

A crisis meeting between Freiburg Kripo and Stuttgart Verfassungsschutz was obviously about politics too – about power, jurisdiction, public image and recrimination. A jungle of interests you had to cut a swathe through before embarking on the actual subject of discussion. You've got to be patient, Graeve had told her when they had a preliminary meeting at half past seven. Wake me if I nod off, Louise had replied.

Answers and *cooperation* – these were the goals they'd set for the meeting.

But first came the politics.

She glanced at Ziller's watch; thirty minutes had passed. At least the tea and the chit-chat were helping against the buzzing in her ears, which was quieter now. And they helped her not think of Esther, of Marc, who still hadn't been found, and of Kilian, who'd texted *I'm OK* at half past four and hadn't been in touch since. At four o'clock the control centre started geolocating his mobile. The text had been sent from the Kappler Tal, barely two kilometres from Esther's house. The phone had been switched off prior to that and immediately afterwards. At least he was thinking straight – anyone able to professionally bug a house might have tracking devices too.

"Having children is just the best," Henning Ziller continued with a broad smile. "You learn to look at the world in a more relaxed way, to think before doing or saying something, because the impact is directly visible on their faces. Don't you think so, Herr Graeve?"

"Indeed."

"Herr Bermann, you have children too, don't you? Remind me, how many?"

"Help me, Louise," Bermann said, scratching his moustache.

"Five," Louise said.

"Five," Bermann said.

"Five!" Ziller beamed. "You must be a *very* thoughtful man."

"Nope," Bermann said.

Louise wondered where the change in atmosphere had come from. Graeve suddenly looked alert, while Bermann was poking fun at himself, as if both men had read a purpose into Ziller's words that had passed her by.

"It's an important criterion for me when recruiting," Ziller continued. "Whether the applicant has children. Through children you learn to take responsibility. The world no longer revolves around yourself but around your charges. Your perspective changes. It's only through children that you grow up and thus become a fully fledged member of this society." He turned to his colleagues. "Am I right?"

Antje Harth nodded earnestly, Michael Bredik made a slight movement of his head. Louise couldn't help think of what Kilian had said: "A couple kissing each other without much passion." She couldn't imagine either of them being passionate. Harth came across as prim, Bredik dull – a shrinking violet and a pen-pusher.

"Frau Harth and Herr Bredik have children too." Ziller smiled again. "Is there another splash of tea?" he asked, holding up his cup.

"Help yourself, Herr Ziller," Graeve said, not moving.

Ziller refilled his cup, still with a smile on his face.

"What a cheap stunt," Bermann said.

Louise looked at him in surprise. "Have I missed something?"

"Keep your cool," Bermann said, patting her knee. "It's not worth getting worked up."

"The truth *is* cheap sometimes," Ziller said.

"He's right," she said.

Ziller looked at her. "And sometimes it's as bitter as high-percentage alcohol."

121

"I see," Louise said.

She'd understood. Childless *and* an alcoholic.

Leaning forwards, Graeve cleared his throat menacingly and put cream and kluntjes in his tea. "Herr Ziller," he said finally, "you're a guest here. Please behave accordingly."

Ziller smiled.

"Any more digs like that and I'll ask you to leave."

The smile grew broader; a smug chortle issued from Ziller's closed mouth.

"Please," Louise said. "This isn't about me."

Turning to her, Ziller raised a hand. One finger pointed at her and behind it the insect sparkled. "That's a serious misapprehension."

"It's about Esther Graf."

"Another error."

"I'm sorry?"

Ziller leaned back, crossed his legs and rested his hands in his lap. The watch strap clicked. "There's one thing none of you have understood. Frau Graf is just a small cog in the machine. Ultimately she's not important."

"Why did she try to kill herself, then?" Louise asked, biting her lip as she uttered these words. Bermann groaned and Graeve cleared his throat again. An open goal.

"Because *you* stuck your oar in," Ziller replied.

"I think we could all do with a break," Graeve said.

The Stuttgart team went off for a smoke, Bermann disappeared saying he had to make a call, and Louise went to the bathroom. When she returned Graeve was at his desk.

"We're not getting anywhere like this, boss."

"I fear you're right."

She wandered over to the windows. The spire of the minster reflected the sunlight and a flock of birds flew across the Dreisam.

To the north of the city a small aircraft gleamed and for a moment it felt as if the buzzing in her head were coming from the plane.

As bitter as high-percentage alcohol.

She put the shame and humiliation to the back of her mind. "I could throw up." She heard Graeve give a friendly snort and turned around. "If I'm the problem I shouldn't be part of the conversation."

"The problem is Henning Ziller."

She gave a crooked grin.

"No self-pity now, Louise. We can't afford it. Have you heard anything from Lubowitz?"

"No. I'll go over to Littenweiler later and have a chat with him. Then I'll pop in to see Esther Graf."

She'd called the hospital earlier this morning and spoken to a night sister. Esther had woken around five and dozed off again soon afterwards. No visitors, no calls so far. They hadn't managed to track down any relatives yet. Esther hadn't answered any questions relating to family.

There was a knock at the door and Bermann came back in. Looking at Louise he raised his arms with a grin, which could mean many things, including: nice to have you back, three months is a long time. Since July they'd only had phone contact and this morning in Graeve's office was the first time they'd seen each other.

"You've really hit the ground running."

She shrugged.

"Two days back on the job and you've already pissed off Berlin Kripo and the Verfassungsschutz." He smiled cheerfully.

So he *had* missed her.

"Yours?" Bermann said, pointing at the mobile vibrating on the windowsill.

Louise nodded, surprised, and picked it up. "Kilian . . . *Do nothing, we're OK, I'll be in touch again.*"

"Thank God," Graeve said. His phone rang and he looked at the display: "Control centre." He took the call, spoke briefly to an officer, then hung up. That text had been sent from the Kappler Tal too. "They're on foot."

They discussed whether to heed Kilian's request or send support. Clearly there was no immediate danger. And yet – one police officer abducted, a second in pursuit on his own . . . Graeve was inclined to request the SWAT team again. Bermann said they should have faith in Kilian's experience as a surveillance officer. Louise was too tired to decide on a course of action.

"Good," Graeve said hesitantly. "Let's keep waiting. Rolf, have you found out anything about our guests?"

"They're from department A."

This was the practical benefit of having a male chauvinist like Bermann on your team. Many of his current or ex-lovers worked in a number of investigative bodies, including, of course, the Stuttgart Verfassungsschutz office. Early this morning he'd given some mysterious individual, probably blonde, the names Ziller, Harth and Bredik, and now he had the answer.

"Which means?"

From the corridor came the sound of footsteps and loud laughter. Bermann lowered his voice. "Counter-espionage, proliferation and economic security." Antje Harth moved to the Verfassungsschutz from Financial Crime at Stuttgart Kripo; Michael Bredik studied business in Sigmaringen before changing track to join the agency.

"Economic experts," Graeve mused.

"GoSolar," Louise whispered.

The door flew open and Henning Ziller came in.

The break hadn't helped; the atmosphere was just as tense as before, even though Ziller was beaming as if he'd just become a father for the third time.

"We're agreed, then?" he said, when they'd all sat down again.

"On what?" Graeve asked.

"That you're going to leave the investigation to us."

"No. More tea?"

"Absolutely."

Ziller lifted up his cup and Graeve filled it. "A suggestion," he said.

Ziller tapped his watch. "I don't have much time, I've got to get back to Stuttgart."

"I understand."

"But it's very important to me that we're agreed."

Graeve nodded.

"We are on the same side, after all. Working towards the same goals. Facing the same enemies."

"We intend to continue cooperating," Graeve said. "You'll get all the findings from our investigation and your people will be integrated into the task force. We—"

"The *task* force?" Ziller sounded alarmed. For the first time this morning a crack had appeared in his façade of self-assurance. "You're planning to set up a *task* force?"

"Of course." Graeve counted on his fingers: "Abduction of a police officer using armed force, unlawful breaking and entering, unlawful remote surveillance, a fugitive suspected of attempted murder probably in our area of jurisdiction, suspicion of further as-yet-undetected crimes."

"OK, OK, *OK*," Ziller said, throwing his hands in the air, where they hovered for a moment before landing on his thighs with a slap. "Just for now let's forget that the situation has been aggravated only because Frau Bonì here breached the rules in a manner warranting a disciplinary investigation . . ." He stopped, seemingly expecting protest from Louise or her superiors. But no protest was forthcoming.

Instead Louise said, "Go on. If this isn't about Esther Graf, then what *is* it about?"

Ziller's eyes became small, his voice quiet. "The security of our state. Do you finally understand? Nothing less than that."

"What state are you talking about?" Bermann asked.

"Sorry?"

"Are you talking about Baden-Württemberg or the Federal Republic of Germany?"

"The Federal Republic, of course."

"How is it about the security of the country?" Graeve asked.

Stretching out his arms, Ziller said, "I do beg your pardon, but I've already said more than I ought to have."

Silence descended on the room.

Louise turned her gaze to the windows. On the ground below she saw a narrow strip of sunlight. How she would love to be lying there now, stretched out in the warmth, sleeping all day long in the soft light. Reinhard Graeve would supply her with tea and biscuits and bring her a fluffy blanket when the sun vanished. She thought of Ben, who was a sun-lover and who she hadn't called back because she loved him. She was, she thought, a strange woman.

Louise looked at Ziller. "Is the suspect from Berlin one of your people? Are we after an undercover Verfassungsschutz investigator?"

"With all due respect," Ziller replied, "only you could cook up such a fanciful idea." He lowered his head like a bull about to charge. "Freiburg Kripo *cannot* set up a task force for this, Herr Graeve, do you understand? The jurisdiction remains with us and you are going to cease all investigation into the matter. Every step you undertake from now could have devastating consequences – for your force, for officers in regional agencies working on this case, for people who are caught up in this through no fault of their own, and for our state, of course."

"Of course," Bermann said.

Louise caught a look from Michael Bredik, who was sitting opposite her. In his face was irritation, although she couldn't tell whether he was annoyed at her, Freiburg Kripo or Ziller himself.

Louise thought of the rumours surrounding GoSolar – insider trading, financial straits, decline in quality. She pictured Ernesto Freudenreich's felt slippers and Peter Schöne's small, staring eyes. The noise inside her head grew louder.

She had to go to bed.

"One last attempt," Graeve said, taking off his jacket and laying it over the back of the sofa. The bells of the minster struck nine. For some unfathomable reason the pilot watch said ten to nine. "No joint task force, instead we'll put together an investigation team solely to deal with the abduction of our colleague. Discussion between our two offices will be between you and me. Our findings will be passed on to the Verfassungsschutz, which will take care of all other issues, such as—"

"Saving the country," Bermann said.

"If it were up to me . . ." Ziller said with a shrug. "But I'm afraid it isn't up to me. The ministry of the interior has ordered that—"

"Which one?" Bermann cut in.

"I'm sorry?"

"The ministry of the interior of Baden-Württemberg or of the Federal Republic?"

"Baden-Württemberg, of course." Ziller didn't bother saying any more; the message was clear: you're out.

"OK," Graeve said. "If you're interested in the task force's findings let me know. The first—"

"There won't be any task force," Ziller interrupted.

Undeterred, Graeve outlined the initial steps of the "Littenweiler" task force. From Kripo's perspective Esther Graf was the only link they had to their colleague's abductors. After forensics had checked her house for traces, task force officers would undertake a search; they already had a warrant for this. Everything else depended on their initial findings. They were also searching for Hans Peter Steinhoff, who might be in communication with one of the hostage takers.

"No, that is not what's going to happen," Ziller said.

"So now we come to the key question," Graeve said coolly. "Does the Verfassungsschutz have information that could lead us to apprehend the hostage takers? If so, you should disclose it, for if you neglect to do so you'll be guilty of obstructing the course of justice while in office."

Ziller raised his eyebrows. "Are you threatening me?"

Graeve didn't respond.

"Kripo threatening the Verfassungsschutz? Freiburg threatening Stuttgart? You . . . you don't even have your own airport!" Ziller burst out laughing.

"Christ, these Swabians," Bermann said.

While Ziller was still laughing Louise got up. "I'm going now," she said. She kissed Bermann on the cheek and thanked him, then she kissed Graeve on the cheek and thanked him. Once in the corridor she hastened up to the third floor, brimming with anger and frustration, with fear mixed in somewhere. *As bitter as high-percentage alcohol*, but it was a release too; only a few minutes ago she'd thought again about a little glass for an hour of peace.

She closed the door to her office, lay down on the floor by one of the windows – where there was no sunlight – curled into a ball and began to weep with exhaustion.

When, half an hour later, she was standing by the sink in jeans and bra, trying at least to salvage outwardly what could be salvaged, Bermann came in and sat on the edge of the desk without saying a word. She let the basin fill to the top and plunged her face in up to the hairline. In the cold water the buzzing sounded like a roar, as if the Niagara Falls were inside her head. She sensed Bermann's eyes on her body, but she couldn't care less. Unfreedom began where you felt harassed by the gaze of other people. She'd never give anyone this power again, and certainly not Rolf Bermann.

At least this still worked, she thought: Bermann could gawp as much as he liked; she wasn't interested.

Louise straightened up and reached for the towel. When she'd put on her jumper she turned around. "Task force meeting?"

"In ten minutes."

"I've had it up to here with meetings."

Bermann raised one eyebrow. They needed her, he said. It was *her* case; nobody else was as well informed. There were questions only she was able to answer.

She pulled her hair back and tied it with a hairband. "Ask me now, then. I'm not going to sit in another meeting today."

Bermann sighed. "OK, tell me all about it, from the very start."

Bonì spoke, and he listened without asking questions. As she was talking, she took the holster out of the drawer and attached it to her belt. Bermann followed her movements with his eyes.

When she was done she put on her denim jacket. "I'm going to Littenweiler and then to GoSolar."

"Alone, I assume."

"Yes."

"You only work on your own, don't you?"

"It's always been like that, Rolf."

Our lone wolf, Alfons Hoffmann had once said. Always alone, even now when everything was fine again. Rubbish, Louise had protested.

Alfons Hoffmann, who hadn't returned to work since his heart attack in August.

"You can do Littenweiler on your own, but you're taking a colleague with you to GoSolar."

"One of the desk worms?"

"We'll see."

"Not Peter, not Ulf, not Annemarie, OK? I don't want any more problems."

Bermann smiled grimly. "Who would we like, then?"

"Illi, Mats or Anne would be OK. Ebbe Rohwe from Berlin – I get on with him reasonably well. He's got good taste in music and that counts for a lot."

They looked at each other in silence. Then Bermann slid off the desk and went to the door. Gripping the handle he turned and fixed his eyes on her.

"If the other officer is there, they're there, if not, they're not, OK?" Louise said.

He nodded.

"Now go on and say it, just so we can get it over with."

"Are you drinking again?"

"No."

"So long as you're not drinking, I'll back you."

"I know."

"If you start again I'll have your guts for garters."

Bermann's expression suggested he still had something to say, maybe quite a lot. She waited for the Bermann word that would confirm this suspicion – *OK*. Only Bermann could make this word sound as if there were other words resonating within it, words such as: "I'm happy you're back. I've missed you. I don't know what's wrong, but I'm worried about you. I'd like you to get back on your feet, because work would be no fun without you."

Those sorts of words.

"OK," he said.

Littenweiler was in sunshine, but as she drove up the road to Esther's house the wooded slope slid in front of the sun. In the cool shade she got out and went up the steps, familiar now. She wondered where Kilian might be and how Marc was. There had been no word for an hour and a half. As a surveillance officer Kilian was an experienced observer. But she doubted he was a match for Esther's guardian angel.

"I hope you thought of bringing coffee," Lubowitz called out from beside the open front door, cigarette in hand. He was wearing a white Tyvek suit, yellow socks and no shoes. Voices were coming from inside the house. Someone swore. Someone laughed. In her mind, Boni briefly saw Esther's exhausted face when she'd opened the door to her for the first time on Monday evening.

On the doormat were huge blue sliders in plastic overshoes – even for someone one metre ninety tall, Lubowitz had enormous feet.

"No, sorry."

"There's a bakery down by the crossroads."

She grinned wearily. Prisoners of a bizarre world of nanotraces, the forensics officers were accordingly eccentric, but nothing could proceed without them. So at crime scenes they had a bit of licence to bark orders at investigators from the real world. "Not now, Lubowitz, I don't have the time. Can I come in?"

"Not yet."

Louise nodded, grateful to be spared the sight of the bathroom.

"We'll be done in an hour, then you can do what you like."

The smoke from his cigarette rose into her nostrils. And there was another smell, which must be coming from the house – blood. Her eyes fell on Lubowitz's trouser legs, which were smeared with red.

"If they knew what a mess it made they'd swallow pills," he grumbled. "The blood shoots a metre high, all the fucking tiles are covered in it." He shook his head and tossed away the cigarette. "The word bloodbath really fits the bill here. Ever thought about that?"

"No."

"It's a salutary sight for suicide candidates."

"I'm sure it is. Found any shoeprints?"

"In the bathroom and on the way to the bedroom."

"Different ones?"

"There's one pattern that keeps cropping up and a heap of prints without any pattern."

"Overshoes?"

Lubowitz nodded. Louise wasn't surprised. The first time – after Esther had slit her wrist – the unknown man had rushed into the house. The second time – when Marc had got in his way – his visit had been prepared.

"I've e-mailed you the prints from Berlin."

"We'll compare them."

"Thanks. Found anything else?"

"What could we find? They were careful."

She waited – Lubowitz liked making his colleagues from the real world wait. There was movement inside his closed mouth. His tongue ran along the incisors, made his cheek bulge and worked on the molars. Louise heard muffled squelching noises.

In the end he shrugged.

Plugs that had recently been dismantled and which might have contained bugs, signs of abrasion on the lock of a desk drawer in which they might have positioned a mini camera – if her hunch was correct. One of his men was checking to see if any transmission devices were left anywhere in the house, but that would take until tomorrow. Louise didn't suppose he would find anything. The three men had had almost half an hour to remove all the bugs and cameras.

"How far do those things transmit?"

Lubowitz shook another cigarette from the packet and lit it. "Bugs work like mobile phones. You listen to everything from the comfort of your own home. You can't do that with cameras unless you've got a directional aerial or signal repeater. They give you a distance of between two and three kilometres, depending on the thickness of the walls. But I don't think there were directional aerials or repeaters here."

"What, then?"

"Rod aerials, Bonì."

"Meaning?"

"Outside, about a hundred metres. Less if there are walls between the transmitter and receiver."

Louise waited for more. Lubowitz seemed far away in his thoughts – or back in the house detecting abrasions on a lock, a fibre on the brown sofa, a hair on a rug. She found him the most inscrutable of all her colleagues.

"What do you mean by 'less'?"

Lubowitz furrowed his brow. "Ten to fifteen metres? No idea, how do I know what equipment they used?"

She let her gaze wander along the fence. There were only a handful of houses close by, but she wouldn't get a search warrant unless she could prove there had been illegal remote surveillance.

"I'm going back in, Boni," Lubowitz said, turning around and putting his covered sliders back on. "Don't forget the coffee next time, OK?"

As the front door slammed shut her mobile rang. An unknown number – the hospital. She was put straight through to Bertram Faller, who said he'd questioned Esther Graf as requested. Graf claimed she'd done it herself and now she wanted to know the identity of the man who'd bandaged her. "Do you know who it was?"

"Unfortunately not," Louise replied. "Did she see the man? His face?"

"Yes."

"Can she describe him?"

"I don't think so, she was practically unconscious."

"Have you asked her?"

"No." Faller's tone left no room for doubt. He wasn't going to ask her either. Nobody was going to ask her, for the time being at least; he would make sure of that. "Are we done?"

"Did he say anything?"

It sounded as if Faller was scratching his beard. "She didn't really understand. It sounded like: *What have you done, what have you done?*"

"He said it several times?"

"Three or four times."

Now she had a hunch as to what connected the man to Esther. Through the bugs and cameras he'd become involved in her life, maybe for weeks or months, and lost his professional distance. She'd become part of *his* life. "Has she had a visit?"

"From whom?" Faller's tone was clear – a sad statement rather than a question. Esther didn't seem to have anyone who might have visited her.

"One more thing," Louise said. Esther must have asked someone at the hospital to report her sick to GoSolar.

"Yes, we called them."

"Who?"

"The personnel department."

"Nobody else? A colleague?"

Once more Faller didn't answer.

She forced herself to remain calm. Faller was protecting Esther as best he could, and Bonì found this honourable as it didn't always happen. In the intensive care departments of many general hospitals, suicide patients were not given the best psychosocial treatment. She had to accept the fact that Faller was putting Esther's interests even above those of Kripo.

For a few seconds at least.

Louise's gaze fell on the front door. Only now did she notice that Esther's yellow umbrella lay in the grass. She picked it up and leaned it where it had been on her first visit.

Then her patience was exhausted. "Faller, last night armed hostage-takers came out of Esther's—"

"Annette Mayerhöfer," Faller interrupted grumpily.

"Thanks. What did you tell her?"

"That Frau Graf has sepsis."

She nodded. Bertram Faller went the whole hog for his patients.

"But there still aren't going to be any conversations."

"Understood. Please pass on my regards."

"Absolutely not."

In the car Louise took out the piece of paper she'd jotted Ben's number down on. As it rang she pondered what to say. *I love you too* was too bold, *What are the women like down there?* was exposing her hang-ups, as was *Lost my phone sounds strange Ben, don't you think?* So maybe, *How's the weather over there?* Or *I've got this sound in my head from a broken light.* What she really wanted to say was, *Don't come home at the weekend, I'm not feeling stable at the moment. Come when I don't need you anymore, but when I just . . . want you.*

It was still ringing. She took a breath – this time she was going to be spared.

But then he finally answered. "Liebermann."

"Hi!"

"Hi." She heard him laugh with relief.

"The connection . . ."

"I've been worried about you."

"The connection is crap, I can hardly hear you . . ."

"I miss you, Louise."

"Are you still there?"

"Yes, somehow . . ."

What *somehow*? she thought, exasperated. *Somehow I love you, somehow I want to marry you?* Just keep your mouth shut, Ben . . . "I've got a pretty tricky case on at the moment . . . Are you still there?"

"Yes."

"And I've got a funny sound in my ears, from a broken light."

"Hmm."

"This crappy line . . . Why do you have . . ."

"Tell me about the case."

". . . to Sarajevo, why can't you go to Zürich or London, at least we could call each other."

No answer.

"I can't hear you, Ben."

"I didn't say anything."

"It's all so *complicated*."

"What are you trying to say, Louise?"

A lot of things, Ben, she thought, but I'd rather say nothing. "I was in Berlin a couple of days ago. On this case, you see. I don't like it. Berlin, I mean. Not my city."

"Let's talk about it when I'm back."

"Are you putting the phone down on me now?"

"No, no."

"Do you have to go?"

"No, I've just got back to the hotel."

"It just sounded like . . . What have you been up to?"

"I went for a coffee with Jim and Antun. Former SIPA colleagues."

She racked her brain to work out what the abbreviation stood for – she was thinking about it only the other day and now she'd already forgotten. Oh yes, *State Investigation and Protection Agency*. And who were Jim and Antun? Was anyone else with them, an Iva or a Tina?

She didn't ask him this, of course.

"I . . . do really miss you," Ben said.

She rolled her eyes. Ben Liebermann was one of those men who said the wrong thing when they wanted to say the right thing. Who showed their emotions, making you feel harassed. At times like this, Louise thought, she occasionally preferred men like Rolf Bermann who said nothing, or an "OK" at most. But those men were only good for a couple of seconds, not a moment longer. The others were fit for purpose. They were the ones you had to hold on to. Men like Ben, who it might not be possible to hold on to, because he couldn't settle down, having to change town, woman, job every couple of years, as if he were a particularly restless descendant of Odysseus.

Ben had fallen silent; she knew he was waiting.

"I happened to listen to Element of Crime in Berlin, 'Die schönen Rosen'. A colleague had it on in the car."

Silence.

"Now I've got the CD on the whole time at home."

Silence.

"That's your lot for today, Benno Liebermann."

In distant Sarajevo she heard a quiet, soft laugh. Louise joined in the laughter, suddenly filled with elation.

Then the conversation was finally over.

10

At eleven o'clock Bonì arrived at Haid business park and pulled up outside the GoSolar building, a modern-looking, four-storey cube of glass and steel surrounded by trees. Towering a few metres in front of the building was a shield of solar panels, angled to catch the sun's rays. The car park, with no more than eleven vehicles in it, was bordered by grass verges and flowerbeds mulched with bark. The employees at GoSolar rode bicycles; the racks along the western side of the building were full. Louise's bad conscience stirred, as it did every few weeks, a hot breeze in her remote consciousness. She was a police officer in the green city and she didn't even *own* a bike; she drove the one and a half kilometres from her apartment to police HQ. You didn't do that sort of thing in Freiburg, her bad conscience said, cursing.

She got out and looked around. No couple kissing without much passion. But the car park was exposed and could be seen from a distance. Someone might be standing behind trees, in a building, and watching her without her knowing.

Bugs and cameras in Berlin and in Littenweiler.

She turned to face the building and stared at the dark-blue façade, shielding her eyes from the November sun with a hand. Inside she could make out figures, while three smokers stood by the entrance. Sinners in paradise.

Her mobile buzzed – a text message.

Come and get us, Kilian had written.

She stared at the screen, puzzled. Come and get us?

From where? she wrote back.

No reply.

It was a moment before it sank in. Kilian must have been discovered and overpowered – presumably sometime in the night. The abductors had left him and Marc in the woods, guarded by one man who'd used Kilian's mobile three times to send messages and buy time. They knew the phone was being tracked, but they'd banked on the fact that Kripo wouldn't intervene.

A car pulled up behind Louise and a familiar voice said, "Your colleague is here."

Soon afterwards Bermann was standing beside her, a grin on his face, his fingers in his pockets like a teenager and a white shirt taut across his muscular chest.

She showed him the text message.

"Shit." He returned to his car to send uniformed officers and, just in case, the SWAT team to the Kappler Tal. A helicopter had to be put on alert too.

"They're better than us," he said when he came back.

"Not better, just quicker. What's the task force doing?"

"On its way to Littenweiler – sends its greetings, by the way."

Louise shrugged. "Maybe I'll make it tomorrow."

"You'll make it this evening. Six o'clock in my office."

"Why not in the task force room?"

"It's still a small task force."

She frowned. A task force that could be quickly disbanded. Reinhard Graeve was planning ahead. He knew he wasn't just dealing with the Verfassungsschutz, but the ministry of the interior and the regional government too. He'd declared war on Henning Ziller, who would bring out the heavy artillery – agency bosses, junior ministers and other politicians. If the pressure became too great, Graeve would have no other option than to capitulate.

"By the way," Bermann said. The phone the unknown man had

called emergency services with was a pre-paid mobile that had only been used for that single conversation lasting 1 minute 57 seconds. It was now switched off and couldn't be located.

Louise nodded. It was probably lying somewhere at the bottom of the Dreisam.

Bermann nodded at the GoSolar building. "Let's keep pretending."

"Pretending what?"

"Pretending we don't know that Kilian and Marc are probably safe. Two abducted police officers – that'll allow you to barge into any supervisory board meeting. Attempted murder in Berlin is a bit small-scale."

"Sounds more Boni than Bermann."

"A dose of Ziller in the morning makes even the most steadfast investigator wobble."

They made their way to the entrance.

"Do you sense it too?"

"What?"

"That we're being observed."

He snorted. "We're becoming paranoid."

They passed through a cloud of smoke, then Louise looked up at a small camera lens by the double doors.

Bermann opened one, ushered her in and said, "You do the talking."

"I thought you were too old to change."

He gave a melancholic laugh. "Today I'm young again."

The foyer that housed the reception was flooded with light and extended up to the glass ceiling. The receptionist briefly spoke on the phone to a "Herr Kleinert", then they were taken by lift up to the fourth floor. In a waiting area with a panoramic view they sat on rattan seats amongst water coolers and plants as tall as the room. On an LED wall behind them a video clip was playing – children frolicking by a waterfall in the sunshine. The sound was muted and a remote control lay on a low table. Beside the screen was a coffee area with an expensive-looking espresso machine. The shadow of an indoor palm danced on Bermann's chest. It felt to Louise as if it were still summer in here rather than autumn.

She blinked in the sunlight. The tiredness had returned.

A blonde woman came smartly over and offered them coffee, soft drinks and biscuits. Bermann grinned at her and they both declined.

"I miss my old colleagues," Louise said. "Illi and Alfons. And the boss, of course. Almenbroich."

Bermann said nothing.

"Even Anne." She tapped her head. "They're all in here and I can't get them to leave. Sometimes I can't believe that other people are now sitting in their offices. I'm surprised it's technically possible."

She waited for a reaction; Bermann just stared at her.

"Oh, well," she said, listening to the buzzing inside her head, which had become an integral part of her body and seemed to adapt to her surroundings. Here it sounded soft and calm – the "eco" variant.

Bonì picked up one of the company brochures arranged on the table. On page two she came across Gerhard Kleinert, smiling confidently at her. She knew this fresh-faced individual from the company's website. According to the text he was fifty-two, a qualified engineer, chief technical officer and one of the firm's three founders.

She showed Bermann the photo. He nodded indifferently. The blonde woman was back, asking for their patience for another moment or two. He nodded and patiently watched her walk away.

Laughing, Louise stood up, went to the nearest water cooler and helped herself. The rattan creaked cosily when she sat back down. Sleep, she thought, just half an hour's sleep.

Eventually Bermann clapped his hands. "Come on, let's go and find the guy."

She yawned. There was actually more Bonì in Bermann than she would have thought possible.

They didn't have to look for long; Kleinert's office was just two doors down. "Wow!" Bermann said mockingly, pointing at the nameplate. Kleinert had two doctorates.

Bermann knocked at the door and opened without waiting.

A large room, furnished spartanly and in muted tones. A desk, low office cabinets and seating area with two abstract paintings that provided the only splash of colour. To the left an orange canvas with lines; to the right a blue one with lines. Louise was still trying to work out what they represented when she noticed that Bermann's hand was darting towards his holster.

She followed his gaze in horror.

Between the desk and the floor-to-ceiling windows stood an office chair with its back to them. She saw the upper half of an inert body, arms hanging from a light-grey suit jacket, a limp hand. Her pulse quickened and the buzzing in her head became shrill.

Bonì pulled out her gun.

While Bermann gestured to her to go to the right and he moved to the left, it crossed her mind that Kleinert had been notified of their presence not even twenty minutes ago, and was still alive then. They'd been waiting outside for a good fifteen minutes, less than ten metres from his office . . .

To the left, a door, to the right Bermann was standing beside another. He slowly pushed it open and she could make out a tiled floor and wall – a small bathroom. Bermann turned back and indicated the door she was slowly approaching. She nodded. Her eyes shot back to the man in the chair. Now she could see more: the left shoulder, the left leg up, a black lead on the arm.

Louise returned her Heckler & Koch to its holster and put a finger to her ear.

"What?" Bermann said.

At that moment the chair whipped round and she found herself staring into the terrified eyes from the GoSolar brochure.

After drinking a glass of water Gerhard Kleinert seemed to have recovered from the shock. He apologised, saying he'd been trying to relax after a strenuous board meeting before calling them in. In his embarrassment, Kleinert briefly looked like a confirmand who'd been forced to wear an oversized suit by his parents.

He stood up, shook their hands, then took his seat again. In the distance Louise could hear piano music, something classical, regular and cool like Bach. Kleinert fiddled with a black iPod and the music stopped.

She looked longingly at the sofa beneath the paintings, but Kleinert didn't invite them over to the seating area so they remained standing where they were, Bermann to his right, Louise to his left. Rather practical, she thought; like this they could put the screws on him.

In fact Kleinert didn't much resemble the photograph in the brochure. Even after life had returned to his body there was nothing fresh about his face. Deep furrows lined the waxy-looking cheeks as they met his nose, and his skin was as bad as a teenager's. Rather than radiating confidence, his eyes flickered about like someone who didn't get enough sleep.

"Everything OK now?" she said.

"Yes, thanks." He rubbed his brow, nose and mouth. "Am I right in thinking you're from Freiburg Kripo?"

"Yes."

He nodded thoughtfully. His rubbery lips were not completely closed; his upper incisors sat on the lower lip. Anatomical features that had probably earned him a lot of teasing at school. "And why . . .?" he said eventually, looking blankly from her to Bermann.

Kleinert wasn't a good actor.

Louise signalled to Bermann to do the explaining. She already had a hunch of what Kleinert would tell them: not the truth, or only part of the truth, or a variant of the truth devoid of information, but not legally compromising. People slit their wrists, were beaten up, taken hostage, had painful sounds and weights inside their head, and then you had to grapple with men like Henning Ziller and Gerhard Kleinert who pursued their own interests and acted as if they were either important or clueless.

Bermann explained that two officers had been abducted at gunpoint last night from the house of a GoSolar female employee. Louise admired his calmness in these situations. Ever the model head of section, a rock in stormy waters, covered in parts by putrid moss and washed smooth in others, but stable overall. Contrary to her, nothing crumbled, the bottom didn't float to the top. The whole thing was firmly anchored and it struck her that you could either hang on to this rock or sit on top of it.

"Taken hostage?" Kleinert said. "For heaven's sake . . . Who by?" He was even more waxen now and looked as if he barely possessed the strength to sit up straight.

Bermann remained vague – three men, no clue as to their identity.

Kleinert shook his head; the disbelief was genuine.

"Are you unwell?" Louise said.

"No, no, just overworked. These men . . . Who could they be? I mean, terrorists or . . . burglars or . . ."

"We don't know," Bermann said.

"Who's the employee?"

"For Christ's sake!" Louise said.

Kleinert flinched.

"Questions, questions, questions. We need *answers*, Kleinert. You know who it is."

"I could . . . request the list of absentees, if she—"

"No," Louise butted in. "She's not on it. She's sitting at a desk in this marvellous solar spaceship, working on the eco-paradise of the future, as she does every day."

Kleinert blinked hectically; Bermann cleared his throat.

Exasperated, Louise turned away and focused on the abstract paintings above the sofa. The orange was too garish, the blue too sombre, the lines forming unpleasantly angular shapes. Now she realised they were supposed to be human figures. On the left a woman, on the right a man, frozen in lines, without a soul. She resisted the urge to take the paintings down and turn them to face the wall.

A mobile rang. She heard Bermann utter a terse "Yes", followed by an "OK". She turned back to the two men.

"The parents have found the boys. They're just a bit dirty and chilled."

Bonì nodded, relieved.

"Why were your officers at my employee's house?" Kleinert asked Bermann. "Can you tell me that, at least?"

"No," Louise said.

"If she's done something wrong, then as her employer—"

"She hasn't."

"No, but why—"

"*We're* asking the questions, Kleinert. *You're* giving the answers – haven't you got that yet? So, do you know who we're talking about?"

"I'm sorry, but with more than three hundred and—"

"Is he trying to pull the wool over our eyes, Rolf?"

Bermann growled.

"What I'm saying is, you're not particularly convincing."

"But why should I—"

"*We're* asking the questions, for Christ's sake," Louise said, rubbing her eyes. "Why is the Verfassungsschutz involved?"

"The Verfassungsschutz?"

"For God's sake, talk, man!"

Kleinert looked at Bermann as if he were hoping for help from the rock in the choppy seas. The rock offered no help.

"Why is the Verfassungsschutz involved?" Louise asked again.

"Involved in what?"

"I don't believe it." Overcome with anger she laughed out loud. Anger at Kleinert, at the buzzing in her head, but most of all anger at herself, because increasingly she was losing control. Certain qualities seemed to have evaporated, such as patience, calm, and the conviction that she would ultimately reach her goal. Qualities she'd sometimes been able to fall back on, even during her Jägermeister period. "Do you know what happens when you slit your wrists?"

Kleinert's eyes grew larger.

"The blood spurts two metres into the air and makes a mess of the tiles."

"Louise," Bermann said calmly. He was looking at her too now, his mouth a line beneath his moustache. She suddenly wondered why he'd gone along with her for so long this morning without intervening. A year or two ago he wouldn't have stood by and watched. Incomprehensibility and anger would have prevailed. Now she had the impression that he was being swept along without being able to do anything about it – or wanting to.

"This guy's making me mad. But OK." She took the photograph of Hans Peter Steinhoff from her handbag and placed it on the desk. "Do you know him?"

Kleinert took his time, then shook his head.

"Sure?"

"Completely."

"It's possible that this man tried to kill your colleague."

Kleinert stared at the photo again. Beads of sweat stuck to the roots of his grey hair. "*Kill?*"

"Do you know him now?"

"No."

146

"Is he lying, Rolf?"

Bermann raised his eyebrows. "No."

"That's what I think too. *Shit.*" Louise put the photograph back in her bag. Kleinert looked relieved, but she sensed he was afraid. He might be a brilliant solar expert, full of confidence, but he gave the impression he'd stumbled into an unfamiliar world and couldn't get his bearings.

"So tell us, what happens at GoSolar?"

Kleinert shifted back in his char. His eyes darted to the telephone on his desk and Louise realised he was waiting for a call, the call that would be his salvation.

The display read 11.41. One minute too late, four minutes too early? She thought of Eberhard Rohwe and "We Will Rock You". That was how all this trouble had begun.

Taking the cordless phone from its dock, Bonì removed the batteries and laid them on the desk. "What about these rumours? Insider trading, financial straits, quality issues?"

Kleinert ran a hand across his brow and glanced at Bermann. Once more the rock was no help.

He picked up the phone, put the batteries back in and said the company was facing serious problems. GoSolar was in great financial difficulties. Because of the rumours of insider trading the banks had blocked credit. Major customers had backed out and orders, both regional and national, might be cancelled. In July the company had engaged a renowned auditing firm. Their report, he said, proved that all the buying and selling of shares by employees had been done correctly. Although this report had been published it hadn't yet influenced public opinion and hadn't been able to persuade the banks to change their mind. As a result, he went on, a project that was crucial for the firm – developing solar cells for cars – had been put back. If the situation didn't change over the next two quarters, GoSolar would be on the brink of insolvency.

"Our CFO is urging us to start a kitty," he said with a sheepish smile. "That says it all, really."

"What's a CFO?" Louise said.

"A chief financial officer."

Kleinert was staring at the display: 11.43.

He drew breath.

"Where do the rumours come from?" Bermann asked, now standing with legs apart and arms crossed in front of his chest. His eyes were small and focused, the hound had smelled the game.

Kleinert hesitated. "I'm afraid we don't know."

"Do you have a suspicion?"

"Nothing concrete, no."

"Anything unconcrete?" Louise said.

Perturbed, Kleinert narrowed his eyes and for a moment she almost felt sorry for him. As an engineer you'd devoted your life to cute little silicon crystals and all of a sudden you had to grapple with damaging rumours and detectives of Bonì's ilk.

"So far as we can trace them back, the first rumours appeared in a French newspaper."

"What do you infer from that?" Bermann asked. "Is French competition behind all this?"

Kleinert shrugged. So far, he replied, French solar firms had not shown themselves to be serious competitors. The French market was nowhere near as large as the German one, and because of the country's official preference for nuclear energy, state support for renewables had so far been low. There were no companies as big or as innovative as those in Germany. People were saying, however, that the Villepin government was planning a statutory feed-in remuneration that would come into force next year, which would definitely boost the French sector. And yet . . . "Look, in France there is a per capita average of 0.44 watts of photovoltaic output, compared to more than forty watts in Germany. There's no . . ."

The phone rang.

". . . comparison between the two markets. Excuse me."

Louise had turned and was already at the door when Kleinert began to explain – another meeting – now – as he'd told them, the company was facing serious problems. A cliché of regret, then she stepped into the corridor. The cliché was repeated, then her nervous system saw reason and let Kleinert's voice fade away in the buzzing between her ears.

She waited beside her car. The November sun shone surprisingly brightly, its reflections off car roofs and the façade of the building flying directly into the pain centre inside her head. Louise screwed up her eyes and tried to ignore the buzzing. In the end Gerhard Kleinert had said very little, but he had come out with one interesting item: "French".

Department A of the Verfassungsschutz was responsible for counter-espionage, proliferation and economic security. Henning Ziller, head of the department, had said it was about the country's security, which perhaps meant the security of the country's *economy*. Was GoSolar a victim of industrial espionage?

But the Verfassungsschutz was only brought into play if a foreign intelligence service was involved. The agency wasn't interested in competitive espionage; in the case of industrial espionage it leaped into the ring with the promise of silence if asked for help. An ideal partner for businesses concerned about their reputation. For the Verfassungsschutz the opportunity principle applied – it *could* investigate if criminal activity came to light, unlike Kripo, which was subject to the legality principle and *obliged* to investigate.

Bermann exited the building and came slowly over to Louise. He was carrying his coat and she could see sweat patches under his arms. His gaze was fixed on her, he looked focused. Not a strict boss anymore but a concerned one, even though he would never admit it.

"What was *that*, Louise?"

"Creative witness questioning."

Bermann snorted.

"I'm just very tired, Rolf."

"Then go and get some sleep."

"And I've got this fucking noise in my head."

"Tinnitus?"

"Rubbish. A broken ceiling light."

"So long as you know what you're doing."

"I mostly do."

Bermann wandered over to his car and she followed him. The indicators flashed with a sing-song tone, as if the car was happy to have him back. As he opened the passenger door and threw his coat on the seat, he said kindly, "Your compatriots again, eh?"

They ran through the possibilities. A French competitor, a French secret service – were the three men from Esther's house members of this? That would explain the bugs and cameras and also why they'd acted with such restraint.

Louise opened the rear door of Bermann's car and sat in the shade. The weight in her head had grown even heavier. "But didn't Kleinert say that the French solar sector isn't a competitor. That their market's too small?"

"Maybe they export."

She nodded.

"Or they're trying to roll out a new product into the market. If they don't have one, then they get the construction data from a German competitor."

"Solar cells for cars?"

Bermann raised his eyebrows in agreement. "And while they're about it they can also seed a few rumours about their German competitor. I mean, it would be very handy if it went bankrupt."

Louise leaned her head and shoulders against the back seat. Even here, in Bermann's car, immersed in the smells of one of his sexual playgrounds, she would have slept if sleep were at all possible. "But a secret service?"

"The Verfassungsschutz wouldn't be in charge otherwise."

She yawned. Thought about two minutes ago and already forgotten.

Louise knew that the idea wasn't ludicrous. Many foreign intelligence services were open-minded when it came to their country's economy; some even had a legal obligation to be active. They provided knowledge relating to foreign competitors and sourced information. The globe was awash with electronic data streams, while the aether was one big babble of voices. Satellites and ground stations gathered gigabyte after gigabyte of words and data. If that didn't suffice, they tapped telephones, intercepted e-mails, eavesdropped on careless bosses or garrulous employees in trains and on planes, approached secretaries in supermarkets, pretended to be interested colleagues at trade fairs, and infiltrated servers or intranets with poor security. American intelligence agencies did this, as did the Russians, the Chinese, the British, the Israelis and – if the rumours could be believed – so did the French, for example their foreign intelligence service: Direction Générale de la Sécurité Extérieure, DGSE.

It happened in Germany too.

But the Americans, British and French were friends. No German politician or official would openly declare that friendly countries were spying on the national economy. Let alone businesses worried about severe damage to their image. The share price! The investors! The banks! Fear made these companies keep quiet.

While preparing for teaching in Wertheim, Louise had read a security report which said only eight per cent of Baden-Württemberg businesses damaged by espionage turned to the authorities or consultants. Ninety per cent of those firms affected didn't even know they were being spied on. This meant thousands, because apparently around a fifth of all businesses were at some point victims of espionage.

"We need officers from D31 on the task force," she said.

"We've already got them."

"Who?"

"Peter Schöne and the hero with the slippers."

The tyrannosaurus and the deer, plus herself. Skirmishes were inevitable. Bermann was going to have fun.

He put one foot onto the running board and leaned his arms on the roof and the open door. His eyes were wide open. Every fibre in him radiated energy and strength. For a moment Bonì found him almost sinister. His body created shade but he was blocking the way out of the car.

She yawned again.

"You need to see a dentist."

"Really?"

"You've got a cavity on the bottom left."

She felt for it with her tongue. It had opened up in Wertheim. She laughed. The boredom had even eaten into her teeth.

"Want me to drive you home?"

"No, thanks. I'll be fine."

Bermann asked if she was going to come to Littenweiler. Lubowitz was finished and had said they were now free to search the house. She shook her head; she wanted to go back into GoSolar.

"What?" Bermann leaned forwards, his head hovering right above hers.

"Don't get your knickers in a twist. Just a chat between women."

"Between women?"

"A colleague of Esther Graf."

"Don't forget we haven't got a search warrant. And leave Kleinert be, OK?"

"OK, boss."

Bermann let her get out. "One more thing." He was going to drive to the hospital at three o'clock. They had to speak to Graf, no matter what Faller said.

Louise briefly pondered whether she ought to watch the spectacle – two alpha males in battle. Faller would win, so she could spare herself the journey. She would try to talk to Esther later, after eight o'clock tonight, when Faller's shift was over.

But Bermann didn't need to know this.

Then she would stand by in case the guardian angel accepted her offer of a conversation.

Bermann didn't need to know this either.

11

An information board in the foyer showed visitors the way. Boni was in luck; she was in building 1, which housed both the management and the research and development department where Esther worked and – she hoped – Annette Mayerhöfer, who Faller had called that morning.

The department was on the second floor. She went up a light-coloured wooden staircase that crossed the foyer. Narrow lines of shadow and light alternated on the steps, creating a disorienting pattern on the wood. She felt slightly dizzy and, as before, the sunlight slanting into the building hurt her eyes and head.

She could see Bermann in the car park outside. He was leaning against his car, on the phone.

The staircase led to a corridor running parallel, at the end of which was an open-plan office. White office furniture divided the space into groups of four desks. Around twenty staff were sitting in front of computer screens, all of them younger than thirty, all men. None took any notice of her. Louise wandered over to a corridor with individual offices, seating areas and coffee machines. As she went past the doors she inspected the nameplates, but couldn't see either Esther's or Mayerhöfer's.

In the corridor on the other side of the open-plan office she found what she was looking for. It said HEAD OF DEPARTMENT in sky-blue letters on the wall. The first office was that of *Annette Mayerhöfer / Esther Graf.*

She knocked; nobody answered.

Wait or leave?

Wait.

She sat opposite the door in a chair set back in a small recess with a water cooler. On a coffee table was a solar magazine. As she was mulling over the meaning of "energy return times" and "solar island systems" she nodded off.

A hand on Bonì's shoulder woke her. She opened her eyes.

She'd put a leg over one of the arms of the chair and was leaning back over the other. Suppressing a yawn, she sat up. Beside her stood a woman with shoulder-length black hair that covered the left side of her forehead. She gave Louise a friendly smile. Narrow glasses, fashionable suit, the blouse with dark stripes open to the middle of her décolleté. Definitely attractive and confident, no doubt determined and clever too. The counterpart to Esther Graf.

On the lapel of the woman's blazer was a name badge. Being found while you were asleep made searching fun, Louise thought contentedly.

"You won't go far here in that position," Annette Mayerhöfer said.

"I'll hand in my notice, then."

Mayerhöfer smiled. "Were you looking for me?"

"If you've got a sofa."

"We have a chill-out room on the third floor."

"That would make the month pass quickly. Coffee?"

"There's a machine over there."

Louise stretched. "Happy to wait here."

"Would you tell me who you are before you send me to get coffee?"

"Don't ask too much of me." Smiling, Louise got to her feet and picked up her denim jacket. "Louise Bonì, Freiburg Kripo. I need ten minutes of your time." She fished her police badge from the pocket. "Latte macchiato, if you've got it, with two sugars, please."

Annette Mayerhöfer stared at her wide-eyed.

"Don't worry, I've just got a few questions."

"I *knew* it."

"Knew what?"

Mayerhöfer lowered her voice. "Not here."

Annette Mayerhöfer was taken on by GoSolar in the year it was founded, 1996. She had experienced the firm's difficult early years, the sector's first boom, the company's flotation on the stock market in 2001, the market slump in 2002, the construction of the building in Haid, the big contracts that had made GoSolar one of the top ten solar cell producers, the next boom. She was thirty-three and one of the company's major assets. Three weeks ago she'd handed in her notice.

"I don't want to watch all of this go to pot, you understand?" she said.

"No," Louise said.

They were sitting in the office that Mayerhöfer shared with Esther Graf, an impressively large room, albeit only half the size of Gerhard Kleinert's. In the middle ran an invisible dividing line, on either side of which were a desk and three shelves on the wall. In Mayerhöfer's half there were also houseplants and a tea trolley with a number of orchids; in Graf's half a narrow metal cabinet, beside which a door lead into the adjacent office.

In her shock Mayerhöfer had forgotten the latte macchiato.

"What did you know?" Louise asked. "And why is the firm going to pot?"

Mayerhöfer tapped her right index-finger on the desk and looked at Louise with a hint of surprise. "Aren't you here because of the rumours?"

"I thought they'd been disproved."

"Officially, yes."

"But?"

"Whether they're true or not, once rumours like that start flying around you've got a serious problem. You need bags of money, energy and expertise to deal with them. And if they still turn out to be true . . ." Mayerhöfer shrugged. She had no desire, she said, straightening her glasses, to work in a business where managers or board members would at some point be convicted of criminal activity. Things had got a bit too comfortable for her here in any case. Ten years with the same firm – it was time for new challenges, for a change, a move. "On January 1 I'm starting work with an energy company in Hamburg. They want to expand into the wind energy sector, and that interests me. Surprised?"

"A little, yes. You spend ten years working for GoSolar and then you change because of a few rumours?"

"Well, it's not only the rumours." Mayerhöfer's finger began tapping a twitchy rhythm: slow, slow, fast.

The rumours had started at some point this year, which had changed the atmosphere in the company. At a stroke the firm's future was uncertain, people were worried about their jobs and the relationship between management and employees deteriorated. Some colleagues complained of bullying-like tactics, sexual harassment and malicious gossip. "There's been something very fishy going on here for months and I'm not going to let it rub off on me."

"Do you think it's possible that the rumours were spread deliberately? By a competitor? To put GoSolar in difficulty and maybe even oust it from the market?"

Mayerhöfer's index finger paused in mid-movement and she frowned. "What do you mean?"

"It's just a thought."

"A rather . . . explosive thought. Is there any evidence to suggest it?"

"Nothing concrete."

"But a suspicion?"

"Just a vague hunch."

"Hmm. Any particular competitor in mind?"

"We haven't got that far yet."

Mayerhöfer nodded; her finger picked up its rhythm again. "To answer your question . . ." It was conceivable, of course; even in the green-energy sector firms played hardball. But she saw no indication of it, and even less reason for it. Nor could she think of a single competitor who might be responsible. "But you wouldn't have reached such conclusions on the basis of nothing, so I suppose we have to entertain the possibility. I'm happy I'm going."

When there was a knock at the door she put a finger to her lips. "Yes?"

The door to the neighbouring office opened and an exceptionally good-looking man appeared, stirring memories of hot summer days – large dark eyes, tanned skin, white shirt, beige flannel trousers and light-brown loafers without socks, as if he'd sprung from a golfing magazine. He also had a warm, friendly smile, which lost none of its warmth when he noticed Louise.

She checked his eyebrows: impressive too.

"Excuse me, Frau Mayerhöfer. Have you already had lunch?"

"Yes," Mayerhöfer replied.

"Shame."

"Go for the lasagne, it's delicious."

"My favourite." The golfer beamed, Mayerhöfer beamed. Then the door closed.

"Wow!" Louise said.

"You're welcome to him, I don't get involved with colleagues. But hurry, half the workforce here is after him, including the guys."

Louise made a dismissive gesture and laughed. Look, but don't touch.

But something in the golfer's brief appearance and Mayerhöfer's answer was puzzling her. Already had lunch . . . She checked the time – half past one. She left Kleinert's office at a quarter to twelve and knocked at Mayerhöfer's door around midday. That meant she'd slept for over an hour, hanging across a chair in a business's waiting area.

Freiburg Kripo really wasn't showing its best face.

Something else had struck her. "Are you not on first-name terms at GoSolar? I thought everything here was ... you know, green."

Mayerhöfer smiled. "The sector emerged from the alternative spirit of Kreuzberg in Berlin. But now companies are getting involved with the top players. Damn, I forgot your latte macchiato. Do you still want me to get you one?"

"No, thanks."

"It's really no trouble."

Louise shook her head. "Is your colleague new?"

"Are you interested, then?"

"How long's he been working for GoSolar?"

"You *are* interested."

Next door to Esther Graf and clearly new, Louise thought. Yes, she was interested.

"Since September," Mayerhöfer said.

"What's his name?"

"Philipp."

"German?"

"Funny question. Yes."

"What about his surname?"

Mayerhöfer cleared her throat. "I ought to have added that he and I won't be colleagues for much longer."

"I understand."

"It's nothing serious. Just a little platonic flirt that needs a non-platonic finale. I don't start anything that I can't suitably conclude."

"I won't get in your way, promise."

"Good." Mayerhöfer's expression was gentle, her clear features had become softer. "A latte macchiato now?"

"No, just the surname, Frau Mayerhöfer."

"Schulz."

Philipp Schulz, office neighbour of Esther Graf, working for GoSolar since September. Louise rubbed her tired eyes. Guardian angel, masked shadows, surveillance, the Verfassungsschutz called into action. And a stab in the dark. "I need to talk to him."

"You really are interested, aren't you?"

"Merely professionally."

"Which doesn't make it any better considering the profession you're in." Mayerhöfer leaned back in her chair. "You're not here because of the rumours."

"Not only." Louise looked at Mayerhöfer, wondering whether she could trust her. If she went by her feelings, then yes. But the past few days had taught her she ought not to rely on her feelings. So she kept it vague – three armed men, two colleagues abducted, attempted murder in Berlin, the name GoSolar cropping up, background unclear.

"And you think it's possible Herr Schulz might have something to do with this?"

Louise shrugged. "I'm shaking the tree in the hope someone comes falling out of it."

Mayerhöfer fixed her eyes on Louise. The softness in her face had gone, she looked distant and controlled again, as if she'd run a risk analysis in her head and then suddenly reconciled herself to the fact that the suitable conclusion of a little platonic flirt didn't always look as you hoped it would.

"I'm sorry," Louise said.

"It happens. Like I said, it's nothing serious. Nothing that can't be replaced." Mayerhöfer's index finger started moving again, tapping its rhythm: slow, slow, fast. "You ought to know the circumstances in which Herr Schulz came to GoSolar. No idea if it's important or not, but it was definitely strange. Interested?"

"Sure am."

Schulz's predecessor, Heinrich Willert, had been dismissed without notice in August. Pornographic films featuring young boys had been found on his office computer. The management had refrained from reporting the matter to the police because Willert had accepted his dismissal. Although he claimed he hadn't downloaded the clips, they were stored in a password-protected area that only he had access to, and they'd been saved over a considerable period of time – never when he was on holiday and never when he was ill. On those specific days at the specific times he'd been sitting at his desk.

"How were they discovered if only he had access to them?"

"Pure chance. We don't switch our computers off overnight. He'd forgotten to close the software he viewed the films on. Early the next morning one of the cleaners nudged the mouse, the computer woke up from standby and that was that."

If GoSolar was being spied on, Louise thought, it was very possible that someone had been planted in the firm to work under cover.

For whom a job might have been freed up.

Bonì left a few minutes later. When she got to the stairs she gazed outside through the wall of windows. A man in beige trousers was cycling rapidly away from the car park. Philipp Schulz seemed to have changed his mind – not lasagne, but a doner or sushi or a sausage from the nearest takeaway.

Or he was on the way to meet someone who had to be told that Kripo had made its way into Esther Graf's office.

But, if so, how did he know who she was? It was possible, she thought, that he'd seen her on a monitor showing images from the hidden cameras at Esther's.

She turned back and went to the coffee machine. A thought was fermenting deep inside her mind, in the compost of her ideas, and like so many of her thoughts during these days of exhaustion it wouldn't come straight out into the open. Morosely, she pressed a finger on a promising-looking symbol.

As the latte macchiato flowed fragrantly into a tall glass, the thought took shape. If she was right, at some point this year a web had been spun around GoSolar and a spy smuggled into the company. But who was to say they would be happy with just *one* mole?

Annette Mayerhöfer was utterly opposed to the idea – difficult technically, dodgy legally, not to mention incredibly disloyal. "No way!"

"But it's just paper."

Mayerhöfer shook her head. "No."

Louise laid her coat once again over the chair, put the glass on the desk and sat down. They looked at each other in silence.

"Shit," Mayerhöfer said.

"I know I'm disagreeable."

"That's a euphemism. You're a plague."

Louise smiled. "A plague on the side of the good guys."

"That doesn't stop you being a plague."

"Keep talking, I'm enjoying this."

"Shit!"

Pointing to the latte macchiato, Louise said, "Like one too?"

"I don't drink milk."

"Espresso?"

Mayerhöfer stared at her.

"I'll get the espresso, you print out the list. Do we have a deal?"

"*Shit!*"

A few minutes later Louise was holding a list of those GoSolar employees who'd been appointed that year. Sixteen names and addresses including the details of Philipp Schulz, as well as those of his predecessor, Heinrich Willert, added by Mayerhöfer by hand.

"If I weren't taking my residual leave on Monday, you wouldn't be getting this," Mayerhöfer said, angrily stirring her espresso.

"I know. Could I use your fax?"

"Is this never going to stop?"

Her index finger pointed to an all-in-one device by the side wall.

"Have you got a pen?"

A biro rolled across the desk.

"Call me if it's raining and I'll bring you an umbrella," Mayerhöfer said.

"I'd rather have a pizza," Louise replied.

On the stairs something else occurred to her that had taken too long to grasp. If Philipp Schulz was part of the web, was he Esther Graf's guardian angel?

12

In the car she called Bermann. He was still at Esther's house with two other members of the task force. So far they hadn't found anything of interest; the search was ongoing.

Louise put down the two front windows. The car had been sitting in the sun for almost three hours and she could hardly breathe in the sticky warmth.

Bermann kept talking. Over the phone Lubowitz had reported forensics' initial findings. They'd identified the same shoe profile in the blood in Graf's bathroom, in the bedroom, on the stairs – only going down, not up – as well as in the hallway. The imprints matched those secured by the Berlin team in the hotel stairwell.

They already knew about the abrasions on the desk lock and the plug sockets that must have just been taken off or put on. There were similar marks in the bulb socket of a lamp in the bedroom and on a wooden shelf in the sitting room. Bermann said Lubowitz had examined these closely and was convinced that Louise was right: Esther Graf had been monitored via bugs and cameras that must have been in every room.

Only two people had left fingerprints: Graf and Bonì herself.

"Did you have dinner there?"

"Pizza with salami and mushrooms."

"Isn't that going a bit too far? Dinner with a witness?"

"What witness?"

Bermann laughed. "By the way, when are you going to show me what you bought at the Turkish market?"

"I'll bring it all to the task force meeting. What's happened to Marc and Kilian?"

They were exhausted, frozen and slightly befuddled, but otherwise doing well. They were trying to act cool and cracking jokes to take their minds off the fact that they'd acted pretty stupidly and had been in serious danger.

Their statements had already been taken.

Marc had bumped into two men on the road below Graf's house. A third had knocked him to the ground from behind. He hadn't seen any faces, he could only describe their clothing.

"Did he hear them speak?"

"Yes, they were German." Marc was insistent that they weren't French or from any other country.

"What about Kilian?"

Bermann sighed theatrically.

Kilian had followed Marc and the three men through the woods for a quarter of an hour until he realised that only two men plus Marc were in front of him. But it was too late; the third man put a gun to the back of his head.

"What's going to happen to him now?"

"We don't know yet. I'll sit down with him, the boss and Schöne later and we'll have a think." Peter Schöne was insisting that a note be put in Kilian's personnel file. He was not at all happy that Boni's methods – investigating off one's own bat, disobeying orders from superiors – were catching on. "At least you get results. Kilian just gets caught."

"For God's sake leave the poor guy in peace."

"We'll see. It won't be that bad."

She started the car and drove off. Bermann enquired about the "chat between women" and she told him about Mayerhöfer, Philipp Schulz and Heinrich Willert. When she'd finished Bermann said nothing. She guessed what he was thinking – what craziness is going through that woman's head now?

"Let me guess. You're on your way to see Schulz?" he said eventually.

"I'm on my way to get a doner from Schwabentor."

"Which is around the corner from Schulz?"

"Well, seeing as I'm in the neighbourhood."

"I'll have lots of extra meat and chilli sauce, please."

Bonì put her mobile on the passenger seat with a sigh. Bermann's sudden friendliness and concern made her feel slightly uneasy. She would have preferred to see Schulz on her own, before paying a visit to Willert. But she was glad that Bermann wasn't losing sight of what was still at the edge of her mind: the terrain was becoming ever more confusing, and if they were on the right track they were pushing their invisible opponent further and further into the corner.

Which meant the danger was escalating.

The doners were just ready when Bermann arrived.

They sat at one of the few tables and ate. After a few bites Bermann's moustache was red and his fingers were dripping. His eyes were focused on her. "What's the overhead light up to?"

"Buzzing and humming."

"It'll get better when you've had a good sleep."

She nodded.

"Oh, before I forget . . ." Bermann chewed and swallowed. He had new information on Hans Peter Steinhoff.

Ernesto Freudenreich had buried himself with two computers, two litres of milk and four jars of apple puree in some basement room where nobody would root him out. He was keeping in touch via the occasional e-mail. A search had turned up that Steinhoff's last print article appeared in 2000. Since then he'd only published online, all of it fairly trivial, mostly football and no more than four articles a year – a trained journalist who had hardly anything published. But what was more interesting was that over the last few years he'd been accredited at lots of international solar energy fairs and conferences.

"Germany, the US, China, Russia, Spain, France and who knows where else. He's not just working for the BND."

"Who, then?"

Bermann looked at her in slight astonishment, as if the answer were perfectly obvious.

She tapped her head. "With this thing in my head, I can't work it out."

"He's dealing in information."

"Is he telling one lot what the others are in the process of developing?"

"Maybe he's only got one customer."

"A French business."

"Or a French secret service," Bermann said.

"What about the guardian angel and his men?"

"Hired by the French to spy on GoSolar?"

She picked up the water bottle and drank the last third in one gulp. The thing in her head was blocking transmission paths, preventing 100 per cent concentration. But hunches were sneaking past its sides, and one of these was telling her that something wasn't right with Bermann's theory. Steinhoff *couldn't* only be the information supplier, or he wouldn't have appeared outside Esther's hotel room in Berlin. The guardian angel and Steinhoff *couldn't* be on the same side or one wouldn't have tried to kill the other.

She rubbed her eyes. Too tired to think. "We need to check out the people on the list."

"I thought that was already happening."

"Not just the names, Rolf. The people."

Bermann frowned.

"We'll do Schulz, let our colleagues see to the others," she said.

"Gently, gently. We don't want to scare anyone off."

He was right. "Apart from Schulz."

"What are you planning to ask him?"

"Where he was at three o'clock this morning, for example."

And she wanted to see his eyes. If Philipp Schulz was the guardian angel she would recognise his eyes.

Shortly afterwards they went out onto Herrenstrasse and headed north. Schulz lived in the attic of one of the narrow houses by the minster. They rang the bell and waited by the front door beneath an oriel. They rang again and, when nobody answered, Louise took a few steps back and gazed up. The house was painted dusky pink, three windows on the ground and first floors. There were three round attic windows too, one of them open.

She looked at Bermann.

"Don't even think about it," he said.

She shrugged. This was the problem. When the boss was here she had to stick to the rules. She couldn't get a key from a caretaker or neighbour. Or see how good she still was with a credit card.

Louise looked up again and for a split second saw a shadow move to the side behind the middle attic window. "He's there, Rolf."

"He's not opening up, so we can't go in."

"Try again." While Bermann pressed the bell she kept her eyes fixed on the window.

Schulz didn't open the door and the shadow didn't reappear.

Bonì went to the door angrily and put her finger on the bell. Nothing. "Shit."

"Andrele's going to be at the meeting this evening. Maybe we'll get a search warrant," Bermann said, gently patting her on the shoulder.

"You don't believe that for one minute."

"No," he agreed.

"What if he does a runner?"

"He can go where he likes. We've got absolutely nothing on him."

"We've got a reasonable suspicion."

"*You've* got a suspicion."

"Don't you want to go and have a beer somewhere, Rolf?"

"Too early."

"Visit a girlfriend?"

"Again?" Bermann stuck his thumbs in his trouser pockets and smiled.

"Christ!"

He laughed, and for a fleeting moment she saw a shockingly high degree of affection in his eyes.

Rolf Bermann's abyss had opened up.

Then his expression became severe, his brows knitted together and a growl issued from his chest: "Where does the paedophile live?"

"In Wittnau."

"Meet you outside the town hall."

She'd been driving for barely five minutes when Bermann called. Heinrich Willert no longer lived in Wittnau and they hadn't yet managed to find out where he'd moved to. Park somewhere, lie down on the back seat, sleep, and I'll be back in touch. Listening to the echo of his voice in her head, she wondered whether he was deliberately trying to get her off the case for a while, to give her a break. But she had no desire to drive to Wittnau to find out. Instead she stopped by the side of the road and picked up her mobile again.

"Wait," Mayerhöfer said. Vivaldi's "Spring" rang out. Then she was on the line again. Philipp Schulz had taken the rest of the day off, saying something had upset his stomach.

Not something, Louise thought grumpily. Some*one*. Annette Mayerhöfer's surprise guest. And now Schulz was sitting behind his bullseye attic windows, nursing his stomach ache by making a few phone calls to arrange his departure. And there was nothing she could do to stop him because her boss thought there was no reasonable suspicion.

Cursing, she moved the seat back as far as it would go. She fell asleep even before she'd finished closing her eyes.

13

Heinrich Willert had been living in Belfortstrasse near the main train station since October. His decline had unfolded at record speed – in August his wife filed for divorce and moved out of the family home in Wittnau. The house was now up for sale; the last two monthly mortgage payments were still outstanding. Willert hadn't yet found a new job.

He lived on the first floor of an old, unrenovated house. Dark-brown façade, crumbling render, graffiti, and beside the bells almost all the names were written by hand. The door to the street didn't shut; Louise pushed it open. No lights came on and the windows were so dirty they barely let any light through. In the gloom Bermann and she climbed the creaky, smooth stairs. Bermann swore continually, tripping once and slipping once on the edge of a stair. Louise moaned. The creaking inflamed the buzzing in her head and made the block vibrate painfully.

On the first floor it reeked of rubbish and damp. Further up the stairs they could hear televisions and reggae.

It was 4.10 p.m., she had slept for an hour and felt almost refreshed.

"No mercy," Bermann growled.

"What?"

"He's a child abuser."

"What if someone framed him?"

"So long as he can't prove it he's a child abuser."

Louise rolled her eyes. When it came to child abuse, in no matter which form, Bermann was not open to argument. It was possible that Willert had escaped punishment only because he hadn't been reported to the police. She suspected what Bermann thought of this and feared what that meant for the interrogation.

Bonì rang the bell.

When the door opened, sunlight came falling onto the landing. Blinded, she screwed up her eyes. In the door stood a slim man, his face in the shadows.

"Freiburg Kripo," Bermann said tensely, stepping forwards. "Heinrich Willert?"

Seconds passed, then the man nodded.

A room about twenty square metres in size with a cooker and a sink, on the floor a mattress with a bedspread, and in front of the only window, a table with three chairs and an artificial marguerite in a plastic bottle, in addition to the tiny bathroom they'd passed on the way in. Willert seemed to be bracing himself against the dereliction in his own way: he wore suit trousers, a white shirt and tie – albeit crumpled and not particularly clean looking – and his hair was combed although not washed.

Willert, in his mid-forties, sat on the mattress, leaving the table to them. His feet were drawn up to his body, his arms around his knees, his face bony and lifeless, eyes rigid. For a moment Louise pictured another tiny room – a bed, a table, a half-empty shelf in Stühlinger. On this bed too sat a man who no longer had a job, but for different reasons. Then she saw the same man sitting on a bed in a hotel room in Sarajevo. He had a telephone in his hand, the joy had subsided, as had his smile, as he wondered what the woman on the other end of the line was trying to say. After a year he still didn't know her well enough to *understand*.

Perhaps, she thought, they should move in together. Surely the independence thing would sort itself out somehow, and the polar opposites of compulsive autonomy and fear of losing him would oscillate around some tolerable midway point.

Assuming the man in Sarajevo still wanted to after their conversation. Nobody could put up with too much chaos.

Before the pendulum could swing back to the other extreme she channelled her thoughts once again to Willert.

"If it were up to me," Bermann said, "you'd be banged up in a cell rather than sitting in this luxury apartment."

Willert didn't respond. His eyes were fixed on the table, his brow was furrowed and he was blinking frantically. Pinned on the wall behind him was a photograph of a woman and two blond boys around fourteen years old with broad grins.

Bermann had noticed it too. "Your family?" He pointed to the picture. "Sweet boys."

No reaction.

"For Christ's sake," Louise said.

Bermann snorted; Willert looked at her in surprise. Then his gaze drifted to the floor, alighting beside his feet.

"Alright," she said. "You can't talk to us because officially nothing happened. No kiddy porn on your computer. There was never a police investigation, only an internal deal. So you can't even tell us you *didn't* download those clips, because that would be an admission that such an accusation had been made and we would have to investigate."

She stood up, went over to Willert and kneeled on the floor a couple of metres away from him. Behind her a chair creaked and a foot scraped on the floor. Bermann standing to attention.

Willert's eyes slowly crept up her body. She wasn't sure if he was taking in what he was seeing.

"And because you can't say that, we can't ask you who downloaded the films if it wasn't you, because it can be proved that you were at your desk at the times they were downloaded. And you can't tell us that someone must have manipulated your computer – someone who's into kiddy porn or someone who arranged for the clips to be found on your computer to get you into trouble. We can't ask you about enemies in the company and you can't say you didn't have any enemies in the company, and that's why you think that this someone wanted to get you into trouble for other reasons, maybe even wanted to get you the sack. We can't ask why you think that and you can't tell us you don't know. And because you can't say that, we can't ask you if it's possible that the reason you got into trouble was so someone else, someone quite specific, would be given your job. And because we can't have this conversation, and because I didn't realise that beforehand I'm going to ask you just one thing: what exactly did you do at GoSolar?"

Willert took time over his answer, as if he first had to understand what all of this meant. Finally he spoke. "I was responsible for the department's security."

Louise sank onto her bottom and sat cross-legged. She could have kicked herself; she ought to have asked Mayerhöfer what Willert and thus Philipp Schulz did at the firm.

Then she concentrated again, insofar as that was possible with the buzzing in her head. Philipp Schulz was responsible for the security of the research and development department – the pieces of the puzzle were gradually coming together to make a picture.

"What were your tasks?"

"Installation and monitoring of video cameras, alarm systems, computerised fuse boxes and so on. Handbooks for staff, background checks on applicants." Willert's voice was high and whiny and didn't go with his clothing, which surely was a conscious sign that he hadn't given up. I'm at the end of my tether, the sound of the voice said.

"For the entire firm?"

"Just for building 1."

"Did you keep an eye on the monitors yourself?"

He shook his head. That job was for the security guards in building 3, who watched the monitors in all departments.

"Were you responsible for IT security too?"

"No."

"Who was, then?"

"Nobody."

"Doesn't GoSolar have any IT security?"

"No. There's a manual with instructions for employees . . . 'Change your password once a month. Don't talk about company matters on public transport.' Those sorts of things."

"Isn't that irresponsible?"

Willert shrugged. "Security is expensive and they don't think the investment is worth it." One year ago GoSolar cut its security budget by half because nothing had ever happened. The outside spaces – access roads, car parks, pavements, lorry areas for collection and delivery – were no longer patrolled, just monitored by a few cameras. Some rooms inside the building had no cameras installed at all – the foyers, canteens, chill-out rooms, underground car parks. There were no bug-proof areas on the entire site and a staff ID allowed access to all buildings and departments.

"In other words: illegally obtaining sensitive data at GoSolar is child's play?"

Willert hesitated. Only now did he seem to understand what she was getting at. "That's going too far. But if you take the time and make the effort it shouldn't be too difficult. Is . . . is that what this is about? Industrial espionage. Is that why they did it?"

"Did what?" Bermann butted in.

Willert didn't answer.

"You're not going to wriggle out of it that easily," Bermann said. "If anyone tells me that paedophile porn was found on your computer, you'll have the public prosecutors at your throat within seconds."

No sooner had Bermann finished talking than the room was filled with the hellish laughter and squealing from several children's mouths. Louise whipped around.

Bermann took the mobile from his coat pocket and the noise stopped abruptly. "Yes?" Deep lines appeared on his brow and his eyes narrowed. "On our way." He got up and went to the door. "We have to go."

She got up too, scanning his face for some clue. From one moment to the next the burning fear had returned – not Esther, she thought, not Annette Mayerhöfer, both of whom might be in danger because she hadn't taken care, hadn't thought about this case with sufficient focus . . . Rather a message from Stuttgart, the Verfassungsschutz, the ministry of the interior, please take your childless alkie off the case before an international crisis breaks out . . .

"Say something, Rolf, for Christ's sake!"

"Be quiet," Bermann replied, stepping into the tiny hallway.

She forced herself to take a deep breath.

"Talk to Esther Graf," Willert said quietly. "One of the departmental head's assistants."

"Why?"

"Louise," Bermann said insistently.

"Wait. What are you saying about Esther Graf?"

Willert had spotted her in the photocopying room late one evening at the end of June without her noticing. When a sheet of paper fell to the floor she picked it up almost in a panic, which made him suspicious. So he continued to watch her for a while. Looking very nervous she hastily made two copies of a document, one of which she put in a folder and then in the safe in the head of department's office. He never found out what happened to the other one because his wife rang and after he'd finished talking to her Esther had already left the building.

"Do you know what she copied?"

"No."

Bermann opened the door to the apartment. "We can sort that out later. Come on, now."

"Did you tell anyone about this?"

"Pete Monaghan, the head of department, the following morning."

"And?"

Monaghan and Willert looked in the safe and found a dozen almost identical-looking folders that Esther Graf had copied and ordered according to the number on the cover sheet – texts of speeches that Monaghan was going to give, technical data from research laboratories and so on. Willert couldn't say which folder he'd seen Esther holding the previous evening. "Herr Monaghan thanked me and that was that."

Louise nodded thoughtfully. So Esther had got hold of company documents. There could be a number of reasons why Monaghan hadn't pursued the matter – perhaps he didn't think it was important, perhaps he simply forgot. Or maybe GoSolar was already working with the Verfassungsschutz, who had taken the matter on board and were keeping tabs on Esther Graf.

"We'll need to talk again," she said.

"I'm here," Willert replied, and for the first time she detected hope in his voice.

She followed Bermann onto the landing. For a moment she could see only his outline until her eyes got used to the dim light. "So? Is my suspicion justified now, Rolf?"

"Don't annoy me."

He hurried on ahead.

"What's happened?"

"Shooting in the woods at Ebnet."

"Hunters, maybe?"

"Animals don't cry for help."

Before she could ask about the details she heard the crack of wood, then the figure in front of her swore, falling first to one side, then the other, as he went sliding down the stairs. Bermann's pale hands flapped in the air and he toppled backwards like a felled tree. Another crack of wood and he kept sliding until he came to an abrupt stop at the bottom of the stairs.

Louise heard him groan.

"Are you hurt?"

"What the fuck?"

She carefully went down to Bermann and knelt beside him. His head was on the edge of a stair and his face was contorted with pain, so far as she could make out.

But he was laughing. "I don't believe it . . ."

"Rolf, are you OK?"

"Yes, yes," he insisted, sitting up. His skin glowed white in the gloom and he ran his left hand over his right forearm.

"Just a bruise."

He was giving off a sour tang of sweat. Only now did she realise that all her limbs had been numbed by a powerful shock. Rolf Bermann, the rock, was lying before her on the stairs like a stranded whale.

She helped him up.

"Fuck's sake," he said, rubbing the back of his head. "I'm going to sue."

"Do that."

"And then I'll get my hands on Willert."

"But first we're going to Ebnet. Feeling better?"

"Yes, yes."

Slowly they made their way to the door. Bermann's steps were short and unsteady, and once he wobbled slightly. She wanted to take his arm, but he refused. Again he felt the back of his head and cursed.

"I'll drive, you come with me," she said.

"Oh, leave me alone." He gave a hoarse laugh. "Do you order your foreign copper around like this too? The poor sod." He felt for the doorknob, twice grabbing at thin air as if his hand were refusing to obey. Bermann didn't have the strength to open the door. Louise helped him.

They stepped outside. In the light of the sun she saw that all the colour had drained from his face.

"You can't drive now, Rolf."

"Don't talk nonsense."

She put a hand on his cheek – it was cold and quivering. Bermann flinched.

"What if you've got concussion?"

"I've got a bruise on my arm and my arse, that's all."

"Get yourself checked out."

"Stop getting on my tits." He made a movement with his hand. "My car's over there. See you in Ebnet."

He turned away and she followed him.

"Louise, bugger off. I'll manage."

"You've got to prove that to me first."

They turned into the first side street. Bermann struggled to get the car key from his coat pocket, then he touched the remote button. Nothing happened. Bermann's gaze drifted across the parked cars, his eyes half-closed, blinking irregularly.

"Over there," Louise said. "In the driveway."

She heard the jolly sing-song, then Bermann opened the door and circumspectly let himself down on the seat. "Shit, my arse hurts."

"I'm more worried about your head."

"Worry about your own head." He tried to close the door, but she held it open.

"Sure?"

"Yes, I am, but if you don't now leave me in peace I *will* end up with concussion."

She smiled. "Alright, then. Where in Ebnet?"

A barbecue area to the east of the village – go through the centre, then take Steinhalde along the woods, then a right up into the

Welchental. "Left, I mean," Bermann said, starting the engine and waving her away. Louise took a step back. The car shot off with an aggressive snarl.

On the way to her car she contemplated going via Schwabentor and trying to get into Philipp Schulz's apartment if he failed to open the door again. She had the ideal opportunity – the boss was on his way to Ebnet and more concerned with his bottom than her methods. But Louise had second thoughts. Steinhoff might be in town, the guardian angel and his people were here, maybe French agents too – and barely a kilometre to the north of Littenweiler, where Esther lived, there had been shooting. It was more than possible that there might be a connection.

14

Ebnet, at the easternmost fringe of Freiburg on the old B31, was in a state of emergency. Louise had seen the blue lights from a distance. A roadblock had been set up at the entrance to the village and another at the exit. Only emergency vehicles were being allowed through. Patrol cars and police vans with Göppingen numberplates were parked on Steinhalde, which had houses on either side – the commander must have requested back-up from the constabulary.

She had to leave the car at the junction and walk up the shady narrow road. On the way she met the occasional uniformed officer who didn't know much more than she did: shots near a barbecue area, the vicinity being combed for the gunman and a potential victim, the canine unit called in. There was a witness, but they didn't know what she'd seen.

Then Bonì was alone for a few minutes. Here, between the hills, dusk set in quickly. The air was cool; feeling chilly, she fastened her coat. She was out of breath and her pulse was racing. Barely fifteen minutes' walking and she was as exhausted as after an hour's jog.

The sound of muffled barking jolted Louise from her thoughts. Through the window of a farmhouse she saw a Doberman with its front paws on the sill, yapping angrily in her direction. On a fenced meadow beside the main building, two men were catching frightened horses. To the left was a car park, beside it a cabin. At a stone table a few metres further away sat Kilian.

Breathing heavily, Louise approached him. She was filled with relief and anger – he'd got away with a black eye but had disobeyed her instructions and had pointlessly put himself in danger. The anger won out and surged ahead, even though they were here for other, more urgent reasons. "You know what I think?" she said acidly. "You're in the wrong job."

Kilian raised his handsome eyebrows in a warning gesture.

She dug a finger into his chest. "One day you'll be lying in some dark street with a bullet hole in your back, and your widow and children will sit at home cursing you."

Kilian stared at her, as if contemplating whether he fancied getting embroiled in an argument. He cleared his throat and said, "You're a fine one to talk."

"You haven't understood the difference, you idiot."

"Which is?"

"Look at yourself, then look at me. You're young and a picture of health. I'm old and a fucking wreck. Nobody needs me and that's why I survive. I'm not reckless, just angry, pig-headed and vindictive. I'm not afraid, or at least I'm not afraid of losing anything, because I haven't got anything to lose. You have!"

"That's lots of differences," he said, standing up.

"Don't take the piss."

Shouting in the distance, a dog barked, two others joined in. The animals were silenced with strict commands that bored painfully into her hearing.

"What about loyalty? Friendship?" Kilian said.

Once again she jabbed his chest with her finger. He took her hand and held it tight. The corners of his mouth quivered and she realised how shocked he'd been by her harsh reaction. "That's precisely the point," she said more calmly.

"I don't understand."

"Watch those old plays . . ."

"What old plays?"

"I dunno, Shakespeare, that sort of thing. Ancient plays."

"What about them?"

"People *die* out of loyalty and friendship. Let go of me!" He released her hand. "You want to be *good*, Kilian. And it makes you block out everything else – your fear, your flight response, your reason. Everything that could save your life when it comes down to it."

"Everyone wants to be good, you included."

"No, I really don't."

"What, then?"

She shrugged. "What do I know? I'm just driven somehow."

Bonì was distracted by movement between the trees. In the twilight she could make out two men in white plastic suits. Judging by the height, one of them must be Lubowitz. When he bent his torso he stood there for several seconds like an acute-angled triangle.

Turning back to Kilian she said, "Message understood?"

He nodded.

They went to the edge of the woods and stepped onto a path. Twenty metres further on, the way was blocked by two lengths of police tape flapping in the wind. In between were evidence markers, one beside a dark, damp patch – blood that had seeped onto the forest floor. The outlines of hands could clearly be seen in the earth, as well as two almost round indents, side by side.

"Shit," Louise said.

The victim had fallen to his knees and then run on, pursued by the shooter.

As they hurried over to Lubowitz and his colleague, Kilian filled her in.

An emergency call had been made just before 4 p.m. A jogger heading up the Welchental from Ebnet had heard shots in the vicinity of the barbecue area and a man shouting for help. Three shots, around a dozen cries for help, all of this within a couple of minutes. Then silence again.

"He didn't make it," Louise said.

"That's what it looks like."

The hysterical witness called the emergency number on her mobile. She ran back to her apartment in Ebnet where she dialled 110 again. She was transferred to D11, then put through to Peter Schöne who was deputising as head of the task force because Bermann was on the road. As an investigator into financial crime Schöne had hardly any experience of operations in the field, hence the big song and dance with the extra officers and canine unit.

The first patrol car arrived at the barbecue area ten minutes after the call had been made – so roughly at the same time as Louise and Bermann rang on Willert's bell.

Putting a hand on Kilian's arm she asked about Bermann. He hadn't seen him yet, Kilian replied, maybe he was with the witness who was being questioned by the task force. They'd called earlier to say the witness had heard a car start up and head north. It must have parked further up because there'd been no vehicle at the barbecue area or car park.

Louise and Kilian had reached the two forensics officers, who were putting more police tape around trickles of blood and impressions in the soil.

"You forgot the coffee again," Lubowitz said.

"I'll have a cappuccino with lactose-free milk," his colleague said. "If you're going . . ."

Ignoring the men's comments, Louise looked at the evidence on the forest floor. "He fell again."

"Yes," Lubowitz said. "And here he was bleeding from two wounds." He pointed to a long imprint that presumably had been made by a body, and to the dark spots beside it. The impressions were deeper where the hips and shoulders must have been. "The first bullet in the left arm or shoulder, the second in the right leg."

He pointed to the path on the other side of the police tape, where more officers in white suits were kneeling at irregular intervals.

"From here he wasn't able to walk properly anymore, he had to drag his right leg behind him. He won't have made it far – two or three hundred metres perhaps. If they didn't carry him away you'll find a body somewhere near here."

"They?" Louise asked.

"Two people were after him. One tall and heavy, the other of medium height and much lighter. Two men or a man and a woman."

He'd barely finished his sentence when a dog barked in the undergrowth to the side of the path. Twigs broke, someone had started running. About one hundred and fifty metres away Louise saw a Rottweiler, behind him the canine officer, then both disappeared amongst the trees and shrubs.

They heard shouting that passed from one man to the next.

"Always the same," Lubowitz grumbled.

"Bloody herd of elephants," his colleague said. "You can forget any evidence."

The voices and noises stopped abruptly.

They had discovered the body.

Louise and Kilian got there after Lubowitz, who muttered to himself as he pushed four uniformed officers to the side. Somewhat apart from them sat the canine officer, stroking the Rottweiler and speaking softly to it.

Even before Louise glimpsed the lifeless body she knew who it was. About a metre from him lay a light-brown loafer. A bare foot, beige flannel trousers, and a white shirt drenched in blood. Philipp Schulz had been shot in the thigh, the arm and the back of his head.

"Just keep away from him, OK?" Lubowitz said, wrapping the end of the police tape around a tree. Louise moved so she could see the left side of the face. The warm smile was gone, the jaw sunken, the eyes slightly open. His muscles were limp and there was no expression on his face. Sitting on her haunches, she recalled the brief instant from the night before outside Esther's house, when she'd looked into the eyes of the man she believed to be the guardian angel.

She could see no similarity.

But in Littenweiler she'd encountered a living human being; here lay a dead man with half-closed eyes.

Bonì thought of Henning Ziller, who'd warned of devastating consequences if Kripo didn't stop its investigation. He'd been proved right. Philipp Schulz would still be alive if she hadn't gone to see Annette Mayerhöfer.

She rubbed her chest and tried to keep her cool. The fact that Schulz – who might not have been Esther's guardian angel but was probably part of the invisible web around GoSolar – had been killed didn't fit the picture at all. Had he panicked after meeting her that afternoon? Maybe he'd wanted to get out and had been prevented from doing so. But by whom? Steinhoff? The guardian angel?

And whose shadow had she seen through Schulz's window?

Louise thought of Ziller again. He'd spoken of a "highly complex case". Nobody had taken him seriously.

Including her.

III

The Spider

15

There patrol cars, ten constables and around thirty onlookers all waiting at a safe distance, plus neighbours in doorways or at open windows – like in Ebnet, Herrenstrasse near the Schwabentor was in uproar too. And she, Louise thought as she stopped by the uniformed officers, their blue lights flashing hectically, always arrived too late.

She and Kilian got out of the car. The sun had set, the sky had clouded over. Gentle rain was falling, but it didn't seem to bother the gawkers. They stood in small groups outside the houses opposite, lit up by a streetlamp and the blue lights whose reflection was cast back by the façades, giving the narrow street a frantic, silent rhythm. One of the faces in the crowd looked familiar, then others got in the way and her faint memory faded. She took a step to the side, but the face had vanished. From the foggy depths of her mind rose the word "dull", and then she realised who the man was: Michael Bredik, one of Ziller's assistants who she'd sat opposite in Graeve's office that morning.

Louise turned to Kilian. "Tell them one blue light's enough. This is intolerable."

The rhythm became calmer.

The uniformed officers had checked out three tenants who had entered or left the building and they'd tracked down the caretaker, who had hurried over from Marienstrasse. Louise briefed them on the situation: the apartment was probably empty, but they had to be prepared for anything.

"No SWAT team?" said a police inspector with red hair and a moustache.

"No time."

She got them to point out the caretaker, who she didn't recognise immediately: Ronescu, the gentle Romanian from her building in Gartenstrasse, in whose kitchen she'd emptied countless bottles of ţuică. The bags under his eyes now covered half of his lugubrious face, the bulges in his skin were larger, and he was more stooped than when she'd last seen him. Dozens of blood vessels on his nose suggested that, unlike her, he was still on the ţuică.

Then she smelled the alcohol.

"Frau Louise," he muttered in astonishment and raised a hand in greeting.

The sound of his voice, the rolled "r" and dark vowels made her shudder. Ronescu belonged to the time *before* – before the detoxification and the withdrawal, before her return to life, before Ben. The time when all her thoughts had revolved around where she could drink in private, where she could hide the bottles and how long her stocks would last.

She took Ronescu's hand. "How are you?"

"Oh, you know . . ." He shrugged. "But you look better. Tired, but . . . healthy."

Louise smiled, aghast. Yes, healthy in that sense, but not in another way. "I need to get into the building, into Philipp Schulz's apartment."

"And you . . . you're allowed to do that?"

"Yes." On the way she'd called Marianne Andrele, the public prosecutor. She'd agreed to the search verbally; the warrant would be sorted out.

Ronescu held up a bunch of keys. "Let's go, then."

"No, you have to stay here."

He showed her two keys before handing her the bunch.

"What's the layout of the apartment?"

190

Ronescu held his hands parallel to each other in front of his stomach. "You start in the hallway." He flipped his right hand outwards. "Here's the bathroom, the kitchen's straight on, and here's the bedroom," he said, flipping his left hand outwards.

With Kilian, the red-haired inspector and three of his constables she discussed the plan of action. Then they entered the building and, pistols at the ready, made their way up to the attic where there were two apartments, one at the back, the other facing Herrenstrasse. Above the bell of the latter it said SCHULZ, on the doormat WELCOME.

The officers spaced themselves out on the stairs, only Kilian stayed right beside Louise. He looked focused and calm, in contrast to her. She hated situations like this. A closed door and nobody knew what was behind it.

Bonì rang twice and said, "Kripo, open up, please."

When nothing happened, she unlocked the door and, with her gun pointing in front of her, stepped into the small hallway lit only by the light from the landing. She could sense Kilian right behind her, hear his slow breathing. Then it was drowned out by footsteps, doors flew open, Kilian in the bathroom, the uniformed officers in the bedroom, she in the kitchen.

Kilian was the first to give the all-clear, then Bonì, and finally the redhead.

She sank into a chair beside a tiny coffee table. Her legs were shaking and she was breathing too quickly. She scanned the kitchen, which was no bigger than ten square metres. No cupboards, no shelf, no fridge, no cooker. Next to the sink was a dirty paper plate with breadcrumbs and a plastic cup, beside it a paper bag from a bakery. Philipp Schulz might have lived here, but he hadn't made it his home.

"Holy shit!" Kilian exclaimed in the bathroom.

Struggling to her feet, she returned the pistol to its holster and put on a pair of overshoes.

The bathroom was minuscule. Kilian had opened the plastic

cabinet above the sink. Three shelves full of make-up applicators, hair dye and colour remover, a container with fake moustaches and various other items.

Once more Eberhardt Rohwe's earlier suspicion was proving true: professionals through and through.

The redhead came into the hallway. "We'll wait down below."

Louise nodded. "Thanks for your help." When they'd gone she looked into the bedroom from the doorway. A single bed, a clothes rail on wheels with shirts and suits hanging from it, an open suitcase with four pairs of shoes, a travel bag and a small television with indoor aerial. How ironic, she thought. Heinrich Willert, the predecessor, and Philipp Schulz, the successor, both homeless in similar ways.

"We need forensics," she told Kilian. "And call Bermann. Tell him to expand the task force."

"Are you ordering him around?"

"Say please, then."

Kilian went into the kitchen and she took a few steps into the half-empty bedroom. If Schulz had stored revealing documents here they would have gone by now. Forensics would find his fingerprints but little else. Whoever was here this afternoon had plenty of time to tidy up. Here and elsewhere. Now, following Schulz's death, he would begin to unravel the web, if he hadn't already started.

Time was running away from them now.

"Forensics are on their way, but I can't get hold of Bermann," Kilian said.

Louise turned around. "What do you mean?"

"He's not picking up."

She took out her mobile and dialled his number. No answer.

As they went down to the ground floor she got Peter Schöne's number from the control centre.

"I don't have the time, Boni," Schöne said dismally.

"Where are you?"

192

"Still in Ebnet."

"With the witness?"

"No, by the body in the woods."

They stepped out into Herrenstrasse. There were a few more onlookers now; the ring had closed around the cars. Amongst them stood the uniformed officers. Ronescu and the redhead were leaning against a patrol car, smoking. She scanned the crowd but couldn't see Michael Bredik.

Schöne growled in her ear.

"Is Rolf with you?" she said.

"He's got a headache."

"Have you spoken to him?"

"No."

"Where is he?"

"At the doctor's. And where are you? Do I really want to know? No, but tell me anyway. I mean, you are a member of my task force even if I never see you in the flesh." Schöne laughed.

"I've just been inside the dead man's apartment."

"You know where it is?"

Bonì groaned quietly to herself. She'd requested police back-up and spoken to the public prosecutor, but had forgotten to notify the task force.

She outlined the situation, adding that she had to speak to the other fifteen people on Annette Mayerhöfer's list as quickly as possible. If accomplices of Schulz were among them they would be going underground very soon. If they hadn't disappeared already.

Peter Schöne said nothing. She was glad his small eyes weren't staring at her.

"Seven o'clock at HQ?" she said.

"I don't get up till seven."

"This evening, Peter. We've got to keep on this."

"Are you becoming hysterical again?"

"Yes." She hung up angrily and turned to the redhead. The apartment had to be sealed off and a patrol car must stay outside the building. He promised to see to it.

She took Ronescu aside. "I have to go."

"All the best, then, Frau Louise."

"Does my colleague have your details?"

Ronescu nodded.

"I'll give you a call. Perhaps we'll find the time to have a drink."

He raised his eyebrows and deep lines appeared on his brow. "You disappoint me, Frau Louise."

"Just water, Herr Ronescu – forever more."

A quarter of an hour later she was in her office with Kilian, reluctantly being persuaded that a major operation was logistically impossible that evening. Interrogating fifteen people simultaneously required preparation on a large scale. Because she suspected that at least one other person on Annette Mayerhöfer's list had infiltrated GoSolar and that there was the danger of them absconding after Schulz's death, it made sense to begin the preliminary work on this at once. Where did these fifteen people live? Who was rushing to get where? Who was meeting who?

The interrogation teams would also need to be brought up to speed and be briefed by her. Strategy and preferred outcomes had to be established, a set of questions worked out, and colleagues also had to know what to do in case the individual in question couldn't be found. And they needed a coordination and communications office, typists and telephonists.

But most of all they needed thirty investigators.

So far the task force consisted of six officers from D11 and D31. Rolf Bermann was at the doctor's, Ernesto Freudenreich had shut himself away in the basement, and Peter Schöne and the two other officers were still in Ebnet. Which just left her this evening.

"And me," Kilian said. "And Marc."

"Hmm." A completely exhausted chief inspector with acoustic and psychological issues, and two young daredevils who'd got themselves caught and had spent half the night freezing their arses off in the woods.

Frustrated, she glanced at the two hundred pages of information Ernesto Freudenreich had put together on the fifteen people from police sources and the internet. Family status, private websites, biographical details, professional career, holidays, hobbies, photos. Of these hundreds of details one or two might harbour a valuable clue – but who was going to start looking for this now? And using what criteria?

Kilian offered to check how many surveillance officers were still in the building. Maybe they could keep a watch on a few of the names on the list. Louise was about to say "Do it" when she saw that the chair in front of her desk was already empty, and heard Kilian's footsteps in the corridor. Her mind must have paused for a few seconds.

Louise rested her chin on her hands. Her head was heavy, her eyes ached, the buzzing resounded between her ears, a merciless echo dashing off cave walls. In her brain names flew around that she could only with great difficulty match with people and details. Hans Peter Steinhoff, journalist from Hamburg, beaten up in Berlin/Philipp Schulz, Heinrich Willert's successor at GoSolar, dead in the woods/ Willert, sacked for child pornography in August, run-down apartment in Belfortstrasse/Gerhard Kleinert, founder and co-chair of GoSolar, lover of dreadful abstract art/Annette Mayerhöfer, Esther Graf's colleague, working on wind power in Hamburg from January/the guardian angel, attempted murder in Berlin, bugs and cameras, saved Esther's life, possibly developed feelings for her through remote surveillance, took Marc hostage, maybe same person as the murdered Philipp Schulz.

Esther herself, about whom she remembered every detail.

Then fifteen other names . . .

Yawning, she checked the time. Just after seven. The bearded doctor – whose name had slipped her mind – was on duty for another hour. But she didn't have to be at the hospital at eight, ten would be OK too. And eleven would mean three and a half hours' sleep.

Then talk to Esther and wait for the guardian angel, if he was still alive.

The door opened, Kilian came in and stopped two metres from her desk. "Six officers. With us that makes eight."

"Six plus three is eight? Oh, well."

"Marc's gone home. He wasn't feeling great."

Louise pursed her lips. Nobody was feeling great during these strange days. Not even Rolf Bermann, who always felt great.

"We could ask Ernesto if anything has caught his eye," Kilian said.

Louise yawned again. "I don't follow you."

"About anyone on Mayerhöfer's list."

"Why are you standing there, looking like a lost sheep? Could you please sit down?"

He grinned. "I smell of beer."

"Why?"

"Because I just had one."

She sighed. "Sit down, Kilian."

Louise wrote a message to Ernesto; the reply came less than a minute later.

It had come to his attention that five names had gaps in their biographies. He'd hit dead ends, information couldn't be verified, no photos, strange coincidences. But he couldn't guarantee anything, three exclamation marks. Only because she'd asked, it wasn't his department, four exclamation marks.

She wrote, *Strange coincidences*, four question marks.

Again she didn't have to wait long.

"Person 1" of the five, a physicist, had purportedly worked at the headquarters of the American Solar Energy Society in Boulder, Colorado, from 2000 to the end of 2004. A photograph on the GoSolar website showed the man, who'd been employed there in the research department since May 2005. Three weeks ago a man with the same name had been arrested by Berlin customs for breaking import rules and resisting a law-enforcement officer – the man in question had failed to declare laptops purchased in the US and a mobile phone in its original packaging, and had actually attacked an officer. The customs photo clearly showed a different man from the GoSolar employee. Two Germans with the same name at ASES in Boulder?

For both photos see file, three exclamation marks.

"I'd be interested to know how he gets hold of this information," Kilian said.

"I wouldn't," Louise replied.

"Person 4" of the "suspicious" new employees had been accredited at the Intersolar trade fair in Freiburg at the end of June 2004 – as a journalist, just like Hans Peter Steinhoff. The two had stayed in the same hotel, a small pension in Kirchzarten. *Coincidence*, four question marks.

"Could be," Kilian said.

"All the same, we're going to pay a visit to both men," Louise said, putting on her coat. Already standing, she typed an e-mail to Ernesto: *Thanks!!!*

"How many of my colleagues do you need?"

"All six. We'll divide into two teams, you're in charge of one, me the other."

Kilian got up. "Cool. I've never been in charge of a team before."

"It's quite simple. You give instructions, the others follow them."

The six investigators were waiting in Kilian's office. Louise left it to him to select the teams. After briefing them she went to the office next door and called Peter Schöne, who was on the way back to HQ.

He sounded edgy but was perfectly friendly. A lack of experience of operations in the field combined with the discovery of a corpse tamed even a wolf.

Maybe he was impressed by her speed, too.

Neither the interview with the witness, nor examination of the dead man's clothes nor the manhunt had brought any results so far, he said. Lubowitz and his forensics team had finished up half an hour ago and were on their way to the deceased's apartment. One more hour, Lubowitz had growled, then they'd be calling it a day.

"Same for us, Bonì. We're knackered," Schöne said. "We'll start again at eight tomorrow morning. If anything happens, the control centre will take over."

She told him what Ernesto had discovered. About persons 1 and 4, who they were going to visit.

"Do you never sleep?"

"Only when there's time."

Schöne sighed. "Rolf send his regards."

"Where is he, actually?"

"Still at the doctor's. They're running some tests."

"What sort of tests?"

"No idea." She heard him yawn. "Eight o'clock tomorrow morning, Bonì. I'd like you to be there too." He cleared his throat. "Is there anything else that has to be done today?"

She asked him to prepare the interrogation of the thirteen remaining individuals on Ernesto's list and fill out the necessary forms – a large-scale operation at the GoSolar premises.

"Not exactly the most subtle approach."

No, she thought. But they didn't have time for subtlety anymore. "Have you heard anything from Graeve?"

"Yes. He said he couldn't contact you. Nobody can contact you. The battery on your mobile is dead."

She couldn't resist a smirk. If there was one thing she made sure of, it was that her phone had juice. "What would he tell me if the battery weren't dead?"

"That it's time to go home."

Graeve must have had to give in; the pressure from above had become too great. At least he'd bought her a few more hours.

"A convoy is on its way from Stuttgart," Schöne said.

"Armoured cars?"

"Very armoured, very black, very expensive."

"Smells like trouble."

"Like a reeking cesspit." The Verfassungsschutz was furious at Freiburg Kripo's behaviour, the ministry of the interior was on the case, and they were getting calls from Stuttgart every half hour. Accusations were coming thick and fast – bungled investigations, people's lives in danger. Freiburg government district was trying to calm the waters. Since that afternoon the Verfassungsschutz had been in charge, and Kripo only a junior partner. Together they would get done what needed to be done.

Afterwards, Schöne said, heads would roll.

The eight of them hurried down the steps and got into two Kripo cars. Louise sat in the passenger seat, made herself comfortable and leaned her head back. Kilian had told her the names of the surveillance officers in her team but she hadn't remembered a single one, even though she'd shaken their hands, looked them in the eye and cracked a few jokes to break the ice. On the stairs she named them according to their features: "Serious", "Saxon" and "Sniffler" – every two minutes he drew the contents of his nostrils into his sinuses.

Serious drove, Saxon and Sniffler sat in the back.

They were on their way to St Georgen to visit "person 4" on Ernesto's little list: Ulrich Meier, who might have met Hans Peter Steinhoff at the Intersolar fair in June 2004.

It wasn't only the names, numbers from the past few hours were causing her problems too. She went through them for the umpteenth time. *Sixteen* people taken on by GoSolar in 2005 were on Mayerhöfer's list. Minus Philipp Schulz, that made *fifteen*. Ernesto had classified *five* of these as suspicious, and with *two* of these five – person 1 and person 4 – he'd been struck by strange coincidences.

Really quite simple, she thought. Sixteen, fifteen, five, two.

Buildings raced past, traffic lights flashed on and went out, and a pale moon sat in the sky. Serious drove aggressively and braked abruptly. Sniffler yawned, Saxon talked about a holiday in Greece. A faint whiff of alcohol hung in the air. One beer per man – the haze of three beers inside the car.

Then time started doing its strange leaps again. No sooner had the word "Delphi" been uttered than Serious was already parking outside a four-storey apartment block. Barely had they got out of the car than they were beside the entrance. Louise had just deciphered the name "Ulrich Meier" on the doorbell panel when a man from the neighbouring apartment on the third floor said he'd twice heard Meier on the stairs earlier that evening. Her phone rang and the conversation was already at an end – person 1 wasn't at home either, Kilian had said.

"What?" she asked.

"So what now?" Serious repeated, holding open the door for her. They were back on the street again.

"Who fancies a night shift?"

Then she was sitting in a patrol car with Serious, on the phone to the chief duty officer, arranging night-time surveillance of the apartments of the remaining fourteen new GoSolar employees. Standing alone outside police HQ, contemplating a visit to persons 2, 3 and 5. Stopping at some lights in Wiehre, wishing she had a bicycle – now and then a bit of fresh air was good for you, especially at confusing times like this. Closing the door to her apartment and wondering when she'd abandoned the idea of going to see 2, 3 and 5.

Lying in bed, setting the alarm for half past ten and thanking all the gods in this universe that she hadn't given in to the temptation of a drink.

Listening to Ben's voice on the answerphone at full volume in the sitting room and falling asleep at some point between *I love you* and *Maybe Sunday?*

16

At 11.00 p.m. Louise entered the hospital. She'd showered, eaten slices of pizza under a canopy in the drizzle and drunk a double espresso. This brief revitalisation would suffice for two or three alert hours.

At the night desk she only had to show her Kripo ID; no questions were asked. The corridor outside intensive care was deserted apart from two uniformed officers from Freiburg North station, and a night sister who was busy with paperwork in a little room with a glass panel. Louise glanced up at the ceiling light. It wasn't buzzing anymore; there was just the sound in her head.

"Repaired earlier," one of the constables said. "It was unbearable."

The other officer was holding a list of names of the hospital staff. Two relatives of patients had visited the intensive care ward after they'd been checked. Otherwise only doctors, orderlies and "hordes of nuns". Nobody who stood out. Nobody for Esther.

Louise waited until the security doors to the ward opened and a nurse came out. Then she went in.

In a small anteroom she disinfected her hands with the dispenser. Then she went through a door into a dimly lit, open space with six beds in which patients were sleeping. Buttons and screens of machines monitoring vital statistics were lit up, and there were quiet beeps at regular intervals. From the ceiling came the gentle whoosh of the air-filtration system.

On either side were narrow areas partitioned off by plastic

curtains. The first four were empty; in the third on the left she found Esther.

She seemed to be asleep. Her hair was stuck to the pillow, her cheeks pale valleys, dark rings beneath her eyes. From her right arm an IV tube led to a bottle of solution, and a screen above it showed the vital functions. On the small table beside her bed were a newspaper, a bottle of mineral water, a glass, a watch, and that was it. Nothing that a visitor might have brought.

She recalled Bertram Faller's question – who would be visiting her?

No parents, no siblings, no friends, no colleagues. Just a Kripo woman no longer able to be considerate.

Bonì wished she hadn't come.

But she knew that she couldn't leave without having spoken to Esther. About GoSolar, about Berlin. That was how it was, that was how *she* was, and had been for a few days or weeks or months.

She hated herself for it.

Get these investigations over with, she thought, then finally have a clear-out, do away with all the debris that had accumulated inside her over the course of forty-five years. A daily coffee with Katrin Rein, her favourite psychologist, or even move in with the woman. Then spend a while chatting to the friendly trees around the Kanzan-an, who knew how to deal with her better than any human being.

The shadowy eyes opened and looked at Louise. Then Esther half sat up, pushing the pillow behind her back. "There's a chair somewhere."

Louise fetched an uncomfortable metal seat from a corner of the room and placed it beside the bed. "How are you?"

Esther lowered her gaze and said nothing.

"If there's anything I can do for you . . ."

"Thanks."

"Would you like me to ring your parents?"

"What for?"

"So they can come and visit you."

"They live in Australia?"

"What about a friend, then?"

A feeble shake of the head.

"Don't you have anybody who—"

"I don't need anybody," Esther said, pulling the covers over her chest and smoothing them. Her eyes wandered to the bandage around her left wrist. After a moment she put her right hand on it. "Why are you here?"

"Because of GoSolar."

"Then let's finally get it over with."

Esther began with Berlin, repeating what she'd already told Louise in Littenweiler: her GP had referred her to his brother-in-law, an anxiety and depression specialist at the Charité. Freiburg wasn't an option, and in any case she saw the trip to Berlin as a challenge, her first step out of her illness – she had a fear of travel, a fear of flying. A fear of being on her own in an unfamiliar city. Maybe it'll do you good, the GP had said.

And so she'd flown to Berlin.

She was only barely aware of what happened in the hotel corridor – at the Charité she'd been given antidepressants to calm her down. Shortly after the commotion outside her door she'd fallen asleep again.

She was woken by a telephone call, a GoSolar colleague ringing to say he happened to be in Berlin too and would like to have dinner with her. She said no. He tried to persuade her, but she stuck to her guns. She wasn't feeling well, either physically or emotionally. She didn't fancy it.

Then her colleague said he *had* to talk to her. About what she was doing at GoSolar. She didn't understand and wanted to end the conversation.

But he knew.

"Knew what, Esther?" Louise asked gently.

"I thought you knew."

"Not exactly."

"I . . . But I can't say it like *that*, I have to start from the beginning."

"OK, tell me about Berlin first. About your colleague. What's his name?"

"Schulz."

Louise froze. "Philipp Schulz? In the office next to yours?"

"Do you know him?"

"Vaguely. Keep going."

Esther ended up being persuaded, and in a panic went to the restaurant Schulz had suggested, an Italian on the U7 line as she – Louise – had suspected. Schulz had acted strangely. She became increasingly worried about his behaviour; it was as if he believed they were being watched and were in danger. When she asked him about this he played it down.

Eventually he proposed a deal: she should cooperate with the Verfassungsschutz, name names, then he would guarantee her immunity from prosecution.

"With the Verfassungsschutz? What exactly did he say?"

"That he worked for the Verfassungsschutz and that I—"

"Did he show you any ID?"

"Yes."

"Have you ever seen a Verfassungsschutz ID before?"

"No."

"So it might have been faked?"

Esther's eyes were fixed on Louise, her small face reflected confusion. "Yes."

Philipp Schulz murdered – that in itself didn't fit the picture Louise had put together, let alone the fact that he might have been working for the Verfassungsschutz . . . On the other hand there was no proof he was part of the web of espionage, despite the circumstances in which he'd arrived at GoSolar – the pornography on Heinrich Willert's computer.

Was it conceivable that the Verfassungsschutz had planted him as Willert's successor? Copied the incriminating films onto his computer and assigned them fake download data to make this possible?

Esther reached for the water bottle, but could barely keep hold of it through sheer exhaustion. Louise took it from her, filled the glass and waited until she'd drunk some.

"How did you react?"

"I . . . I ran away. I know that was silly, but Schulz was behaving so strangely and I didn't know how to tell him everything. I thought he wouldn't believe me anyway and then I felt ill and was worried I was going to be sick . . ."

Soft footsteps approached from the open section of the ward. A small, shapeless silhouette glided by. When the sound had faded Louise asked, "Did Schulz contact you again in Berlin?"

"No."

"Have you seen him since?"

"In the office, on Monday and Tuesday."

"Did he say anything else?"

Esther shook her head. "He just looked weird." She swallowed hard, as if she were fighting back the tears.

Louise resisted the urge to sit on the bed and try to comfort Esther. Even back in Littenweiler she'd felt the need to wrap her in blankets, lift her up and carry her to somewhere where she was safe from the world. Look after her like you look after a distraught child. She wondered if the man who'd saved Esther's life felt the same, if he'd sensed her neediness via the bugs and cameras. A pretty woman whose profound longing for affection and protection was evident.

"What exactly did . . . does Schulz know?"

"He said he knew I was *spying*," Esther said, wiping the tears from her eyes. "That I was copying documents and showing a *conspicuous interest* in technical details."

"Did he go into any more detail?"

Esther shook her head.

"Is he right?"

"No! I'm not *spying*! It's all a dreadful mistake!"

"Can you tell me about it now? About the mistake?"

Back in April Esther was approached by a colleague. Louise knew this man's name too; she'd rung his doorbell only a few hours ago: person 4 – Ulrich Meier – St Georgen.

Meier told her the firm was planning to set up a hi-tech security department to protect the company and their IT system. A separate, large department with software, technical and security experts. First, however, they wanted to get an idea of what and where the weak spots inside the company were. An external security firm would then use this analysis to develop a strategy. A task force which he, Meier, was a member of had been set up to carry out the risk assessment. The team had been tasked with collecting the relevant data by the end of the year.

One person in each department had been asked to do this job. GoSolar would become a business that was equal to the challenges of the coming years, protected against know-how theft, plagiarism, spying and similar threats. As with its solar products, the company wanted to set new standards in business security too.

"And you said you were willing to be involved?"

"I felt . . . flattered. Ulrich asked *me*. Me, not Annette, she's—"

"Annette Mayerhöfer?"

"Yes. She's fantastic. So intelligent. She gets her own way, she's not afraid of anyone."

"Is she your superior?"

"Not really. But she takes responsibility, says what she thinks, unlike me. She wants to make it to the top, whereas I'm quite happy with things as they are."

"You know she's handed in her notice?"

"Yes." Esther admitted that she was anxious at the thought of a new colleague starting; she couldn't imagine work without Annette. They were in perfect harmony – one reliable and thorough in the background, the other determined and forceful in the foreground.

One in the shade, the other in the sun, Louise thought. "What exactly did you do for Meier?"

Over several months Esther photocopied internal documents with technical data, calculations, market research and estimated sales figures, or sent them to an external e-mail address that Meier had given her. She also passed on minutes of meetings, records of conversations with joint-venture partners and suchlike.

"About which product?"

"Have you heard of 'DriveSolar'?"

"Yes, solar panels for car roofs, right?"

Esther nodded. Ulrich Meier had wanted her to obtain information about this project alone, because it was so important for GoSolar and the task force had to know how such sensitive data was being protected. Esther kept the photocopies in her desk until Meier approached her in the staff canteen or came to sit by her desk. Later that day she would take them in an envelope to the ladies' toilets in her department and slip it between the loo-roll holder and the wall in a particular cubicle.

"Who picked them up?"

"I don't know."

"Who apart from Meier did you talk to about the task force and the . . . planned security department?"

"Nobody."

"Why is 'DriveSolar' so important, in fact? Solar cells for car roofs is hardly a lucrative market, is it?"

Not over the next few years, Esther replied, but in the near future. Until now there had only been one competitor, and GoSolar wanted to get into the market early. In cooperation with a car manufacturer and a supplier in Saxony-Anhalt, the company was building a factory designed for the fully automated mass production of car modules. Currently, with a traditional crystalline cell module, you could barely power the interior lights when the engine was off. But the research department was working flat out to improve efficiency, as well as developing semi-transparent cells for the side and rear windows. They were also working on thin-layer modules that could eventually be stuck in sheets onto the bodywork.

With a smile Louise rolled her eyes. *Crystalline, thin-layer* – it was all Greek to her.

But she couldn't cheer Esther up. Head bowed, she stared at the empty glass in her hand. "It *is* all a mistake, isn't it?"

"It looks that way, yes."

"Have I done anything illegal?"

Louise shook her head reassuringly.

"But what does the Verfassungsschutz want from me, then?"

"Oh, they're only interested in GoSolar. I mean, you know the rumours. Insider dealing and so on."

"Did they . . . how do you say it? Infiltrate Schulz in?"

"I'm assuming so."

"So why are *you* here? Are you working with the Verfassungsschutz?"

"No. I just want to find out exactly what happened in Berlin. The identity of the man who had the room next to yours."

Esther nodded and seemed to believe her, even though her answer explained barely half of what had happened in Berlin and Freiburg.

Louise waited for further questions, but none came. Perhaps because Esther was anxious to avoid upsetting the construct, so she could still believe that Ulrich Meier had asked her to help the task force. That she'd been helping rather than spying.

Their eyes met. Esther held Bonì's gaze for a few seconds, then lowered her eyes. Louise realised at once that the construct was already broken. Esther knew she was caught in a trap.

Hence the suicide attempt.

In the open section of the ward a woman had started crying and a man's voice was muttering some words of comfort. Louise had got up and was pacing up and down within the plastic rectangle. Philipp Schulz in Berlin, apparently working for the Verfassungsschutz – a dreadful thought. This would mean that it was no mole who'd been murdered – which would have been bad enough – but a colleague. And how wrong she would have been! There had to be plausible alternatives.

But she couldn't come up with any, no matter how hard she tried. She thought it unlikely that in Berlin Schulz had merely been testing Esther's loyalty to the phony task force, or trying to find out whether the Verfassungsschutz had approached her. Why would he have made Esther panic? And since the group had been keeping her under surveillance for weeks, maybe months, they must know if she was in contact with the Stuttgart office.

Bonì sat down. "Did Schulz question you about the fight in the hotel?"

"Yes." He asked what she'd picked up. Whether she saw the victim or the aggressor. If she could describe the man from room 35.

There were many possible scenarios to account for what had happened in Berlin, Louise thought. But Philipp Schulz meeting Esther that evening, having almost killed Hans Peter Steinhoff at the hotel in the afternoon, was not one of them.

"Did you see the man who bandaged you in your house?"

"Only in a blur. I wasn't . . . properly awake."

"Did he hide his face from you? Was he wearing a mask?"

"No."

"Would you be able to identify him?"

"I think so. If he was right in front of me."

Louise leaned back. She was puzzled to feel a wave of relief pass through her. Esther's guardian angel and Schulz were not the same man. He was alive.

Sometime later she woke with a start. Twenty to twelve; she'd nodded off for a few minutes. Esther was asleep too, her head turned to the side. She was still holding the glass. All Louise could hear was the soft beeping of the monitor and – like irregular, distant echoes – that of the machines in the open section of the ward.

Louise stretched. The uncomfortable metal chair that consisted only of edges and hard surfaces had dug painfully into her in several places.

When she detected a movement out of the corner of her eye, she turned her head – and jumped. Beyond the dividing curtain, scarcely four metres away, stood a figure. A man peering in at them.

Once again she'd been found while asleep.

She got up tentatively, to let the man know she'd noticed him and wasn't going to react. For several seconds both of them stood there without moving, separated only by the plastic curtain. Because the man was making no move to come in or leave, she knew she wasn't mistaken – Esther's guardian angel had turned up to her rendezvous.

In the end he slowly backed away, then turned and walked off silently.

Glancing at Esther and checking that her pistol was in its holster, she followed him.

17

When Louise emerged into the open section of the ward, the man was nowhere to be seen. She turned to her left, towards the second security door – that was the direction he'd headed. More curtained-off beds, then visitors' toilets, a locked broom cupboard and some staffrooms – open, but empty. She didn't expect to bump into him here. He was careful and experienced; he'd wait for her somewhere he felt was safer. She had to find this place.

She pushed the security door and held it open with one hand. On this side too, there were two officers sitting on chairs by the wall. Louise didn't know either of them.

"Louise Bonì, D11."

They got up and one said, "Marić, and this is Heller. Freiburg North."

Nobody had entered or left the ward in the past twenty minutes, apart from a nun who'd come twice and gone twice.

Louise asked Marić to describe her.

Short, plump, old – the shapeless silhouette from earlier. She didn't think the guardian angel could have found the time to transform himself into a short, round nun.

She unfolded the plan of the building that Kilian had been given by Bertram Faller. "Where are we?"

Marić showed her.

"Have you got a pen?"

She marked the spot. According to the plan the ward had two entrances, both of which were being watched. The guardian angel can't have climbed in through a window; they were all closed and the ward was on the second floor. There must be a third way in.

She asked Marić to have a good look at the plan.

"Only two security doors, that's for sure," he said after a while. Then he pointed to the heading – "NEW BUILDING". "Is there an old part as well?"

"Shit, you're right." A few years ago the hospital had acquired a new building that now housed the intensive care ward, along with other departments. She'd read a newspaper article about it. All of a sudden a picture came to mind: people in white gowns holding up champagne glasses, and in the middle of them a bishop dressed in black.

A new structure which had been built on to the old part. Somewhere there must be access between the two.

She told Marić and Heller that a wanted suspect was in the building – don't arrest him, but be vigilant and keep me informed.

"Is he dangerous?"

"Probably not."

"*Prob*ably not?" Heller echoed scornfully.

"That's life." She shrugged.

In the dim light of the ward she studied the floorplan. The old part of the hospital was attached to the new building on its western wing, and ran southwards, the horizontal bar of an "L", if her memory of the layout of the hospital as a whole was correct. He couldn't have used the passageways beyond the second security door because Marić and Heller were there. There was really only one possibility: the last room on the south side before this exit from the ward – a nurses' room, according to the plan.

She put the floorplan away and rubbed the sides of her head in exhaustion. The polyphonous beeping of the machines in intensive care had intensified the buzzing in her head. Acoustic relatives who seemed to be swapping messages.

The nurses' room was empty, the light off. Dull yellow moonlight seeped in through a window. In the middle of the western wall was a door. She opened it and felt the wall for a light switch.

Wooden steps – she was in the old part of the hospital. Two entrances being guarded, the third had been overlooked; the mistakes were mounting up. Four policemen and still Esther had been unprotected.

Because the door could only be opened with a key on the other side, Bonì took a dirty mug from the sink and placed it on the ground between the door and the frame.

She looked around hesitantly. There was nothing to suggest that the man was anywhere in the vicinity.

Wait, or keep searching?

She sat at the bottom of the stairs. If he wanted to speak, he would find her. Especially if she fell asleep again, she thought.

He came a quarter of an hour later.

The lights on the stairs had gone out every couple of minutes and she'd switched them on again each time. When she sank back onto the wooden floor for the final time he was standing on the steps above her. He was wearing a face mask and holding the Walther in his gloved right hand, as he had outside Esther's house in the early hours. This time it was pointing downwards.

She recognised his eyes too.

"Your gun," he said softly.

Louise stood up, took her pistol by the barrel and handed it to him. She had no idea what to do, what she was hoping to achieve. Once again she'd failed to work out an objective or a strategy.

"Mobile too?"

"There's no reception here. Close the door."

With her foot she nudged the mug into the nurses' room and pulled the door shut. "I assume you know who I am?"

He nodded.

"In that case it's only fair if you tell me who *you* are." Louise tried to remember what he'd called himself in Berlin, but couldn't. She'd been in this situation once before, in the summer of 2003. The man who'd forced his way into her apartment had used her neighbour's name – Marcel. "Come on, any old name will do, it's not that hard. Make one up."

"Mike."

"Would you take off your mask, Mike? I don't like talking to people who hide their face from me."

"Don't forget that you wanted to meet me." His voice hadn't changed; it was still calm.

"And you've come. Your mask."

"Not yet. Sit down."

Bonì willingly flopped onto the floor again and leaned her back against the door. "Let's start with the outcome," she said. "At the end of this conversation you need to have convinced me that you're not a killer."

"No," Mike said. "At the end of this conversation you need to have offered me a deal."

Mike came down the stairs and sat by the wall opposite her. He put both pistols on the bottom step – not much of a concession as he could grab either in a second if Louise got any silly ideas.

She was too tired to get any silly ideas.

But she was sufficiently awake to bear in mind that Philipp Schulz's killer might be sitting opposite her. "Show me your hands."

Mike took off his gloves and held out his hands, turning them slowly. They were slim but strong, his fingers curved almost elegantly. No visible gunshot residue but she couldn't be certain without an electron microscope. She leaned forwards and smelled the traces of sweat, metal and gun grease on his fingers.

He handed her his gloves, she sniffed them – nothing.

Nor was there any sign on his coat that he'd fired a gun. "Now the Walther," she said.

"Sit on your hands."

She obeyed with a weary smile and Mike held the gun under her nose. But he could have used another pistol. Could have been wearing other gloves, a different coat.

"Let's begin," he said, putting the Walther back on the step.

Louise rubbed her eyes, tried to concentrate. "Correct me if I'm wrong. Since the start of the year Hans Peter Steinhoff has been infiltrating moles into GoSolar on behalf of a French solar company. You're not one of them." She pointed to Mike. "Maybe you organised the whole thing with him, maybe you're just his hatchet man . . . But what I don't understand is why you beat him to within an inch of his life in Berlin. Was it a minor difference of opinion between spies?"

The face beneath the mask moved. Then Mike said, "One thing at a time."

"Alright. What's the name of the French firm?"

"You won't get them."

"With you as a witness I will."

"I'm not available as a witness."

"Not even against Steinhoff?"

He shook his head. "I'm talking to you and that's it."

She sighed. This would be the perfect time for a bit of theatrics. To stand up and leave, or at least to pretend to, to show she needed more than an informal chat. To see whether Mike would hold her back.

But she didn't have the energy for theatrics.

"Was the secret service involved? The French one, I mean?"

"It provided information. Do you intend to prosecute them too?"

"Oh, we'll see."

He laughed quietly.

Above them was a noise, a shuffling in the distance. Mike's eyes drifted to the ceiling, then returned to Louise when the sound had faded.

Her legs were going numb so she changed position. "Steinhoff's people had two jobs. First, to get information about 'DriveSolar', and second to destroy the atmosphere within the firm." She waved her hand about. "Bullying, sexual harassment, slander, rivalry, rumours, and so on."

She waited for Mike to contradict, but he said nothing.

"Because Esther is right at the source, in the research department," she continued, "one of Steinhoff's men used a pretext to get her so that she would provide him with data and information. At the end of June a colleague, Heinrich Willert, saw Esther making copies of documents. Willert told the head of department, whose name I've forgotten, but he didn't take it any further. Is that because he's one of Steinhoff's people?"

"No," Mike said.

The lights went out, Louise felt for the switch and they came on again.

"Your people found out all the same."

"Yes."

"You downloaded kiddy porn and made sure it got found?"

"He'd become a threat."

"Well, he's not a threat anymore. He's sitting in some run-down apartment, thinking of the past when he still had a family, a job and a nice house."

Mike didn't respond.

"You don't care, do you?"

"We don't have time for ethics, Frau Bonì."

"There's always time for ethics."

"Then let's talk about your visit to Esther."

Louise shrugged. "Do you mean the pizza? I was hungry." She tried

217

to hold his severe gaze, but couldn't. He knew he was right. And that was why she was sitting here, still on the case.

"Go on," he said.

"GoSolar employed someone to replace Willert: Philipp Schulz. To begin with I thought he was one of yours, but I was mistaken. He was with the Verfassungsschutz."

The masked head nodded.

"Did you know that from the start?"

"I only found out in Berlin."

"And you were in Berlin because you'd been monitoring Esther?"

"In October she made two calls from a phone box. Then she booked the hotel and her flight."

Suspicious enough, as far as Steinhoff and Mike were concerned. What Louise didn't understand was why Esther had been under surveillance. Did Steinhoff have doubts about her reliability?

"She was the weakest link in the chain," Mike said. "She's not one of us."

"And she's psychologically fragile."

He nodded again.

"All the same. Quite a lot of effort, it seems to me."

"Steinhoff was insistent we keep tabs on her."

"Well, well, he's paranoid too. I mean, think of the price that's been paid." A product that was not guaranteed to earn millions, not even in the future. And yet, Philipp Schulz had to die, Heinrich Willert was living a life of isolation and Esther Graf had been driven to the point of suicide. Not to mention the immense sums of money it must have cost to infiltrate GoSolar with those people. "You can't tell me it's at all proportionate."

"Depends on your perspective," Mike said.

"Murder isn't a question of perspective."

"You're right."

"Is that all you've got to say?"

"Keep going, Frau Bonì."

Louise stared into the dark eyes. Surrounded by the black mask, their expression was impossible to construe. "So, Esther flies to Berlin. You book into the same hotel, install your little devices, observe her and follow her wherever she goes. You must be well organised."

"We had help."

"What about the Verfassungsschutz?"

"They were on to her too."

"And they didn't notice you were there?"

"No."

"Were you in the Charité?"

"Yes."

"That brings us to the thing with Steinhoff. You're going to have to explain that to me."

A silly mix-up, he said. His business partner had met Steinhoff before, but Mike hadn't. He'd only spoken to him over the phone and so didn't recognise him.

"Did you think he might pose a danger to Esther?"

"Yes."

"OK, so you go along the corridor and beat the living daylights out of him."

"Like I said, it was a silly mix-up."

"But who would have an interest in harming Esther? The Verfassungsschutz? Hardly."

Mike took his time to answer. "I overreacted."

"Like with Philipp Schulz this afternoon?"

"One thing at a time, Frau Bonì."

She changed positions again; now her left buttock was feeling numb. "Why was Steinhoff at the hotel?"

"He wanted to talk."

"To Esther? Why?"

"Not to Esther. To me." Mike cleared his throat. There were more misunderstandings. Everyone was on edge on account of Esther's mysterious telephone calls and her trip to Berlin, especially Steinhoff, for whom a lot was at stake. Not only money – this was *his* operation and he was keen to avoid failure at all costs. He couldn't bear the waiting and had come to Berlin to see the surveillance of Esther for himself. He was so flustered he got the wrong room number.

"And he didn't tell you he was coming?"

"He got the wrong telephone number too."

Louise laughed in disbelief.

"He left a message on an answerphone," Mike said. "But it was a Saturday. Nobody listened to the answerphone until the Monday."

She shook her head. Mike's attack on Steinhoff had launched the Kripo investigation – professionals who were tripped up by numbers and silly mix-ups.

And their emotions. A pretty, fragile woman and a secret observer who'd lost his professional distance and overreacted.

"An answerphone in an office?"

"With a view of the river."

"The Spree? The Dreisam?"

Mike didn't answer.

The light went out and Louise slapped her hand on the round switch. "So, you leave the hotel, and one of your people hides Steinhoff in the toilets. That evening Esther meets Schulz. Did you eavesdrop on the conversation?"

"Yes."

She stretched and rubbed the back of her neck. "OK, now you know the Verfassungsschutz has a man at GoSolar. The same strategy, but not quite as efficient as you lot. Then I turn up at Esther's in Littenweiler. Let me guess: panic breaks out."

Mike ignored her comment. They decided to drop Esther and wait, he said. Schulz and Esther needed to be kept under surveillance, but so long as there was no acute danger, there was no need to take any further action. The identities of the people who'd infiltrated GoSolar were fake, but their cover stories would withstand a superficial check.

But then "the Esther thing" happened.

"Her suicide attempt?"

"Yes. We had to end the surveillance and get the equipment out of there before—"

"Hold on. You saw it on camera?"

"Yes."

"Where were you?"

"Nearby."

"Where exactly?"

Mike shook his head.

"Whatever. Anyway, you saved her life and someone ought to thank you for that. Esther won't get the opportunity, so let me do it." She pulled a face. A small hint of sentimentality on the verge of exhaustion.

Mike splayed his gloved fingers as if to say: What difference does that make now?

"So, you wanted to fetch the equipment, but you couldn't get into the house because my colleague was there."

"Yes." From that point on chaos prevailed, everything escalated, he said. The confrontation with Louise and the SWAT team outside Esther's house, the escape into the woods with two hostages, GoSolar as the focus of the Kripo investigation, the Verfassungsschutz alarmed, the moles busted . . .

And then Schulz's murder.

"It's time to take the mask off now, Mike," Louise said.

Not how you would imagine a guardian angel, more a ghost in the night. Closer to forty than thirty, unshaven for a week, light-grey patches in his black hair, drawn face. A fellow insomniac – reddened eyes, sensitive to light, blue rings beneath them, grey skin.

The light went out, the light came on.

"What happened with Schulz?"

Mike's dazzled eyes were on her. "I don't know."

"Not a good position for a deal. Who killed him?"

"I can only guess."

"Guess, then, for God's sake."

"Steinhoff panicked. He intercepted Schulz somewhere and took him to Ebnet. Perhaps he wanted to find out what Schulz knew. Or prevent him from informing his colleagues. Schulz didn't talk, so Steinhoff killed him."

"Without discussing this with you or your partner?"

Mike nodded.

"And you haven't spoken to him on the phone since?"

"I can't get hold of him."

"One glitch after another . . . There were two perpetrators. Were you the second man?"

"No."

"Who was it then?"

"I don't know. None of my people."

"You mean the moles at GoSolar?"

"I mean the two men you saw me with outside Esther's house. There's no way it would be one of the moles. They're physicists, engineers, chemists. Not killers."

"They're criminals. They're using fake identities, stealing data, ruining a business, its employees. Maybe they kill too."

"No," Mike said.

Louise leaned her head against the door and stared at Mike, who returned her gaze. She waited for a feeling, a voice from her intuition, but nothing came. She had no idea whether he was telling the truth or lying. "Why are you here? Why are you talking to me?"

"I want a career change."

"What work is it you do?"

"We help."

"By spying on people and ruining firms?"

"If that's what our client asks for."

She knew which career he meant. Business detective. They operated in a legal grey area, occasionally overstepping the boundaries of legality. It was a booming industry and there were enough experts with the necessary training. Ex-intelligence agents, ex-police officers, ex-soldiers, as well as hackers, technical experts and so on.

But killing a Verfassungsschutz officer?

"I want Steinhoff," she said.

"That's the deal. You get Steinhoff and I disappear."

At that moment the door to the nurses' room was yanked open. Louise toppled backwards, landing between the legs of a man. She saw an outstretched arm and a pistol aimed at Mike. On the wooden steps she heard footsteps, voices shouting, "Don't move!" She looked up. Mike's arms were outstretched; he looked paralysed. Halfway up the stairs stood Antje Harth, who was also pointing a gun at him.

Harth and Bredik – the Verfassungsschutz had sprung into action. Nobody said anything.

Then came a crisp click that tore through the silence, and the light went out.

"Don't shoot!" Louise exclaimed. She got to her feet, knocking against a leg, and felt for the switch by the door.

The light came on.

"Shit," Antje Harth said.

Mike had grabbed both pistols from the step; one was pointing at Harth, the other at Bredik.

"Stay calm, all of you," Louise said.

"Put the weapons down," Bredik ordered.

Mike raised his eyebrows. "How did they get here?"

"No idea," Louise said.

"Weapons down!" Bredik repeated.

223

Mike didn't react.

"Let's just calm down, OK?" Louise said. In her head a crazy mechanism had got into gear, which was counting the seconds until the light went out again. Two minutes? Three? She cursed herself for not having gauged how long it stayed on for. She had to anticipate that Mike would take advantage when it went dark again. He had plenty of options – leap to the bottom of the stairs, take Harth, Bredik or herself hostage. She had no doubt that he'd manage it.

The only question was whether Harth or Bredik would shoot.

She had two or three minutes left to convince Mike that their agreement still stood. But her mind was filled with the buzzing and the counting mechanism, making it impossible to think with any clarity.

Boní turned to Antje Harth. "We need him, he's going to bring us Steinhoff."

Harth's face, which Louise had thought rather prim in Graeve's office, now seemed contorted with tension. Sweat was running down her forehead and cheeks, and she was blinking furiously. "Have you arrested him?"

"No."

"Is this the man who tried to kill Steinhoff?"

Louise sighed. "Who beat Steinhoff up, yes."

"You're under arrest," Harth said to Mike. "You're accused of attempted murder and the murder—"

"Please," Louise said in despair. "He's got nothing to do with your colleague's death."

"Who says?"

"I do."

"Can you prove it?"

"No, but I believe him."

One minute thirty? One minute? No, she thought: longer. The counter in her head was going by her racing pulse.

"Unlike Steinhoff, he didn't have a motive."

"What was Steinhoff's motive?"

"Panic."

Harth snorted. "Not very convincing."

"There were two suspects," Bredik said to Mike. "Who was the second one?"

"He doesn't know," Louise said when Mike didn't reply.

"Not very convincing either," Harth said.

"We have to take him with us, Bonì," Bredik said.

As Harth was cautioning Mike, his eyes were on Louise. She raised her shoulders, hoping he would understand the message: I don't know anymore, do what you think's right, I trust you.

One minute? Thirty seconds?

Less than five seconds later the lights went out. Harth and Bredik cursed, shouted warnings; Louise closed her eyes and waited. An arm clamped her chest and pressed her to a body. Her own body was turned right around, she felt a jab, heard Bredik yell, rapid footsteps on the wooden floor, a muffled sound as someone fell. Mike's breathing in her ear, the barrel of a pistol against the back of her head. Wrenched backwards, her elbows hit the doorframe and she cried in pain. Suddenly the light of the moon was on her face, then the door flew right past her nose and slammed shut.

Without relaxing his grip Mike pushed her through the dark nurses' room. She could smell unwashed clothes, an unwashed body and sweat. "Left or right?" he asked.

Marić and Heller were sitting by the left-hand exit of intensive care; they could cause problems. "Right."

Mike let go of her by the door to the nurses' room. They went out and walked quickly through the ward, past the curtained-off beds where Esther was, then through the open section. There was no sound apart from the soft beeping of the machines and the whoosh of the air-filtration system.

In the anteroom where you disinfected your hands Louise opened the security doors. From the startled look on the faces of both uniformed officers she knew they'd realised who the man beside her was. Two hands reached for their holsters.

"It's OK," she said.

The officer on the left, an old police sergeant, stared at Mike. He didn't look convinced.

"My gun?" Louise said, putting out her hand.

Mike gave her the Heckler & Koch.

"It's OK," she repeated.

The older officer nodded.

They kept going, Mike in front. He led Louise into a side corridor, turned off again and stopped beside a lift that said: FOR STAFF USE ONLY.

She held out her gun. "You can have it back."

"Why?"

"I'm tired. I'll end up confusing it with a pencil and hurt myself."

They took the lift down to the basement, hurried through the deserted laundry and storerooms full of shelves with clothes, towels and bed linen, and stopped beside a fire door. Mike took out a key and opened it. A stone ramp led to a tarmacked path, beyond which lay the grounds of the hospital.

"Wait," Louise said, and went down the ramp. The wind was blowing and she felt a cool drizzle on her cheeks. So far as she could make out in the dark, they were alone.

Mike appeared beside her. "Through the park."

They kept clear of the paths to avoid making any noise, wandering along the side wall through wet grass and beneath bare trees. They would only be visible from the hospital building if someone looked closely: two shadows emerging from the darkness for a mere few seconds when caught in the light of a park lamp. Louise held her side, feeling a stitch, and kept her head bowed; inside it the buzzing was raging. Mike had slackened his pace – a considerate man, at least, she thought, albeit too wilful. In the distance, two nuns dressed in white beneath an umbrella on a night-time walk, but no sign of any more intelligence agents, even though it was inconceivable that Bredik and Harth would have come on their own. Only the childless Chief Inspector Bonì employed such methods, thereby endangering protracted investigations into highly complex cases and stirring up catastrophes; although for the most part she made the right decisions.

At least she ended up in the right places, she thought, where the decisions landed.

"I can't go on anymore."

Mike turned around. "Just another fifty metres."

"Ten, then that's it."

He didn't respond.

Eventually they came to a wrought-iron gate. Louise leaned against the wall, panting, while Mike got another key out of his bag and unlocked it.

"It wouldn't surprise me if you had one to my apartment too," she said.

Again there was no reply. A guardian angel without a sense of humour.

And without trust. He made her give him her mobile, switched it off and removed the battery.

"No more surprises," he said.

A few streets further on they got into an old blue Golf with a Freiburg numberplate.

"Where are we going?"

Mike gave the name of a hotel in the old town.

"Is Steinhoff there?"

"Yes."

"I'm going to need back-up, then."

"You've got me."

"What about the second man?"

He shrugged.

"Can I have my pencil back?"

She was given her gun.

Mike drove at a normal speed, making sure they didn't attract attention. After a few minutes Louise sank into a restive doze. Garish images flashed through her mind – angular naked bodies on orange and blue.

Then she saw a body lying on a red background and she woke with a faint cry.

18

The small, shabby hotel was in the northern part of the old town. Sitting at reception was a boy with acne scars. As they approached him Mike said, "Ask for Ralf Schuster."

Louise nodded. Schuster, Schulz, Meier – the list of the most common names was getting longer and longer, as if the group around Steinhoff and the Verfassungsschutz had been reading the same spy handbook.

She flashed her ID and the startled-looking boy gave her a spare key.

They walked up to the fourth floor. Kitsch paintings of local attractions decorated the walls – Schauinsland, the Kaiserstuhl, Freiburg minster, the Black Forest, vineyards, Staufen, where Faust is said to have died. Filled with a sudden longing, Louise realised how much she wanted to show Ben all of this. The Breisgau was her home, after all, and yet virtually all he knew of it was a bare apartment in Stuhlinger, a chaotic one in Wiehre, a car park in St Georgen, as well as a few pubs and restaurants. It occurred to her that she'd had similar thoughts when driving back from Colmar in the summer, vowing to show him this beautiful region between the Black Forest and the Vosges. I need to make up for lost time, she thought; Ben would be gone in a few months.

But first, the Schusters, Meiers and Schulzes.

They'd reached Steinhoff's floor. Outside the hotel they'd briefly discussed what they were going to do. A simple plan with a couple of alternatives. Mike would call Steinhoff and ask if they could meet at the hotel as he was nearby. If Steinhoff said no they'd surprise him in his room. If he wasn't there or wasn't contactable, they'd wait for him there.

They went into a toilet and Mike dialled the number. After a while he shook his head.

"Shit," Louise said. "Call him again."

Steinhoff didn't answer the second time either.

Their eyes met. Apart from tiredness she couldn't see anything in Mike's face, no agitation, no duplicity, no worry, no emotion at all. Maybe he was leading her into a trap, maybe he'd keep his promise. She had to live with this uncertainty.

"Let's go in."

Mike unlocked the door, Louise peering over his shoulder. When he pushed the door open, she detected a specific smell she knew only too well – blood and excrement. "Careful, Mike!"

The light went on; the room seemed to be empty.

She'd been anticipating a dead body, but all she found was the chaos of a man who wasn't interested in order. Clothes were scattered everywhere, empty beer bottles on the bedside table and television set, personal items, newspapers, chargers, two laptops, three mobiles on the unmade bed, chairs and the narrow desk.

And the smell, which was getting stronger and stronger.

They found Steinhoff behind the bed, lying on his stomach. He'd been shot in the head and the back.

It was half past one in the morning by the time several police cars and an ambulance arrived. Louise was sitting in the foyer on a chair that smelled dusty and old, trying desperately to keep her eyes open. She'd questioned the young receptionist but not got any useful information out of him. He'd begun his shift at ten o'clock and hadn't set eyes on Steinhoff – Ralf Schuster. Around ten people had entered or left the hotel in the past three and a half hours, half of whom the boy knew, the others must have been recent arrivals.

Louise filled in her colleagues and asked them to question the guests in the neighbouring rooms. She would wait for Peter Schöne, who the control centre had got out of bed, and then drive to the Dreisam, where she was due to meet Mike.

One final meeting, he'd said.

The main thing is that you turn up, she'd replied.

She couldn't imagine he didn't have at least an idea of who was responsible for the killings of Philipp Schulz and Hans Peter Steinhoff. Together with his partner and Steinhoff he'd been spinning the web around GoSolar since the start of the year – preparing the operation, looking for apartments, getting hold of tap-proof mobiles, selecting suitable spies and waiting for the right moment to infiltrate them, watching Esther and organising meetings when necessary. He knew everyone involved and together with Steinhoff had been holding the strings the puppets danced from. It was hard to believe there was anyone working in the background he had no knowledge of.

The French? she'd asked.

They can't afford a murder, he'd replied.

Secret service?

Not in it anymore.

"Bonì," someone growled above her.

She opened her lids and stared into Peter Schöne's small eyes, half hidden by bags.

"Now I know why I'm with D31 rather than D11. There's a dead body here every day and you don't get any sleep."

Schöne was slumped on the sofa opposite, having listened with a deep frown to what had happened since Bonì's phone call in the early evening. As deputy leader of the task force he was expected upstairs at the crime scene, but he didn't seem to be able to gird himself.

She thought of how aggressive he'd been at the meeting in his office on Tuesday afternoon, accusing her of prowling around his department, asking if she was getting hysterical again. Now he was sitting apathetically, longing for his bed.

"Do you trust this guy?"

She shrugged.

"I'd offer to come with you . . ." He pursed his lips sheepishly. "But I wouldn't be a great help." A fly pitter-pattered slowly across his shoulder as if his tiredness had rubbed off on it. He didn't notice the insect.

"That's OK. Will you look after everything else? Forensics, the public prosecutor, GoSolar tomorrow morning . . . *this* morning."

He nodded with a sigh. His bed would have to wait.

An officer came in. They'd found two cartridges and both bullets – one in the bedroom wall, one in the wooden floor beneath Steinhoff's body. "Certainly not a Walther P5," he said. "Is that good enough for you?"

"Yes." It wasn't proof, of course, but it supported her assumption that Mike wasn't the killer. If he'd had a second firearm on him, she thought, he'd have taken it out at the hospital rather than bending down for the pistols on the step. It took longer to bend down than to take a gun from a pocket.

"What about the people in the rooms next door?"

"They heard nothing and saw nobody."

"Thanks."

When the officer turned to go, the fly flew off.

"I think I'll go upstairs too," Schöne said.

They stood up.

"Hear anything from Rolf?" Louise said.

"Unchanged."

"What do you mean, 'unchanged'?"

Schöne hesitated. "Didn't Rita call you?"

"No." Louise sank back down into the chair. Her body was covered with a cold tingling.

"Hmm. She was going to call you."

"What's happened to Rolf?"

"Well, he's got a haematoma." Schöne rubbed his splayed hands on his waist and cleared his throat, as if he didn't like being the one who had to deliver the bad news.

"In his head?"

He nodded and sat back down too.

Bermann had aborted his drive to Ebnet because he had a bad headache and felt sick. He waited in the car for ten, twenty minutes, but didn't feel any better. He then took a taxi to HQ and sat at his desk. Eventually he was persuaded by colleagues to go to casualty. On the way there he briefly lost consciousness. The doctors said he probably had concussion. Then he passed out again. A thorough examination that evening revealed he didn't have concussion but a traumatic brain injury with a haematoma.

Bermann was now in a coma.

Louise left the hotel at a quarter past two. Peter Schöne had dissuaded her from going straight to see Bermann in hospital. There's no way they'll let you in, and there's nothing you can do anyway. He'll be fine, he's got a hard head.

A head with a crack in it.

As she sped through the empty night-time streets towards Kaiserbrücke, Louise kept playing the moment over in her mind when Bermann fell on the stairs after they'd questioned Heinrich Willert. No matter how much she wished it could be different, the scene always ended the same way: with a dull thud when the back of Bermann's head crashed onto the stairs.

Then she saw him stagger to the entrance, to the car, tumble onto the seat. She knew she couldn't have stopped him driving, no matter what she said. He'd never have admitted to her that he didn't feel well.

You can't drive now, Rolf.

Don't talk nonsense.

Get yourself checked out.

Stop getting on my tits.

That's what their relationship was like – Rolf Bermann and Louise Bonì, a complicated story. Had it been Schöne or anyone else with him at Willert's, he might have accepted some help, might have agreed to be taken to casualty right away, would have been operated on two hours earlier.

Two hours that could prove decisive.

19

Again Mike took his time.

Louise had been sitting on a bench by the Dreisam, near Kaiserbrücke, for twenty minutes, trying to banish her worries about Bermann.

A quarter to three, light rain falling, the damp coldness seeping through her clothes and into her bones. The Dreisam looked wider than usual; the autumn rains had raised the water level. Apart from a cyclist, nobody had passed her on the towpath, not a soul was to be seen.

She pulled up the collar of her denim jacket and warmed her hands in her armpits. She strained to keep her head up.

Louise didn't doubt that Mike would keep the appointment. He must already be close by, watching her, checking to see whether she'd come alone. Whether she'd been followed by the Verfassungsschutz without realising it.

Another quarter of an hour passed, then she heard a slight rustling in the leaves behind her.

He sat next to her. Rainwater ran down the front and sides of his head; his dark eyes were inscrutable.

"Attempted murder, unlawful remote surveillance, falsification of documents, breaking and entering, resisting a law enforcement officer, incitement to other crimes – give me one good reason why I shouldn't arrest you."

"Because your pistol's out of bullets."

She took the Heckler & Koch from its holster and ejected the magazine. Empty. A feeling she'd been missing stirred inside her – anger. He'd allowed her to enter Steinhoff's hotel room unarmed.

Closing her eyes, Boni let the anger seize hold of her. It warmed her from the inside and brought with it another sensation she'd been missing: she felt alive again.

"Besides, your colleague already tried."

She looked at him. "You're right. I'd forgotten. So we should add resisting arrest to the list."

From the Dreisam she heard a lively babbling and from the bridge the sound of an engine, but otherwise it was silent. This was a lonesome place at three in the morning if you happened to be sitting here with a man who was more ghost than someone made of flesh and blood. Of whom nothing was concrete apart from his bizarre connection to Esther and his desire to get out of the business.

And his nervousness – time and again he glanced at the other side of the river, turned to the left, to the right. A ghost who was never calm.

"Have the moles gone back into their holes?"

"Yes."

"All of them?"

He nodded.

"How many were there?"

"Eight."

"Eight at GoSolar?"

"Yes."

Of course the task force would try to track them down. Not all would be found, but some would; and not in the next few days, but in the coming weeks or months. The rest would remain undetected and go about their daily lives protected by their real identities until someone planned a new operation, spun a new web. Industrial spies were highly coveted; espionage was booming and difficult to prove.

The old fury was roused. You caught one and had to watch impotently as others disappeared back into their boltholes. This web had been broken, but beneath the surface the system remained full of holes.

She tried to compose herself. What happened in the next few hours was important; everything else belonged to a distant galaxy. She had no idea where she would be in a few weeks or months, but she did know where she wasn't going to be: in her office at police HQ.

It was also important that she had Ben close by. And, in the distance, Rolf Bermann's voice booming down the neon-lit corridors of Kripo.

Louise looked at Mike. "Who killed Schulz and Steinhoff?"

"I don't know."

"Who are you covering up for, Mike?"

He didn't reply.

"Someone else is involved in this operation, aren't they? Someone I know nothing about."

"No."

"What about your business partner? Did *he* commit the murders?"

"No."

"How can you be so sure?"

"Because I've known him for years."

"That means nothing."

"In this case it does."

"Who could it be then?"

"We're going round in circles here."

Louise threw her hands in the air. A residue of anger remained, but she sensed that exhaustion was gnawing away at it. "I need a name, for God's sake. A clue. That's why you're here, isn't it? Because you want to help me find the killer."

Mike nodded thoughtfully.

"Let's start at the beginning. Steinhoff approaches you or your business partner. What does he want?"

"Organisation, manpower, equipment. A strategy."

"How does he come across you?"

"He asked around."

"In the business you want to get out of?"

"Yes."

"And you spin the web of espionage together?"

"Yes." Mike's gaze scanned the riverbank opposite. Only now did she notice that his right hand was inside his open coat.

"They sleep at night, Mike."

"Who?"

"Verfassungsschutz agents."

A surprised smile darted across his lips.

"So, you work out a strategy. Where do you get your information about GoSolar from? I mean, you have to know exactly how you're going to infiltrate the company. Where you can plant your people."

"Most of it came from Steinhoff, the rest from us."

"Through observation?"

"That sort of thing."

"And where did Steinhoff get his information?"

"He knows people."

"At GoSolar?"

Mike hesitated. "Maybe."

She leaned back and clasped her hands in her lap, as if this was how she could protect her vague thoughts from the chaos in her head, where images, words, sounds and events churned about. "He had someone in the company from the beginning," she said. "Someone whose identity only he knew."

"And who killed him to avoid being found out?"

"I can't think of anything else."

"Too much coincidence."

"What do you mean?"

"Steinhoff gets the job from France and just happens to have someone at GoSolar to help him?"

Louise didn't reply.

238

"He would have informed us," Mike said, turning to her. There would have been too great a risk that one of the moles might have unintentionally put the others in danger because they didn't know about each other. Quite apart from the fact that they would have saved themselves a lot of work if Steinhoff had named his contact.

"And what if it was the other way around? If Steinhoff was hired by someone from GoSolar? If the French aren't involved at all?"

"My business partner was at a meeting with French people."

"Well, well. Which French people?"

He gave a meagre smile. "Solar French people."

"All the same," Louise said. "In every web there's a spider."

"Sometimes three – Steinhoff, my partner and me."

She shook her head. The three of them had spun the web, but someone was working in the background, someone who'd remained invisible to everyone except for Steinhoff. Not just anyone, not some little cog in the wheel, but someone who'd committed two murders to protect themselves.

They didn't speak for a few minutes. Louise ran through the possibilities again and again. Steinhoff, the French, a contact at GoSolar. She was convinced the answer was merely a question of the right chronology.

The French, the contact, Steinhoff.

The contact, Steinhoff, the French.

"You know what this boils down to?" Mike said.

She looked at him in surprise. "No. What?"

"Who is involved apart from us? Who's been probing GoSolar for months? Who's tried to hamper your investigation?"

"You can't be serious."

He shrugged.

"They don't kill, Mike. Those are colleagues, many of them used to work for Kripo. They don't go to Stuttgart and become murderers and kill their own people. And we're not in some fucking banana republic."

"There's no other explanation."

"There *has* to be." There wasn't much Louise would stake her life on, but on this she would: Steinhoff's and Schulz's killers weren't Verfassungsschutz agents.

Then Mike froze. He bowed his head, held his breath and raised a hand as a signal to keep quiet. Louise strained as hard as she could to listen, but heard nothing.

He stood up. "We've got to go."

"What? Why?"

Without replying he hauled her up and pushed her towards the bridge. She slipped on the greasy path and would have fallen if Mike hadn't still been holding her arm. Bonì was seized by fear, fear of Mike, fear of whoever might be lying in wait for them, ever more fear, and she realised for certain that this was no longer her game, that she'd reached the limit of what she could bear.

"I want my bullets back!"

"Later! There's no time now."

They ran to the bridge, Louise in front, Mike right behind. His hand was still clutching her arm and wouldn't let go, no matter how hard she tried to shake him off.

"For Christ's sake!" she hissed. "I can run on my own!"

The hand released her.

Only to grab her neck seconds later. "Duck!"

"What?" Glancing round at Mike she understood when she saw him running with his head bowed.

There was still nobody on the path behind them.

Again she slipped, again he held her.

Then they were at the bridge. In the narrow strip of darkness beneath the stone roof they stopped. "My . . . bullets," Louise panted.

Mike didn't respond. He stood with his back to her, watching the stretch of riverbank they'd come from. Against the light of a street-lamp his shoulders moved to the rhythm of his breathing, his hands down by his sides, the right one holding the pistol.

"I want my bullets, OK?"

He turned around quickly and for a moment his face loomed in the darkness. Before she could react he nipped behind her. He put his free hand over her mouth, pressed her to his shoulder, and his right hand hovered beside her face.

She heard the pistol being cocked very slowly.

"Would you be quiet for one minute?" he whispered into her ear.

When she nodded he took his hand from her mouth.

"My bull—"

Mike's hand suffocated the rest of the word. In a panic Louise began to struggle, making a grab for Mike's arm to loosen his grip, but she couldn't get herself a millimetre of wiggle room. A hysterical voice yelled in her head, You've fallen into a trap, Bonì, without thinking, without back-up, you've relied on your luck one too many times . . .

Suddenly she heard a bang, then some mechanical noises. At that moment the streetlamp nearest the bridge on the other side of the river went out.

A shot from an automatic reloading gun, the report dampened by a silencer . . .

Having yanked his arm up, Mike aimed at the lampposts. "Left pocket," he whispered. Feeling behind her back she found his coat pocket and took out the bullets.

"Don't say a word, OK?" Mike moved away from her.

Louise loaded the magazine as quickly as she could. "Can you see anyone?"

Again he didn't reply, just pulled her silently behind him. Holding her breath she cast an eye over the riverbank opposite. Still there was nobody to be seen, just the path, a grey-white strip just before the bridge, then it disappeared, only becoming visible again on the other side of the streetlamp that had been shot at.

"Down!" Mike whispered. "Onto your stomach!"

They dropped to the ground. A flash of light from the other side, another bang, a dry echo replied directly behind them. Chips of stone fell onto Louise's head and neck. Cursing, she put both her hands around the grip of the pistol and aimed, without being able to see much more than a patch of black around thirty metres wide.

"Not yet," Mike hissed.

"Do you think I'm going to wait until he's standing in front of me?"

"Keep your face down!"

Pressing her forehead onto the path she felt sharp stones digging painfully into her skin. More shots rang out; the bullets dashed against various points of the bridge. More chips, the whirr of ricochets.

Then nothing.

Above them the drone of a motorbike, a dog barking from a nearby house. Louise heard the rain on the towpath, the Dreisam babbling – but no noise from over there. She turned her head until she had a view. Still nobody to be seen.

"Has he gone?"

"No."

Mike had put the mask over his face and his gloves on. Now he blended almost perfectly into the night. "Stay here and keep down, no matter what happens," he whispered.

"I can't promise that."

The barely visible body beside her started to move, rolling almost silently to lie flat on its back, feet pointing towards the river. Louise heard Mike's deep breathing and was still wondering why he was now looking upwards rather than across the river, when the Dreisam roared barely a metre away, gave a sort of gasp and then spat water at her. Louise dimly saw Mike's head rise up, the pistol hover in the air, then fingers tugged at her hair as if trying desperately to pull her into the river. There was a flash from the barrel of Mike's pistol, accompanied by a loud bang, which resonated thousands of times off the concrete. Just above her came a cry, the fingers let go of her hair, the Dreisam briefly roared again and water rained down on her.

Mike was already on his feet and hurrying downstream when Louise finally got up, but only to her knees. She couldn't go any further, there was no strength in her shaky legs. Her eyes were drawn to a silvery glint in the grass – less than thirty centimetres from her was a combat knife.

She struggled to her feet and stumbled out of the shelter of the bridge arch. Echoes from the shot kept exploding in her ears. Mike was moving slower, aiming his pistol at the river, and now stopped. Someone was swimming in the water, a black body shrouded in inflated clothing rapidly making for the opposite riverbank.

Louise covered her ears with her hands and waited for the fatal shot. But it didn't come.

They watched in silence as a slender man climbed out of the water near the bridge. He was holding his right arm where Mike's bullet must have hit him. Seconds later he had vanished into the bushes. He reappeared for a moment up on the road, then he was out of sight.

She didn't doubt that this was the man she was looking for. The man who with Steinhoff had hunted and killed Philipp Schulz in the woods at Ebnet. Who'd shot Steinhoff in his hotel room hours later.

Louise rubbed the top of her head. The pain and echos were ebbing only slowly, and beneath them the shock cowered. He'd missed her by a whisker.

A joke for Lubowitz: by a whisker.

"Do you know him?"

Mike took the mask off. "No."

"Was he after you or me?"

"You know too much and I talk too much."

She felt for her mobile. "Do you think he'll try again?"

"Not straightaway. He's right-handed."

Sirens sounded in the distance; patrol cars were already on their way.

"Good shot, by the way. Thanks."

"It could have all gone pear-shaped, seeing as how jittery you are." She shrugged. "Are you never frightened?"

Mike didn't reply.

As she took her mobile from her pocket she focused on the other riverbank. The fear and pain had released a thought. Words that, somewhere beyond the exhaustion, were beginning to coalesce as questions for Mike.

"Bet you anything there's someone else."

He gave her a disparaging look.

"That guy isn't the invisible spider in the web."

"No?"

"He's a professional, isn't he?"

"An arrogant professional."

She nodded. "A contract killer. Not the client."

An hour later Louise was sitting on her sofa, trying to formulate the questions for Mike in her head. She'd opened the windows and balcony door but hadn't switched on the light. The humid night wind swept through the room. On the answerphone the red light was flashing. She let it flash; Ben would have to wait.

By the riverbank she'd called the chief duty officer. Uniformed officers and the crime squad had arrived, and roadblocks had been put up around the city centre. Like Mike, she suspected they wouldn't find the man – however arrogant he might be, he was still a professional. At least the roadblocks and patrol cars would force him to stay undercover.

She looked at Mike, sitting at the dining table. His face shimmered in the faint light of the streetlamp. One hand was on the table, the other in his lap. He hadn't moved in the ten minutes he'd been sitting there. Louise sensed he was uncomfortable. Like Gerhard Kleinert, the founder of GoSolar, he seemed to have fallen into a world that was unfamiliar and uncanny. An apartment, a home. Chaos on the floor, a woman on the sofa.

"How did you know your moles' cover had been broken?"

"From Steinhoff."

"How did he know?"

"No idea."

"What did he tell you?"

"That you knew the names and we had to abort the operation."

Louise cleared her throat. A tingling sensation emerged at the back of her neck, then spread to her shoulders and arms. She was very close.

But one step at a time.

"Which names?"

"Those of our people."

"What did he say, exactly?"

Mike ran a hand across his face. "That you knew the names and we had to abort the operation," he repeated. For the first time she detected a hint of irritation in his voice.

"Did he mention a list?"

"No."

Dropping onto her side, Louise nestled her head on a pillow and pulled her legs up. The air had turned cold, the exhaustion was overwhelming. "Did he call you?"

"Yes."

"When?"

"In the afternoon."

"When precisely?"

Mike took his time before saying, "Around two."

She yawned. "Check, Mike."

From her half-closed eyes she watched him take out his mobile and begin to search.

"Thirteen forty-nine."

"At thirteen forty-nine Steinhoff called to say I knew the names?"

"Yes."

She nodded in satisfaction.

Bingo.

All she needed now was the proof.

She closed her eyes completely. "One last favour, Mike."

20

As on the previous day Gerhard Kleinert was sitting at his desk; and as on the previous day he looked as if he were at the end of his tether. Pale, trembling and deeply unnerved, he glanced from one visitor to the next, not seeming to understand what was happening. As on the previous day he pretended to be the executive steamrollered by events, and proved to be a bad actor.

Unlike on the previous day it wasn't Louise and Rolf Bermann standing beside him, but Kripo chief Reinhard Graeve – to his left – and Henning Ziller, Antje Harth and Michael Bredik from the Verfassungsschutz – to his right. In front of him was Marianne Andrele, the public prosecutor, whose terse questions had set the tone of the meeting so far. Louise herself had withdrawn to the only place she could bear to listen to this conversation from – the minimalist sofa beneath the orange and blue bodies, five metres from Ziller and six from Kleinert.

She'd slept from half past four to seven o'clock, then taken an ice-cold shower, washed her hair and put on some clean clothes: blouse, skirt, pumps, blazer. If she were to go under this morning then at least let it happen with some elegance.

Half past nine and still nothing from Mike. Bonì felt a touch of nerves, nothing dramatic, just a touch deep in her insides. She was even too tired to be nervous, although she'd decided to go for broke this morning. She didn't really care whether she went under or not. Her main concern was that Richard Graeve and she were spared from looking ridiculous.

She didn't know when Mike had left her apartment. Shortly before she'd fallen asleep, she'd seen him still sitting at her dining table. By the time the alarm went off he'd gone.

One last favour, Mike.

I'll see what I can do.

If he wanted to, there was a lot a man like Mike could do, she thought. He could beat someone to within an inch of their life, he could save lives. Secretly spy on people, switch sides to be with the good guys. Somewhere in-between lay the path he wanted to take from now on. Maybe he'd realised this path would be easier to follow if he agreed to Chief Inspector Boni's last favour.

Yes, Kleinert was saying. He and the CEO – currently at a conference in the US – had approached the Verfassungsschutz a few months ago because they suspected they were being spied on by a foreign firm. Yes, in agreement with them the agency had begun to obtain information on members of staff. Yes, after Willert had been fired, the Verfassungsschutz had used the opportunity to insert Herr Schulz as his successor. No, Willert's computer hadn't been manipulated for this purpose. Yes, Herr Schulz had suspected Esther Graf of being involved in the espionage.

Yes, no, yes, yes, no and, in-between, sober questions from Andrele, who'd put her hair up with too much spray and was dressed all in dark blue. She was standing with her back to Louise, a sturdy pillar with her eyes fixed on Kleinert.

Today a pillar, yesterday a rock.

From home Louise had rung Rita Bermann, who'd spent the night at the university hospital. Rolf had undergone an operation late the previous evening; there had been complications. He was still in a coma and in a critical condition. They were going to operate again early this afternoon.

Louise was still finding it hard to believe that there was a crack in Bermann's hard skull that now threatened his life. For years he'd been shrouded with an aura of invincibility. He'd always been there, ever since her first day in the serious crime squad, and he would always be there. Anything else was inconceivable.

And yet the yelling children, barking dogs and television voices had fallen silent, replaced by Rita's tearful voice and the whispering of his parents in the background.

"It would have all blown over," Henning Ziller said, making the insect watch strap click, "if Freiburg Kripo – especially Inspector Bonì – hadn't got in our way—"

"This isn't the time to discuss jurisdiction," Andrele interrupted.

"A total disaster!" Ziller continued, incensed. "Bonì starts investigating and what happens? A suicide attempt, two murders, she allows the killer to escape arrest, his accomplices—"

"The *suspected* killer," Andrele says.

"Technically speaking, yes."

"Can you prove his guilt?"

"It won't be very hard."

"Has he made a confession?"

"Not to us," Michael Bredik said.

"Bonì?"

Louise cleared her throat. Andrele turned to looked at her. Graeve and Bredik followed suit. "He's committed a number of crimes, but not murder."

Ziller's face turned red and he threw his hands in the air.

"So we've got no proof, neither for his guilt nor innocence," Andrele said. "Is there a search out for him?"

"Of course," Ziller said. "Two men have been killed, one of them an agent of ours with a wife and two small children. He's the only possible culprit."

"No," Louise said.

"Who else, then?" Ziller bellowed.

"The man who shot at us."

"And who's that?" Andrele said.

"I don't know."

Ziller laughed.

"But I know someone who does."

For a moment there was silence in the large room.

"Who?"

"Someone from GoSolar."

"Impossible!"

"Careful, Boni," Andrele said. "No accusations without proof."

"Surely you're not accusing *me*?" Kleinert said, leaning to the side so he could see Louise behind Andrele.

"Boni," Andrele warned her again.

"How do you come to that conclusion?" Graeve asked.

Louise turned to him and spoke slowly and thoughtfully. Step by step – that was a good motto for her last few hours of service. Step by step, to avoid tripping up right at the end.

Esther Graf, she said, had been selected as a spy by Steinhoff's people because most of the useful documents from the research and development department landed on her desk at some point. Although she'd agreed to cooperate under false pretences, they'd kept her under surveillance from the outset – at home, in the office, out and about. Mike's excuse for this was that she was the weakest link in the chain because she wasn't one of the group and she was also psychologically fragile.

But there was another possible reason: Esther had been working alongside the person who'd initiated the entire operation. Had she become suspicious or been contacted by the Verfassungsschutz, it could have put this person in danger. By means of the surveillance, Steinhoff had ensured that any such development would be picked up early.

"And this person—" Ziller began.

This time Kleinert interrupted him. "Are you saying a GoSolar employee instigated all of this?"

"In cooperation with a French competitor." Louise allowed her gaze to roam over those assembled in the room. Nobody seemed convinced. Andrele and Graeve appeared thoughtful, while the others looked back at her sceptically.

She continued. "Esther was also the perfect spy for another reason. If GoSolar or an investigating authority had found out that most of the data was being stolen from her department, she would have soon been identified as the suspect. Nobody would have looked for another spy – the invisible spider who also ordered the killings to prevent them from being exposed."

Ziller smoothed his hair. "The invisible spider? Are you getting histrionic now, Bonì?"

"Can this be proven?" Andrele asked.

"I hope so," Louise said.

"And you think I've got something to do with it?" Kleinert said, his voice cracking as if on the verge of a hysterical fit.

"Bonì," Andrele said. "Let's have the proof first, then the charge."

The proof . . .

I'll see what I can do.

She hadn't got the impression that it would take Mike hours. But maybe she'd already been half asleep and hadn't heard everything he said. It struck her that she'd asked something else, and her question was about a river and an office . . .

In the office with a view of the river?

Yes.

Now she remembered why she'd asked.

Not in Freiburg, Mike had said.

But in the office with a view of the river?

Yes. If my . . . business partner hasn't tidied up.

And what if he has?

Then I can't help you anymore.

Louise checked the time – ten. She had to expect the worst.

But maybe it was possible to force one's fate. She got up and went to the door. "Come on."

"Where are we going?" Andrele asked.

"To see the spider."

Ziller laughed; the others just stared at her. A group of six people with very different interests, who at that moment all seemed to have the same thought: What is this crazed woman fantasising about now?

"You want proof," Louise said. "Let's see if it works."

Andrele lowered her head and gave Bonì a severe look over her narrow, golden-rimmed glasses. Louise turned to Reinhard Graeve, who wasn't making any move to break away from the group either. In his expensive suit he looked more like a GoSolar executive than a Kripo boss. She sensed that in his restrained way he was striving to stand his ground in the power struggle between Ziller and Andrele, and in the general chaos of the investigation. She knew she wasn't helping much as the chaos was partly down to her particular style of investigating.

Nonetheless, she expected him to stand by her.

"Come on, boss."

He didn't move. "Who do you suspect, Louise?"

"First the proof, then the charge." She essayed a smile, with no success. Her gaze swept Ziller, who seemed to be enjoying silent victories; Harth, who was again caught in her primness; and Bredik, who looked at her with sympathy. She wondered whether these last few hours would bring a final humiliation, whether everything really would have to unravel, even her affection for Graeve and her respect for Andrele.

This would be her fault too. Not only had she crossed her own boundaries, but also those of the people she worked with.

"Boss . . ."

"Later, Louise. We're not finished here."

She nodded, opened the door and closed it quietly behind her.

*

Opting for the stairs, Louise went slowly down to the third floor, crossing the foyer. The murmur of voices drifted up, and far below a telephone rang at reception. Outside, in the middle of countless police cars and the large, black, intelligence service vehicles, stood her red Peugeot, a mingy, forlorn dash of colour amidst the official lustre. Let's go home, it called out to her, and for a moment she found the idea enticing. Go home, put all of this behind you, the humiliation, her reckless gamble, her final few hours.

At a stroke the vehicles were gone, the car park almost empty. Rolf Bermann was leaning against his car, mobile phone to his ear.

Then Bermann was gone too.

On the second floor she could hear the murmur of voices more clearly. Again a telephone rang at reception, soon joined by another one. Outside, the order of the rows of cars was upset by rapid movement. A boy was running right across the car park, zig-zagging past the cars. On the path that led to the entrance to the building he was stopped by a policewoman.

Louise paused.

The policewoman was standing in the way of the boy; all Louise could see was a slim arm rising and pointing to the road. Then the policewoman turned and took the boy under the solar panels to the entrance.

Louise went over to the balustrade. Ten metres below her the two entered the building. Now she recognised the policewoman: Hesse from Freiburg South station, who she'd met during the Merzhausen case. One hand was holding a rectangular silver object, the other was holding the boy. She spoke to a uniformed officer; he pointed her to Peter Schöne, who was sitting in a green armchair a few metres away, sipping coffee.

Schöne took out his phone.

Her mobile rang.

"Post for you. Where are you?"

"Right above you," she said.

A man who looked very tired and smelled bad, a friend of Chief Inspector Louise Bonì. Give her this, he'd said. She's expecting it.

Louise stared at the digital recorder in her hand.

"What should we do with the boy?" Hesse asked.

"Let him go."

Hesse hesitated. "Do you remember me? Merzhausen."

"Yes," Louise said.

"I can't forget it. The fire, the two children."

"Not now, Officer Hesse."

Louise turned and followed the corridor that led past the open-plan area to the departmental management offices. The sky-blue letters on the wall, HEAD OF DEPARTMENT, then the sign with the two women's names: *Annette Mayerhöfer/Esther Graf.*

21

Annette Mayerhöfer was standing beside one of the shelves in her half of the office, holding a folder. Removal boxes were piled up by the side wall, one of them open – the tips of orchids were peeping out.

"Your last day . . ." Louise said.

Mayerhöfer put the folder back on the shelf, pushed her glasses up her nose then offered Louise her hand. "Yes. And not a moment too soon, either. We're going bankrupt."

"So quickly?"

"Yesterday afternoon the regional government cancelled its orders. That in itself amounts to tens of millions of euros that we'd budgeted for. Sooner or later the federal government is bound to do the same."

"What about 'Drive Solar'?"

"Dead as a dodo. Our partners are jumping ship." Mayerhöfer shrugged. "This whole year has been toxic for our image. Now an employee has been murdered and the papers are saying that Kripo and the Verfassungsschutz are investigating. No medium-sized company can survive all that."

"You made the right decision, then."

"Yes, but I've known that for a while."

"Where are you going again? Hanover?"

"Hamburg. But not until January."

"What are you going to do till then?"

"Holiday. Then the move – that's going to take a while." Mayerhöfer smiled. "Lots of shoes, lots of clothes. Nice outfit, by the way. Looks better on you than that denim."

"Thanks. For special occasions."

"Is it your birthday?"

Louise shook her head.

She wandered over to the floor-to-ceiling windows. About a hundred metres away was building 2, behind that to the left, building 3 – almost identical cubes, only considerably smaller than building 1 and without the solar module on the south side.

"What about your case?" Mayerhöfer asked. "Making any progress?"

Louise didn't reply. Outside the building of the firm next door stood a man who seemed to be looking up at her, a shadow in a sun-drenched forecourt beyond a wall of bushes.

A man who looked very tired and smelled bad, a friend of Chief Inspector Louise Bonì.

She raised a hand. The shadow returned the greeting.

Then he crossed the forecourt, vanished around a corner and didn't reappear. Louise felt a stab of regret. She'd have liked to find out more about him, show her gratitude for his help. And she'd have liked to know how things would turn out for him. Whether he'd get in touch with Esther one day, without bugs and cameras.

Then, recalling the list of crimes that Mike had committed, she was surprised she didn't care about them. As if he'd warranted absolution through his help alone.

Louise turned around. Too much had got mixed up.

"Yes, I am making progress. May I?" she said, pointing at Esther Graf's desk chair.

"Of course."

She sank slowly into the black rolling chair. The backrest gave way, putting her at an incredibly comfortable angle. Even the buzzing in her head abated slightly. Bonì closed her eyes. "There's a colleague of mine," she said, "Ernesto Freudenreich. Odd chap – he wears felt slippers in the office and he's hidden himself in the basement so he can have his peace and quiet. He prefers working online, but he'll make the occasional phone call too. He made a lot of calls this morning." She opened her eyes. "You're not going to Hamburg, he says. No company dealing in wind energy there knows your name."

Not a muscle twitched in Mayerhöfer's face, but her eyes did look a tiny bit more wary.

Louise took the digital recorder from the inside pocket of her blazer. It fitted comfortably in her hand; her thumb and forefinger were exactly where the buttons sat. She stroked the surface with her fingers. The device looked new; she suspected it had been bought only that morning, in some nameless town between an office with a view of the river and Haid in Freiburg.

"I don't know what's on it," she said. "Maybe you'll be lucky."

Bonì placed the recorder on the desk in front of her and pressed PLAY.

. . . watch all of this go to pot, a woman's voice said – Mayerhöfer. *You understand?*

No, a second woman's voice replied – Louise.

Mayerhöfer had sat at her desk and was slowly sweeping her black hair out of her face.

What did you know? And why is the firm going to pot?

Aren't you here because of the rumours?

I thought they'd been disproved.

Officially, yes.

But?

Louise fast-forwarded. It wasn't her conversation with Mayerhöfer that was important, but what happened afterwards.

Only last night on the bank of the Dreisam had it occurred to her that Esther's office might have been kept under surveillance as well as her telephone and computer. Mike confirmed it – two bugs and a camera, which had still been working that afternoon. At around midnight his people had cleared out the office. Nobody had listened to the recordings from that day, of course.

. . . already had lunch? The voice of a dead man – Philipp Schulz.

Yes.

Shame.

Go for the lasagne, it's delicious.

The click when Schulz closed the door.

Wow! Louise.

You're welcome to him, I don't get involved with colleagues. But hurry, half the workforce here is after him, including the guys.

Mike or one of his people would send the daily recordings made during Esther's surveillance by e-mail to his business partner late in the evening, and for security reasons they were deleted in Freiburg. In her dozy state Louise had asked him to have the file in question sent to her. It wasn't possible, Mike replied. Maybe she asked again, maybe not. At any rate she realised why he had to get hold of the file himself: his partner didn't know he wanted to get out, that he'd spoken to her.

She fast-forwarded again.

. . . my residual leave on Monday, you wouldn't be getting this. Mayerhöfer.

I know. Could I use your fax?

Is this never going to stop?

Have you got a pen?

The sound of footsteps, then a whirring when the piece of paper with the names of the GoSolar employees fed into the all-in-one device.

Call me if it's raining and I'll bring you an umbrella.

I'd rather have a pizza.

A brief goodbye, then silence.

Seconds passed, during which Mayerhöfer's eyes wandered across the room, finally coming to rest on Louise.

She returned the gaze while she waited.

Less than twenty minutes after she'd left Mayerhöfer's office the previous day, Steinhoff knew that she had the names, including those of the eight moles – he'd notified Mike at thirteen forty-nine. He could have found this out only from Mayerhöfer.

Or, she thought, from someone who had in fact been listening in to her conversation with Mayerhöfer and who picked up the phone at once. Or from someone who'd been monitoring Mayerhöfer's computer commands – she'd compiled the list from the personnel department's data.

Louise could feel herself begin to sweat. More and more doubts were surfacing. Apart from her Hamburg lie, Annette Mayerhöfer hadn't made herself at all suspicious. She would have been the perfect missing link, the last piece of the puzzle that would reveal the complex picture. The picture that Louise had formed . . . But maybe there was another, quite different picture which for unfathomable reasons she'd never wanted to see, and which was far more a reflection of reality than hers.

A nightmarish idea that made her feel sick in the stomach. She felt like getting up and going, to avoid having to watch this idea become reality. She wanted to go home and hole up – but all of a sudden she no longer knew where home was. It wasn't the apartment on Annaplatz, nor Ben's apartment in Stühlinger, her mother's little house in Provence, Kehl with her father and new brother.

Home somewhere.

Annette Mayerhöfer's distinct outlines had dissolved, becoming blurred and shaky. Louise let the tears run, she didn't care, and nor did she care that the buzzing seemed to flow out of her head along with the tears, leaving peace and lightness up there. Now she just had to find the energy to get up, say a few final words to a colleague, get into her car and get to Wiehre in one piece.

To resist the urge for a glass. To sleep.

Later, to stroke the cheek of a man in a coma, and tomorrow to fall into the arms of a man coming off a plane.

To pack a suitcase and go home somewhere.

From the recorder came Mayerhöfer's muted voice.

She's got the names . . . No . . . Hans . . . Just listen to me for a sec, would you? . . . Hans! . . . The operation is being aborted . . . Right. Tell your people they've got to disappear . . . What? . . . Where's he going? . . . Shit, you've got to get him out of the equation! She mustn't talk to him, she thinks he's one of ours, and if she finds out . . . Yes, yes, I know, I'll send you Claude . . .

That was the end of the conversation.

Louise dried her cheeks with a tissue and blew her nose. Mayerhöfer's eyes were still fixed on her unblinkingly.

Once again her voice on the recorder, this time she was speaking French to Claude, a slender man in dark clothing climbing out of the Dreisam, an arrogant professional, hastily being told to get in contact with Steinhoff and take Philipp Schulz out of the equation. Then, as soon as the opportunity presented itself, to do the same to Steinhoff himself.

Louise stopped the recording. Her tears continued to flow. "For Christ's sake, *you* should be the one howling, not me."

She sank back until the soft padding of the chair held her. The public prosecution department wasn't exactly going to be thrilled about this sort of evidence – an illegal recording of words spoken in confidence. At least it hadn't been made by an investigating authority, which would have been disastrous, but by criminals, which would probably mean the evidence was admissible in court. In this part of the world the fruit of the poisonous tree was delicious.

But others could grapple with all that.

"All the fuss about Philipp Schulz . . . a flirt, a non-platonic finale . . . Nobody's pulled my leg like that in a long time." Bonì laughed, impressed and slightly aggrieved. She'd been thoroughly intimidated, had danced on the invisible strings pulled by Mayerhöfer, just like Steinhoff, Mike, Esther and all those others involved.

She turned her head to look at Mayerhöfer, or at least to be able to see the dark blotches. Even as Bonì reeled off the reasons for arrest – suspicion of incitement to two murders, of forming a criminal association, of violating the confidentiality of the spoken word, of violating §17 of the law on unfair competition – Mayerhöfer remained poker-faced, as if she didn't care. Louise suspected that the impression was deceptive. Mayerhöfer was doing a cost–benefit calculation.

During their conversation yesterday she must have realised that the operation and she herself were in danger. Within a few seconds she'd switched from a diversionary tactic – flirting with Schulz – to cooperation: abandoning the flirtation and talking about Heinrich Willert without having to. A risky attempt to keep her options open for a few more days by offering substantially more than had been asked of her.

Maybe it would have worked if Louise hadn't asked for the list of names. At that point Mayerhöfer knew that the operation wasn't merely in danger; it had failed.

She'd remained calm and come into the office this morning, planning to disappear for ever a few hours later. A huge mistake, as it turned out, but she couldn't have known that.

"What I still don't understand . . . solar cells for cars – that's a niche market at best, or have I misunderstood? I mean, it's not going to earn any money for years. Did two people have to be killed and a firm ruined for that?"

"Keep going with the tape," Mayerhöfer said by way of an answer.

Louise pressed PLAY.

A few seconds of rustling, a whispered "*Shit!*" Then Mayerhöfer's clear voice, again speaking French: It's over, we don't have much time, but we've got what we need and GoSolar won't survive this, no, no danger at the moment, all evidence pointing to me is being eliminated and by the time they suspect anything I'll be with you . . . I'll be in touch tomorrow evening, *je t'aime.* The voice had turned soft, as if the words "*chez toi*" had triggered an automatic change of mode. Like pure acoustic stimuli bringing about a change in sound because some neurobiological law demanded it.

Mayerhöfer's index finger pointed to the recorder. "That's it."

Louise pressed the STOP button. She guessed why she had been encouraged to listen to this last telephone call. Another calculated step: a woman in love who had been talked into committing a crime. Mayerhöfer seemed to sense that Louise had been on thin ice these past few days when it came to love.

"You don't send two people to their deaths because of *love*," she said. "That doesn't seem like you."

"Of course not. Success only comes if you're determined. In one year I would have been on the board of . . ." Mayerhöfer raised her eyebrows. "I'd have been sitting on some board, earning a packet."

"And speaking French all day long?"

"Do we have a deal? I'll testify and you get me a reduced sentence?"

Louise shook her head. "Not for murder."

"But wouldn't a confession help?"

"Depends on the judge."

"That's the deal, then. Yes, I would have been speaking French all day long."

"I can't promise you anything, Frau Mayerhöfer."

"It's my risk."

How happy she was, Louise thought, that soon she wouldn't have anything more to do with people like Annette Mayerhöfer. All those cold-blooded or hot-headed criminals who set themselves up to rule over life and death, and who'd inhabited her days and nights.

Who'd held the strings she'd had to dance from.

"What's the company?"

"Soleilfrance."

Louise shrugged. She'd never heard of it, but that wasn't surprising. "And you've got a private connection to Soleilfrance?"

"Ever since a holiday in Nice five years ago."

"What's his name?"

"Georges Lapierre."

For a while there was silence. Mayerhöfer seemed to be waiting for further questions, while Louise was wondering whether she was being manipulated again; it was becoming easier by the moment. Somewhere in the middle of her body the exhaustion had turned into total feebleness and had started advancing in every direction, gobbling up her last reserves. Soon, she thought, she wouldn't even be able to stand up from the chair without assistance.

Je t'aime, Mayerhöfer's voice said inside her head. Less than twenty-four hours later she had betrayed Georges Lapierre.

Mayerhöfer appeared to have read her mind. "Nothing that can't be replaced."

"That's not love, then."

"For me it is. Five wonderful, exciting years that led to a fascinating plan. The plan failed, the love will be a delightful memory. In reality it isn't important anymore. What use is it to me in prison?"

Propping her elbows on the armrests, Louise pressed her fingers to her temples. She was having difficulty keeping up with Mayerhöfer. Rapid, deliberate sentences, as if they'd been planned in advance, just like the changes in strategy. What confounded her most was that Mayerhöfer didn't seem in the least angry, disappointed or anxious. Even though she'd lost, it didn't appear to bother her.

Even in defeat, victory was hers.

"Did you and Georges plan the operation on your own?"

"With two partners from Soleilfrance."

"Who you'll name?"

"Yes."

"Was French intelligence involved?"

"Not actively. Georges has good contacts, the DGSE provided information."

"About GoSolar?"

Mayerhöfer nodded. "What the listening stations picked up over the years."

"Were you responsible for the organisation in Germany?"

"I laid the foundations. Everything else was Steinhoff's job."

"How did you know him?"

"I didn't. I was looking for someone suitable and came across him." Actually she'd had her doubts, Mayerhöfer said. She found Steinhoff too restless, not strategic enough, too impulsive. But his connections and knowledge of the sector convinced her. And time was of the essence. The status of the solar industry in France was going to improve in the foreseeable future. In 2006 a new feed-in tariff was going to come in, and an environmental programme was in the pipeline that would be launched in 2009. "Soleilfrance had to be brought up to speed."

"But with solar cells for cars?"

"Yes, it's a niche market at the moment, but it's also a potential market of the future. There are millions of cars on the roads. The winners will be those who come up with the right product at the right time with the right partners. Those who arrive too late will be out of it. One single firm, Sunways in Konstanz, is supplying the global market. GoSolar, or Soleilfrance, would have joined them as the second. We know that other companies are working on similar ideas. We've heard that within seven years Toyota will have a production-line car that will be fully powered by solar energy via cells on the roof and integrated into the bodywork."

"Like 'DriveSolar'."

"Correct."

"Would Sunways have been your next target?"

Mayerhöfer rocked her head from side to side. "We did consider it. But it would have been more difficult."

"Because there wouldn't have been an Annette Mayerhöfer in the firm."

"Exactly."

"Do you know the real names of the moles?"

"Not off the top of my head. They're in my lawyer's safe, you'll get them later."

"What about Willert?"

"It was a good plan, but the Verfassungsschutz was quicker."

"Who else was involved apart from you and Steinhoff?"

"A business detective agency in Frankfurt. Reuter Business Security, run by Wilhelm Reuter and his son, Mike."

So, an office with a view of the Main, a father for a business partner – and a supposedly invented name that was genuine. Bonì didn't let her surprise and bafflement show. If Mayerhöfer named all those involved when she was interrogated by Andrele, Mike's chances of getting off scot-free were poor. Mayerhöfer couldn't prove that he'd worked for Steinhoff because she hadn't spoken to him personally. But the moles would incriminate him. Maybe, she thought, she could prevent the worst with a call to Frankfurt.

"Who's Claude?"

"Our go-to guy."

"Who was going to kill me?"

"Don't take it personally, Frau Bonì. I wanted to buy some time. And I wanted to know who the man was you had a rendezvous with by the river at three in the morning."

"Did Claude follow me from Steinhoff's hotel?"

"Yes."

"You were actually willing to factor in two more deaths."

"If you've got the chance to earn two million euros per year plus a share of the profits, and land a huge coup in a few years' time . . . I like money, and I don't like it when someone tries to take something away from me."

"I took away your money and your freedom."

Mayerhöfer smiled. "Yes, I don't suppose we're ever going to be friends."

Louise put away the digital recorder and picked up her mobile, weighing it in her hand. She couldn't handle this conversation any longer. Mayerhöfer's cool friendliness, her sober explanations, her invulnerability. For the first time in all these years as a police officer she was desperate to see doubt in the eyes of a criminal, and this wasn't a pleasant realisation.

Mayerhöfer was still pulling her strings.

She dialled Andrele's number and asked her and Graeve to come down to the second floor. Proof, a confession. An empty victory on her last day.

"It's time," she said.

Mayerhöfer got up. "Can I take my orchids with me?"

"They'll be sent to you."

"Thanks." Smoothing her blazer, Mayerhöfer went over to the metal cabinet, her high heels making a faint clacking sound on the carpet. It was a muffled sound, but energetic all the same. She took out a handbag, touched up her lips and eyelids in a mirror on the back of the door, and combed her hair. Then she put on a light over-coat and said, "What about you?"

"I'm going to stay here for a bit."

There was a knock at the door, then Marianne Andrele came in followed by Reinhard Graeve. The door stayed open; outside two uniformed officers were waiting.

Andrele looked at Mayerhöfer, then at Louise. "A woman?"

"Yes." Louise turned to Graeve, who said nothing that could have made up for her disappointment earlier. He looked at her with small, saddened eyes, as if not even proof and a confession could make up for *his* disappointment.

Bonì brought him and Andrele up to speed while Mayerhöfer

stood there stoically, as if it wasn't her they were talking about, but a distant acquaintance.

"The tape," Andrele said.

Louise gave it to her.

Andrele smiled fleetingly. "What should we learn from this? That we can rely on you. It won't be forgotten." Turning to Mayerhöfer, she pointed to the door. Mayerhöfer went ahead, stumbling very slightly when she twisted her right ankle, but recovering immediately.

The tiny signal that Louise had needed.

The door was still open, the footsteps faded into the distance.

"Would you like me to take you home?" Graeve said very softly. He'd moved over to Louise and seemed to be staring down at her from a great height. Now he did look friendly, but stiff too, as well as exhausted and deeply concerned. She wanted to cheer him up – never mind, Boss, it happens every time and neither of us has it easy with me. But she didn't say anything.

Home to somewhere, she thought. Her vision having cleared up only minutes earlier, now Graeve's outlines were blurring and her cheeks were wet once more. When she felt something gentle and light on her shoulder, she wondered what might have landed on it, until she realised that only the hand of a Kripo boss could feel like this.

Louise shook her head. "Take me to Rolf."

The hand felt firmer, the blurred face slowly came closer until it was level with hers, as if Graeve had kneeled down. When she heard him speak she wished the block was still inside her head, preventing his words from getting through. The hospital had called a few minutes earlier. Rolf Bermann had succumbed to his injuries.

Epilogue

Above Basel, aeroplanes glistened in the strong blue of the afternoon sky, a silent slow-motion dance in the distance. Ben's connecting flight from Munich was delayed by half an hour; she waited on a bench outside the arrivals hall, watching the sky gradually being enveloped by dusk from the east. With every minute that passed the planes' navigation lights shone more intensely, their fuselages becoming less distinct until they suddenly disappeared, leaving only red, green and white dots of light in great number. She thought she ought to go in now, seeing as she'd been waiting for one of these descending aircraft. But then her eyes were held once more by the colourful dots slowly approaching from one side, and slowly departing on the other, as if they had all the time in the world or were extremely tired. She tried to figure out the rhythm in which the colourful lights came and went, imagining them approaching from all directions and forming a single thread somewhere high up in the darkness, before descending. They rose back up into the air in another single thread, before scattering in all directions once more and eventually fading into the darkness.

Later on, in front of her stood the man she wanted to keep, if he would wait. Nobody can put up with that much chaos, she thought, not even her. Before making decisions about the future they needed to bear this in mind; something had to be sorted out before that future could be embarked upon.

They gazed at each other without exchanging a word.

Then Ben put down his bag and sat beside her, allowing her to be what she was, coming down into her abyss without disturbing her, just as he had done a year ago in Štrpci in Bosnia.

And like then, the molecules were leaping about wildly.

"I need to talk to the trees again for a while," she said.

Ben nodded.

"And then I'd like to go on holiday with you again."

He smiled, and she knew that he would wait for the few weeks or months she needed to tidy up, to finally clear away the rubble that had accumulated in her over forty-five years.

"Somewhere snowy?"

"No way."

"Good."

"And then . . . Well, then I'll go back to work again, I suppose."

Gazing up at the colourful specks of light flying off into the sky, she found a white one that looked just like all the others, and yet seemed special. She kept watching it until she couldn't see it anymore. She saw a face before her and said farewell.

Acknowledgements

I'd like to thank everyone who helped me with this novel, in particular Chief Inspector Karl-Heinz Schmid (Freiburg Police HQ), Inspector Roland Braunwarth (forensics laboratory) and Superintendent Arno Wöhrle (head of the financial crime department), both from Freiburg government authority, Dept. 6, Baden-Württemberg Police HQ, Senior Chief Inspector Iris Tappendorf (head of VB III 1 of Police HQ 2, Berlin), Bernd Litzenburger from Solon SE, the press office of *PHOTON*, the solar power magazine, the Baden-Württemberg security forum for the 2009–10 SiFo study, everyone else not mentioned by name here, as well as Annina Luzie Schmid for her valuable help with the text.

OLIVER BOTTINI was born in 1965. Four of his novels, including *Zen and the Art of Murder* and *A Summer of Murder* of the Black Forest Investigations have been awarded the Deutscher Krimipreis, Germany's most prestigious award for crime writing. *Zen and the Art of Murder* was shortlisted for the 2018 CWA International Dagger. He lives in Frankfurt. www.bottini.de

JAMIE BULLOCH is the translator of Timur Vermes' *Look Who's Back*, Birgit Vanderbeke's *The Mussel Feast*, which won him the Schlegel-Tieck Prize, and novels by, amongst others, Steven Uhly, Robert Menasse, Romy Hausmann, Sebastian Fitzek and Daniela Krien.